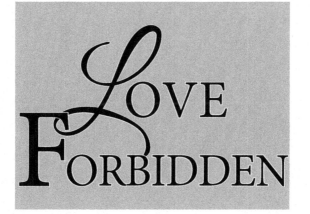

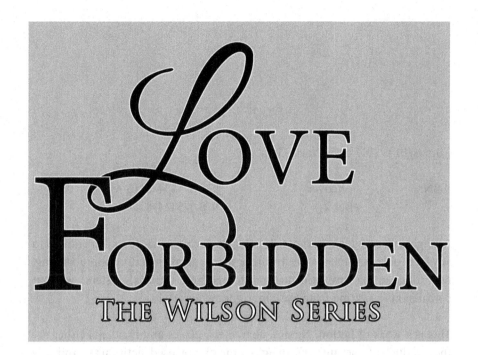

VICTORIA GEM

To order additional copies of this book, contact:
Xlibris
800-056-3182
www.Xlibrispublishing.co.uk
Orders@Xlibrispublishing.co.uk
768278

Chapter One

Belle's First Scene

I T'S NOT EASY BEING THE owner of a big event planning agency, as a matter of fact it is the opposite, but I make it work, safe to say, I am the best in the business.

Right now I am in my office which in London, it is huge, with black lino flooring, the moment you step out of the lift, you have walk a good ten feet to get to me black oak desk, with a black leather chair on my side of the desk, and two chairs on the other side. To get my computer to surface, I push a button.

On the far right hand corner, there is a sofa and two arm chairs, with a table in between, it is good for casual planning of an event. On the right wall near my desk, there is a mantel piece with a coffee brewer and five mugs.

My grey walls are plain, no paintings no pictures, nothing. Which is the way my Dad left it.

On the left wall there are two filing cabinets with a third on the way.

Because I am considered the best in the business, I deal with a lot of high rollers, Mayor's, Lord's, Ambassadors, Secretaries of Defence, other MP's, high end business men, the list could go on. One thing I have learnt in my experience, men are greedy, even when they have everything they still want to try for more.

I am not going to lie, I have had affairs and lots of them. I have broken up marriages and families.

But I never see myself as being in the wrong, why? I'm not married, I don't make any moves, I just have an effect on men. I have nothing to lose, I'm not married and I don't have a family. And I have this logic that if the men cared about their wives and families, then they wouldn't have had affairs to begin with.

And I lose nothing, because no matter what I do, how many men I sleep with, how many marriages and families I ruin, it doesn't change the fact, I'm the best at what I do, I am in the elite, a high roller.

I've spent my whole life in the spotlight, my Nan who's still alive, is still the life and soul of the party at seventy nine, she is a retired actress, and stage performer.

My Mum was an actress, but she died of cancer when I was sixteen, she was only forty five, and my father before he became the best event planner in London, was the police commissioner, but he died of a heart attack when he was sixty five.

My step mother runs a modelling agency with her two brats, I have nothing to do with them, as a matter of fact they always hated me, and after a couple of months of trying the hatred became mutual.

At the age of twenty five, I am still a wild child.

Right now I am bent over my desk, being mercilessly pounded on by my latest endeavour Fox Mason, he's forty, he has light brown Elvis style hair, deep brown almond shaped eyes, which right now are hooded with lust, his lips are thick and downturned, his nose is sharp and pointed, he had a rectangular jaw, he has a goatee, that seems to make him look younger. He is muscular but skinny, his narrow hips are very much in action.

We met at a private function, and have been meeting to have sex for the last month.

He's still in his grey suit, only his trousers and boxers are round his ankles.

I have on a black dress that would sit just above my knees, if it wasn't up around my waist right now, my black panties are around my ankles, I still have my stilettos on.

Fox is barking like a dog on every massive pound he gives me, I'm screaming on every pound, I was hoping for once a man would

2

take me gently, I long for that connection. Instead of someone taking me like they have some kind of claim over me.

Guess that is the downside to my colourful lifestyle, my controversial way of living is plastered all over every newspaper and magazine in London, when an affair is exposed. The more powerful the man I sleep with, the more they feel like they have to prove. They only seem to get rougher, or take longer pounding into me. I am craving gentle, but fear that will lead to love, so I will settle for this.

Fox climaxes on a roar that resonates around the office, when he's done he collapses on top of me, he's breathing hard, and his grip on my wrists is fierce.

I don't know if he doesn't know I didn't climax, or if he doesn't care. He soon will both know and care.

"You're losing your touch. Looks like I need to find a new endeavour." I say cockily, knowing it will get some kind of reaction.

He growls angrily in my ear, and finds enough energy to give me one more vicious pound, "OHH!!" I scream as I climax hard, my head starts to spin, and I feel as if I am free falling.

"Don't ever say that to me again!" He spits nastily. His voice is really deep and husky.

I soon snap out of my post climax bliss, "Oh someone is pissed off, you will soon leave me when your wife finds out."

"Do you see a wedding ring?" He spins me round to show me his hands, and there is no ring.

"Means nothing." I retort, "They are easy to take off."

I shove him off me, pull up my panties, and walk away from him while he's adjusting his trousers, he circles round to face me, he holds out his jacket, "Check the pockets, you will not find a ring." He orders.

"Then it is in the glove compartment of your car, or if it's not there, then it's at home somewhere your wife won't think to look. Most men I sleep with do not bother taking them off, I still let them fuck me." I say surely.

"Wow you really have a suspicious mind."

"Look Fox married or not I don't care, it's not like I have anything to lose, so married or not it means nothing to me." I press my lips

3

together, "If married men choose to fuck me, that is their choice, it's their life, it's their marriage, it's their family. That's not my problem, if they really cared about their wives, or their families, then they would have kept it in their pants. I'm not the one doing the hurting, it's the scumbags cheating on their wives that's doing that. If it wasn't me they had an affair with, it would have been another girl. I fuck them, I use them, and then when I'm done with them, I dispose of them. They think exposing the affair will make me want to be with them, because they think they are in love with me. But all exposing the affair does, is have me labelled a scarlet woman, and it pisses me off."

"Good speech." He replies, "But I'm not married. I just like fucking you."

I consider his words, then look him in the eyes, "Promise me you're not married. I already told you, I don't care."

"I promise." He reiterates, he approaches me and puts his hands on my hips firmly.

"If you're lying, this is over. I don't abide lies." I say firmly.

"I'm not lying, I promise." He kisses me hard, "I have to go to work, I will call you for a hook up, or you call me if you need a good seeing to."

He then leaves, he's not married, and it's me he calls when he wants sex. If he's telling me the truth, I could see a future with him.

Oh what am I saying? I shake the idea out of my head. It's too much to think about on a hot summer morning, but on the plus side it's Friday. But right now, it's ten in the morning, and my day has barely begun, I need a coffee to get me through the day, before I can head off for a weekend off.

The people that work for me work on commission, the more events they plan the more money they make, if they want to work weekends then it's their choice, but I personally prefer my weekends being about me and my family.

I like to see Nan and friends on weekends, Bailey and M.K are as good as family to me, they live with me, so I like spending my days off with them. I wonder what they make of Foxes claim be single, M.K will probably will think it is a load of bullshit, but then again she always does.

Bailey might tell me to give him the benefit of the doubt.

So after a long day at work, it feels good when I can shut my computer down, leave my office, my building, head to my car and start driving home. I'm in my black luxury land rover, the front of the car comes with drive assist, even auto drive, so the car parks itself, I can connect my phone to the cars computer, there is even a compartment I can just slide my phone into, so that it charges, there are even two cup holders, one for me and my passenger.

The rear seats, come with foot rests, they even massage you as you ride, there's a folding table, that comes out of the centre console, so you can work as you ride, there is also a compartment that keeps your drinks cold, and controls for the massage chairs. The interior is made up of the finest leather and wood.

I pull up outside my house, when I learnt my father left me his estate, I put it on the market, and bought this house, as much as I loved my father my old house was too dark for my liking, I wanted something lighter to make feel secure both mentally and physically, this house gives me the perfect balance.

There is a gate that act as a barrier, so no one can take a wrong turn and drive into my estate, in order to open the gate, you use a Bluetooth control key, only myself, M.K, Bailey and Nan have one, but they are easy to come by if I need more, it is a simple case of connecting it, and the typing in a code on the gates main panel, to authorise the connection, then only the keys with the authorisation will work.

My house is a six bedroom house protected by a ten foot wall. My estate is about the size of a football pitch. There is a six foot wide driveway, from the iron get to my house.

Six feet to the right of that there is yellow, aqua and sky blue slate, tiles that are only about four feet wide, curving off to the right gradually, about ten feet down the garden is a patio about ten feet by ten feet with fine oak light brown chairs, with cream leather seats four of them sit around a black marble fire pit, good for summer nights. Six feet behind the fire pit, there is a red stone stove, oven and grill, brilliant for when it is too hot to cook indoors. All of my furniture is King Louis, both outdoor and indoor.

Now the house itself is quite modern, it is only about ten years old, it is made up of the finest cream bricks, the roof is made up of sky blue slate, the window and door frames are painted an aqua blue, there are two garages with doors of the same colour as the door and window frames, there are two garages, one long one to the right of the house and one small one to the left of the house. The smaller garage is used to store the outdoor furniture in winter.

The ground floor window to the left of the front door is the lounge, and is about seven feet wide, and four feet in height. The window fifteen feet above the door, is four feet long and two feet wide, and is the window to the only bathroom in the house. Above the lounge window and about six feet to the left of the bathroom window, is a six feet by six feet window, which is Bailey's room, and above the right garage door, is another six feet by six feet window, which is M.K's room.

On entering the house, you will see there is a theme, which is the beach, with a carpet the same colour of sand, the bottom half of the walls are an aqua blue, with darker shades of blue to represent the sea, and the ripple, the top half of the wall is sky blue with clouds to represent the sky, every room has the same theme, it makes the place seem light.

If you go straight ahead there is a staircase in the lobby, on the back wall just to the right of the staircase, there is a door which leads to a room that Nan sometimes stays in, just to the left behind the stair case there is another door which we use as a cleaning closet.

If you turn left two feet away from the front door there is another door which leads to the lounge, two feet away to the right of the front door, is another door that leads to my study, so I can work from home if I need to.

If you go up the stairs you have the choice to turn left, or right, if you choose to turn left you will find two doors, the one is four feet away from the staircase, and that leads to the bathroom, the second door is straight ahead and that leads to Bailey's room, and there is a door on the right wall which is the spare bedroom.

If you choose to turn right there are two doors on the left wall, about ten feet away from each other, the second door leads to my room, the only door on the right leads to M.K's room.

Only three bedrooms are in use, my room and M.K's room have en-suites, the third is downstairs in Nans room.

My best friends Bailey Moxxam and M.K Townsend both moved in with me when I bought this place two years ago, we have been friends since boarding school. Apart from Nan, Bailey and M.K have been my biggest supports are valued as much as Nan, they are my family, they know about my string of affairs and have never judged me, they might have given me kicks up the arse, but they have never judged.

Both of them work for me, Bailey is in charge of the legal aspect of things. M.K on the other hand is in charge of getting venues ready for an event, she has an eye for detail, so whether an event is outside or in, she makes sure everything has a place and is in it at the time of an event.

I know my friends are home, as they like to say bye to me if they leave work before I do, and I passed Bailey's little royal blue mini convertible as I was coming in, it's her pride and joy.

I don't bother to greet them, I just want a bit of time on my own. Whenever I spend time with Fox Mason, I always wind up feeling drained, and because I saw him before my day even began, I now feel exhausted.

So I just go up to my room, which has the same floor and walls as the rest of the house, straight ahead of me when walk in is a King Louis king size bed, it is made up of the finest oak, painted white, with a white leather and gold frame, the sheets and pillow cases are sky blue.

All of my bedroom cupboards, cabinets and wardrobes are made up of the finest oak, painted white with gold frames, and they have pink orchids painted on them as well.

I have a bedside table to the right of my bed, which has a lamp and a draw which holds the book I am reading. On the right wall is a big six feet high, ten foot wide walk in wardrobe, for a woman who stands at five foot four inches it is ideal.

Four feet to the left of my wardrobe is a door that leads to my en-suite, which too is painted white, with a gold frame and handle with pink orchids painted on it, on the back wall just before the bathroom door there is another wardrobe which I use as a linen cupboard.

On the left wall there is a large window which is about seven feet high and twelve feet in length, the room itself is twelve feet high and twenty square feet wide.

There is also a door in the centre of the big window that leads to the balcony equipped with King Louis loungers all three of them cream leather. If you turn left on the balcony you will see a set of steps, which lead to the kitchen.

Bailey, M.K and I have had many a night on these loungers, talking, laughing and drinking the finest wine. When the weather turns, all of the furniture goes into storage.

Just before the window inside there is a single lounger where I like to sit and read. Only my room has a balcony, so M.K and Bailey tend to sneak into my room to use the balcony stairs, as it is the quickest way into the kitchen, they know I don't care.

Every bedroom has the same kind of design, I am a bit meticulous like that.

Exhausted I just throw myself onto my bed and brood, (yes women do that too). It is something I do after a lot of my encounters with Fox Mason.

My brooding doesn't last long when my friends breeze into my room.

Bailey Moxxam, the bright and smiley red head, with her straight hair in a bob style, droopy hooded grey eyes, thin pink lips, a soft subtly curved nose, with a square jawline. She looks so nice in her grey pencil dress and a black belt around her stomach to show off her pear figure, she looks more serious than she is, she is fun, light and the comforter of the group.

M.K Townsend on the other hand, keeps her chestnut brown hair so it sits just below her shoulders, with full oval lips, round thin jawline, button nose, protruding round sapphire eyes, you would think considering she is already padding around barefoot, in a pair of black cotton pants, and a neon pink vest top that says 'Need Coffee'. You would think she was the more laid back out of the three of us, but oh no, she is feisty, fiery, and not one to back down from a fight, she has punched reporters and paparazzi in the aim of protecting me, she is the protector, my self-proclaimed bodyguard.

I am more like the pacifier of the group, Bailey and I tend to be the only people that can cool M.K down when she is on one. I do think we have all rubbed off on each other, Bailey knows when it is time to get serious like me, M.K knows when it is time to comfort like Bailey, I try to be gentle and light like Bailey, only Nan, M.K and Bailey see that side of me. I also try to be protective like M.K.

"Thought we heard you come in." Bailey constant soft and slightly high pitched voice, gives her tone a constant touch of song, it is nice to listen to.

I give my friends a weak wave, but do not sit up.

"Uh oh, she has seen Fox again." M.K has a kind of toneless voice, it makes her seem hard and uncaring, but only the people that know her see the real her. "Why do you screw the guy if he makes you feel like this?"

"Because the orgasms are out of this world."

"Care to fill me in on what this, 'this' is?" Bailey asks.

"When I know, I will tell you, until then answers on a postcard please." I answer tiredly.

"Well considering you are thinking about how you feel about this guy, this is more than a casual affair." Bailey ever the analyst, she always feels the need to pick apart every affair I have ever had, she can be quite comical about it.

"He isn't married, or if he is he is not admitting it." Bailey sits on the bed to the right of me.

"I have a bad feeling." M.K remains standing with her arms folded, something she always does when she is in serious mode.

"You always have a bad feeling about the men I sleep with." I remind her.

"That is not a bad feeling, that is knowledge that history will repeat itself, the guy will fall for you, you will toss him aside, he will expose the affair to try and win you back, and you name will wind up in every newspaper and magazine in London. This is different, you are going to get hurt. Just be careful that is all I am saying Belle." I know when M.K is being deadly serious, because she says our names when she finishes saying her piece.

"You know what we need, a night out." Bailey chirps.

"What? No I'm tired, it has been a long week." I protest.

"No Bailey's right." M.K puts in. "Get your glad rags on Belle, we are going out, even if it is for a couple of drinks."

I let out a huff of annoyance but my friends take it a sign of victory, they know I have relented, "Fine but am seeing Nan over the weekend."

Nan is the only blood relative I have and no matter what I do, she is never anything but proud of me, her daughter's daughter, the only blood she has left.

Chapter Two

Parker's First Scene

I AM SAT WITH MY friends Sam and Wayne.

Sam is happy go lucky, always smiling and joking, with baby blue droopy hooded eyes, soft surly curved nose, thin lips, a well-define, oblong jawline, skinny but lean frame, he has dirty blond hair, which he likes to keep brushed up, with his sides and back shorter than the top, he is always running his hand through his hair, to keep it out of his eyes, but it seems to add to his charm, he dresses smart/casual, right now he is in a pair of medium blue jeans, that fit just right, and a white long sleeve tight polo shirt, he has no trouble pulling the ladies.

Wayne on the other hand is always sharply dressed and likes to woo the ladies, with his deep brown protruding eyes, light brown hair with short angled fringe, he has a perky pointed nose, square jawline, even straight lips, strong body form, his whole outlook screams success.

We all work at a modelling agency, run by Imelda Hawthorn, we began modelling as teenagers, going from bad, good or wild boys, to bad, good or wild men, so at twenty we are pretty well off.

We are all sat with a bottle of Fosters each, having a light conversation and a few laughs. All in all it is my kind of night, except there is something missing, and I know what it is too, I am missing the warmth of a woman by my side, or the warmth of the knowledge that a woman I love and who loves me, is at home waiting for me when I get home.

I have money, I have travelled with the modelling agency, and I have had the flings and the one night stands, so at twenty years old I am ready to settle down.

"He's daydreaming again." Sam observes elbowing me back in the room, his voice always has a cool tone, it is a bit quiet, but you can hear him alright, "You always daydream about having a woman and love on a night out."

"Why settle?" Wayne always asks me the same question, "You can have plenty of women. So why settle?" Wayne has a very detached tone, and a voice that is rough and gravelly.

I am not getting into this with him, "I got bored, I want more." My short response should put an end to the matter.

"I personally see nothing wrong with it mate." Sam gives me a friendly slap on the shoulder.

"It is my round." I inform my friends, as I make my way to the bar.

It's Friday night, it's busy and loud, I weave my way through the crowd like a champ, when I eventually make it to the bar, I have to yell to a young and pretty barmaid, she is very attractive, with her long blond straight hair, baby blue eyes, her subtle heart shaped jawline, heart shaped lips, that are coated with red lip stick, her small subtle nose, she is too heavy, on the make-up and way too heavy on the eye shadow, eyeliner and foundation, she is in an all black uniform.

"Three bottles of Fosters and a large whiskey please."

"Coming right up." Her voice has a natural purr.

While I am waiting for the drinks, I turn to scan my surroundings, everything is so lively, people are having fun, it is a nightclub called The River, a name I can fully understand, there is always a flow of people.

I turn to the entrance to watch people come and go, and that is when I see her, Belle O Neil, a true vision of beauty, her father used to be the police commissioner, when he retired he got a massive pension, bought an events planning agency, and ran it until his death a couple of years ago, Belle's life has been a bit of a whirlwind,

I don't think she ever grieved for her father, I do know she and Imelda don't get on.

You see the evidence of Belle's controversial lifestyle in all of the tabloids in London, I know she has had affairs and lot's of them. She is very hard to resist, this is the first time I have ever seen her in person, I mentally pray my semi doesn't turn to a full on hard on.

With her raven hair up in pins, to show off her big round golden eyes, that are truly stunning, her sleek oval jawline, her thin upturned lips have a natural redness, her cheeks have a natural to them, she doesn't have to wear make-up, her eye lashes are full and thick, she is naturally flawless, she has a slightly curved nose, and a straight figure, which all adds to her perfection.

And here is a bonus, she has on a long red dress, that is a bit revealing but tasteful. She is with a couple of people, they are talking but I only see her.

She looks nothing like the pictures you see of her in the papers, tonight she has colour in her cheeks, she doesn't seem drained, she seems happy and content.

As she begins scanning her surroundings, our eyes meet, something in me clicks, as our eyes linger on each other, I have no idea what she sees in my eyes, but whatever she sees has her looking away on a tremble. Have I made her uncomfortable? I need to know Belle, there is something about her. I need to know her.

Belle

I have just gotten to a club call The River, with my friends and wow it is packed, but it is Friday night after all, so no surprises there. When we get our glad rags on, we really do get our glad rags on.

M.K has on a black jumpsuit that is quite tight, to show off her tight toned bum, there is a slit down the front centre covering her breasts but showing off her tight toned mid-section, with black lipstick, black eyeliner and eye shadow, she looks appealing in a dangerous sort of way. I am sure there is someone out there for her, who likes that sort of thing.

Bailey has on a royal blue dress that sits mid-thigh, showing off a pair of great legs, with royal blue lipstick, eye shadow and eye liner, she is OCD about colour co-ordinating her clothes and make-up.

We have that in common, I am OCD about my house, she is OCD about her outfits.

"Wow it is packed." Bailey seems shocked.

"Well duh it is Friday night." M.K points out.

"Seems to be a lot of cute guys around here, a lot of them are around our age, and not over a decade older."

"Oh M.K" I roll my eyes, "Not that again, look I get you, you don't like Fox, I got it the first two hundred times you have said it, it is only a bit of fun. Can we have fun now?"

"If you say so, it doesn't change the bad feeling I have, I am not judging you, I am judging him. Not only do I think he is bad news, I also know he is over a decade older than you, in my opinion he is sex addict who has to look for women half his age, that can keep up."

I can't help but laugh at M'K's bluntness, "Duly noted, now enough about Fox, let's have some fun."

"Yeah let's do it." Bailey chirps.

I then look around the club, and realise I am under very close scrutiny, and I know who by as well, Parker Wilson, he works for my step mother, Imelda Hawthorn.

He has a Caesar style haircut, longer on the top, shorter back and sides, it is casually ruffled to give him a mix of boyish and roguish affect to his look, he has a strong oblong jawline, a strong sloped subtle nose, those full lips, I have fantasized about those lips, they are so full and perfectly straight, they always look so kissable.

I know from his photoshoots he has a masculine body, rippling with well-defined toned muscles. He has on a white shirt with the sleeves rolled up, and the two top buttons undone, which gives him a laid back look, he has on a pair of light blue jeans, leaving his most flattering feature until last, his eyes, which a lovely shade of green, round and protruding, they usually have a playful look, or a smouldering look in his photoshoots.

But right now he is looking at me, in a very intense way, it is not a look of lust or of want, it is more a look of wonder. I try to stare him out. But I suddenly feel something, right in the pit of my stomach. So I have to look away and dammit I tremble.

He is still staring at me, I am tempted to check my dress or my skin for burn marks, his stare is that intense.

M.K is quick to notice the attention, "Is that Parker Wilson looking at you as if he had X-ray vision?"

"Oh is he?" I try to act coy.

"Oh yeah, that is an intense stare. Bit weird." Bailey says coolly, "Wait he works for bitch tits right?" Bitch tits my step mother's nickname created by M.K, the name stuck.

"Yeah, he is the one she fancies." M.K confirms for Bailey, "She buys the magazine because of him."

How the fuck did she know? I am quick to deny it, "I don't have a thing for him, firstly he is like six years younger than me, secondly I buy that stupid magazine to support my father's widow."

Bailey then snorts, "Yeah right. Support a woman who wants to see you fail. Pull the other one Belle."

"And actually he is four years and eight months younger than you, but if it makes you feel better, you can round it up to five. And you do fancy him, you have done since he did the Free and Randy shoot. Boy he did look hot in that though." Bailey muses.

"Changes nothing." I retort.

"So what he is younger than you? He seems like a good guy. What does age have to with it? You sleep with guys fifteen years your senior. And they are married. Maybe it is time to find a young and single model, no pun intended. Going by the look in his eyes just then, he is out for more than sex."

"Well then maybe I am not the right girl for him."

"You never know if you don't try." M.K advises.

"Tell you what, I wouldn't kick him out of bed." Bailey muses.

"You have him then." I retort.

"Erm guys we are about to have company in the form of Parker Wilson." M.K is quick to inform.

Parker

I can't help but approach her, the way she looked away, I am like a magnet right now, she felt something like I did. It wasn't a spark, but this is some kind of chemistry and it is sizzling, before I have even spoken to her.

As I approach I notice her friends, the woman to her right looks dangerous, in all black and with a serious look that seems to be welded onto her face.

The woman to her left seems bubbly and light, with her theme colour seeming to be royal blue.

I give the three of them my best smile, the woman on the left gives a little sigh, the woman on the right does nothing, Belle is trying her hardest to look anywhere but my face. She is making me very curious.

"Ladies can I get you all a drink?" I ask confidently.

"Sure you can." The woman on the left chirps.

Scoring a sharp look from Belle, the other woman does nothing.

The woman on the left then says, "I'm Bailey, this is Belle and M.K, we're sisters but without the blood ties."

"Pleasure to meet you. Parker Wilson." I shake Bailey and M.K's hand. But Belle is reluctant to reach out, when she finally does, I bring her hand to my lip. Her is soft like silk, for the first time she looks at me, she is trying to sum me up. She soon quits and yanks her hand away. Curiouser and curiouser.

I approach the bar with the ladies, "So what will you have?"

"A large whiskey on the rocks please." M.K answers.

"Southern Comfort with lemonade please." Bailey second.

"A bottle of Bulmer's pear cider." Belle now answers and has reverted back to no eye contact, "I feel like slumming it tonight." Her voice is as smooth as honey, she seems to have a softness to her tone, even if it is cold right now.

I don't know if 'slumming it' is her real intention, or if she is just saying that because she thinks I might not be able to afford her tastes, it is hard to tell whether she is being thoughtful or offensive. "Order anything you like, trust me honey I can afford it." I smile.

"I just did, a bottle of Bulmer's pear cider please." She sounds annoyed but sticks to her guns, I like that. Even though she is annoyed, you can't sense it in her tone.

"I am going to powder my nose." I hear Belle inform her friends. Bullshit, she is going to take a breather from me.

As soon as I get the drinks and they are set down on an empty table I say, "Excuse me, I am just going to use the restroom."

I then go off in pursuit of Belle.

Belle

Of all the nerve of that man, and Bailey I could kill her, 'Sure you can buy us all a drink, you are a total fucking stranger. But why the hell not?'

I wash my face with cold water, and give myself a mental pep talk. As soon as I feel composed, I go to leave the toilets, and only bump into the very man I came in to avoid.

"What the hell are you doing?" I try to be assertive, "This is the ladies." I remind him.

"Why are you uncomfortable?" Well he is direct, got to give him something for that. His voice is soft and even, but I can imagine it going very deep when he is angry, I have never known a man with the kind of voice you could fall asleep listening to.

"Because you are in the ladies bathroom, holding me hostage." I answer coldly.

"Ha hostage I like that, allow me to elaborate, you can't bear to look at me, but then when I kissed your hand you were curious, so you looked at me until I looked at you, then you didn't look at me again, you even snatched your hand away as if my touch burned you. And now you are gripping the sink because your legs feel like jelly."

I had no idea I was gripping the sink. God what is he doing to me, I only know him through his pictures, "You work for my step mother." I say matter of factly, it is a weak excuse though.

"So what?" He retorts.

"She could have sent you to spy on me. She is always trying to tarnish my reputation, not that I need help with that."

"There is more to it than that. You feel it too, the attraction, it is like a magnet, you don't want it, but it is there, like or not."

"I feel nothing." I argue and lie.

"Oh really?" He challenges, "Well then what would you do if I were to do this…" He takes my arms and pulls me into a nearby cubicle, he keeps his hands on my arms and kicks the door closed.

But I am silent, I don't even yelp, I had no idea a man could be so gentle, it is the kind of gentleness I crave, I look in his eyes, they are intense but he is calm.

"If you felt nothing you wouldn't have let me do this to you, you would have protested, my grip on you is light, you can leave any time you want, you are choosing to stay. What if I did this?" He goes to kiss me, and fuck I get ready to kiss him back, when nothing happens I open my eyes, he is serious, "I will kiss you, and you will know it is coming. Your friends will be wondering where we are, so best get back out there."

He then just leaves the toilet like nothing happened. What the hell was that? I get my bearings and steel myself for seeing him. Two can play at that game.

Parker

She didn't shudder at my touch that I didn't imagine. She didn't hesitate when I was going to kiss her, she was going to kiss me back. That I didn't imagine either. Our encounter has not only made me certain of our attraction it has made me very certain that it's very mutual.

Belle O Neil wants me as much as I want her. I go to my friends, "Sorry guys love calls." Is all I say as I walk off.

I blend into the crowd so that they can't see where I'm going, but I meant what I said, in a sense at least.

As I get to Bailey and M.K all I can say is, "Sorry ladies, I got caught up, being one of the most attractive men in London has it's downfalls."

"It's cool, drink up it's my round." M.K drawls, she is still being standoffish with me, I know she is only involving me in the round because it's the polite thing to do.

Soon Belle re-joins the group, she is quick to down her drink, "M.K put your money away, I will get this round." She relays what we all had and even orders me a drink. "And a shot of vodka please." She finishes. She doesn't even look at me when she passes me my drink.

As soon as she gets her vodka she downs it, "Another, however many I can get with this." She orders the barmaid, flinging her a five pound note. The barmaid gives her two shots of vodka, and Belle adds the change to the tip jar, and downs both the shots in less than ten seconds.

"Whoa Belle slow down." Bailey exclaims, "Carry on like that we are going to wind up carrying you home."

"Somethings up." M.K concludes and then goes to talk to her friend, who is on a mission to get drunk as soon as possible.

Belle is ordering another drink when M.K steps up to her, I don't hear their exchange, but I do notice how intently M.K is listening when Belle is talking, when Belle's finished talking M.K kisses her cheek and whispers something in her ear.

She then breaks away from Belle to go to Bailey, who she tugs out of my earshot, but I know she is filling Bailey in on her talk with Belle, who is throwing down another shot.

"You might want to slow down." I tell her.

"Why don't you piss off?!" She snarls at me.

"A lady is not meant to swear."

"A gentleman is not meant to corner ladies in the toilets, yet you still did that."

"You made me forget myself. Usually I am a gentleman when it comes to women and ladies." I speak with absolute honesty and truth, I even feel the need to repeat, "You made me forget myself."

"Look Parker, you hardly know me, only M.K, Bailey and Nan know the real me, as for everyone else in London, including you. You know about what the papers and the magazines say about me. Let me guess you saw me here and thought easy pickings. Am I right?"

"Not at all I would never think that." Looking at her now I don't see a woman who is easy pickings, I see a woman who is shutting herself off from all but three people and I want to know why.

Soon M.K and Bailey are back, they are remaining close to Belle, "What do you want to do Belle?" M.K asks. Even Bailey is serious, they have gone into protective mode.

"Finish your drinks, if you want to get a bottle of wine or two, then they are on me. But can we leave please?"

"Yeah of course we can." M.K answers quickly.

"I will wait outside."

Before her friends could protest, about her leaving the bar on her own, she is already out of the door, with me in hot pursuit, I have a bit of time before they finish their drinks.

When I get outside, Belle is leaning back on the wall, she has her right thumb and forefinger on the bridge of her nose, she looks utterly shattered. Did I drain her that much?

I don't hesitate, I can't hesitate, "Alright for starters." She looks at me but there is nothing, no anger, there is nothing but a blank stare. What's wrong with her? "I don't see you as easy pickings, so get that ridiculous idea out of your head right now. I know I don't know you. I have no idea what I thought when I saw you, other than, all of those pictures I have seen in the papers and magazines, don't do you justice." She sighs deeply and gives me a weak smile, "You seem very sad Belle."

"You don't know me Parker." She reaffirms my words, "And trust me, you don't want to know me either." I can't work out if she is saying that for my own good or her own, it could be either or both.

Before I can respond M.K and Bailey come out, they are quick to get to Belle, all three of them politely say goodnight, then they all begin walking down the street, M.K has her left arm over Belle's shoulders, Belle has her arm around M.K's waist, Bailey has linked arms the other side of Belle.

I am not going to let this go, I'm determined to know the real Belle. I want to know everything about her. 'I will see you again.' Is my silent vow, to both myself and her. I know where she works, I will see her again.

Belle

We have just gotten home, and I feel so exhausted. How has one encounter with someone drained me so much? What the fuck is this feeling anyway? I became so overcome by need, it is like that feeling of burning desire just knocked the energy right out of me, I want that feeling again, but I am not too happy with the person providing it, Parker Wilson he is a child, he proved it tonight, he is immature, and thinks he can have any woman he wants, well he is not having me.

"Well that was an eventful evening." Bailey chirps.

"One word for it." M.K replies blandly.

"So he literally just dragged you into a cubicle in the ladies and went to kiss you?" Bailey asks again.

"Yes, and I was going to kiss him back, but then he stopped."

"Why did he stop?"

"I have no idea, but all I do know is I was going to kiss him back." I admit, not only to my friends but also to myself for the first time.

"You were going to kiss him back?" M.K asks shocked.

"Yes, and no before you ask, I have no idea what came over me, I just felt this wave of desire hit me like a truck, for a moment I wanted nothing but him, but then when he made it clear he wasn't going to kiss me, I just felt drained, like all of the energy had been sucked out of me, like it took everything I had to just want him."

"Oh fuck." Bailey muses.

"What?" I ask.

"Alright let's piece together the night, you stared each other out, he made you feel awkward, we both saw that, he obviously knew that, because he came sniffing round you after that, he then follows you into the ladies, drags you into a cubicle and goes to kiss you, he even looked worried when you were both outside. I think he was performing some kind of experiment and Belle you gave him the answer he wanted."

"Yeah well I am not too sure I got the answer I wanted, he is a child."

"He was actually named the most mature young adult in London, and that is not an easy title to gain." M.K informs me.

"Yeah well then he will have no problem finding another woman then will he?" I shrug.

"I think that is going to be a challenge for him babe, you didn't see the look in his eyes when you looked away."

Something in the way M.K made that statement makes me think that Parker is not going to be an easy man to avoid. But here is the million dollar question: Do I want to avoid him?

Chapter Three

I AM AT WORK, I did see Nan over the weekend. And we had a blast. But now it is Wednesday. I haven't seen hide nor hair of Parker Wilson since Friday night. I part of me feels relieved about that, the other part of me feels very disappointed.

I am minding my own business working away, when I hear my lift ding to say that there is someone coming in, there is only one person that I have given permission to come straight up, and not bother going to reception. And that is Nan.

I look towards the lift, and I see the woman herself stroll out of the lift, her short hair is wavy and white, I have her round golden eyes, oval jawline, thin lips with a natural redness, slightly curved nose, the only difference is, she has deeply set wrinkles, straight and ever so slightly round figure, she has on a long black dress.

"Nan!" I say standing up to go and greet her, "Why don't you get the receptionist call up and tell me you are here? You don't have to come up." I make sure I get to her as she is level with the sofa in my office.

"Belle O Neil you fuss too much." She says as we embrace, "You look just like your mother."

"And just like you." I muse, "Please sit down, I will go make coffee, stay where you are."

I go and pour coffee, "So what brings you here?" I ask when I make it back to her, with two cups of coffee in my hands.

"Have you had lunch?" She asks, her voice is a bit worn and frail, but the softness is still there.

"No not yet. Why do you ask?"

"Are you too posh to have dinner at Tesco Express with your old Nan?"

"I am never too posh to do anything with you Nan." I smile.

"Well then what do you say to dinner with me, when we have finished our coffee?"

"I can juggle some stuff and then I am all yours." I chirp.

"You work too hard." Nan scolds.

"Yes Nan you tell me that every time you see me."

"I don't like the man you are sleeping with." She retorts.

I look at her in awe, "How do you know...?" Then it hits me, "M.K told you about Fox."

"Yes she told me about Fox, of all the men, you had to pick a man who has done nothing but accept handouts."

"Do you know if he is married? He isn't telling me if he is."

"Oh him. No woman will keep him, he likes to own his women, which is why I am here, you need stay away from him." Nan warns me.

"I can't believe M.K came to you. God she is unbelievable." I moan I am so pissed off with her.

"No she is concerned. She is being a good sister." Nan sees Bailey and M.K as family as much as I do, "And she know that I wouldn't approve." She informs me.

"You never approve of the men I sleep with." Dejavu, I had the same conversation with M.K.

"That is because the men you sleep with are married and total and utter numpties."

I can't help but laugh at that, "Who says that word anymore?" I giggle. We finish our coffee, "Are we going for lunch then?"

Nan nods, we both stand, Nan links arms with me, we leave to go to Tesco Express for our dinner, it is not too far from my office, ten minutes in the car.

When we get there we go straight to the café, I grab a prawn mayonnaise sandwich, and Nan grabs a Caesar salad pot.

We go and sit down, "So how is business? You seem busy."

"Yeah, business is good, as long as people keep getting married, having birthdays, having kids and dying, then business will always be good." I reply.

"Oh Belle." Nan laughs, "The things you come out with."

I then laugh with her, I wasn't actually kidding, but it is good to see her laugh.

Then someone calls my name, as soon as I see him approaching in an all-black suit, I tense up right away, but not in the way I imagined, I am both maddened and happy to see him, I have been dreading seeing him, but at the same time hoping to see him, Parker Wilson.

"Who is that?" Nan asks.

"Parker Wilson." I sigh.

"Oh wow he is good looking and clearly likes you. You have not slept with him as well have you?"

"What? Nan no I have not."

"Well then this one wants to date you, court you, woo you. You should let him."

"Alright Nan shh, before he hears."

Parker

I was minding my own business, I walked into Tesco Express with a clear idea of what I wanted, when I heard someone shrill the name Belle, I turn to the direction in which the sound came from, she is so beautiful, the laugh is a smooth as her voice, the look in her eyes screams love.

I call out her name and approach, I can't help it, I need to meet the person that caused that wonderful look on her face and in her eyes.

The grey skirt suit Belle has on hugs her figure well and screams success.

As soon as she looks up and sees it was me that called her name and that I am approaching she tenses up, I notice that some words are exchanged, then they change the subject, to the upcoming event Belle is planning.

"Ladies." I notice the woman is what Belle will probably look like in fifty years' time, "Let me guess, Belle's Nan? I would have said Mum, but I know the sad truth behind those circumstances."

"Yes she is my granddaughter, she calls me Nan. Everyone else calls me Evelyn. Never Mrs O Neil."

"Pleasure to meet you. Belle you look very lovely today."

"Thank you Mr Wilson." She is trying to be official.

"Parker." I correct, "Mr Wilson is too official for you Belle." She glances up at me, only because she knows I am staring at her, but I can't help it.

"Please do sit down." Evelyn insists.

I don't hesitate, feigning clumsiness, so I move my chair closer to Belle, if I was any closer I would be on her lap, she has nowhere to go, she is right near the divider.

"So Parker, what do you do for a living?"

"Well for now I am a model, I have been for about ten years, my contract runs out when I turn twenty four, where I plan on using my money to open my own hotel." I inform.

"How old are you now?"

"I'm twenty." I answer honestly.

"Young AND ambitious. Had made his own money." She says to Belle, eyes wide and gloating.

"Yes Nan, I have ears and they work just fine." She retorts.

"She is a cheeky one. How do you know my granddaughter?" Ahh the meet the family interrogation, I expected it.

"We met on Friday night, we were both out with friends. So we have not known each other for very long, but I am trying to be friends." I stroke her leg.

She stands up, "Did you want to do some shopping Nan?"

Her Nan is confused but says, "Yes I do need to grab some bits. Would you like to join us Parker?"

"Yes, yes I would." Anything to spend more time with Belle.

"I will grab a trolley." Her Nan says.

"No Nan you finish your lunch, sorry I didn't mean to rush you." She kisses her Nan's cheek, "You with me."

I follow her as she demanded, "You love your Nan." I state.

"Yes I do, and I have just been incredibly rude to her, something that I never do. Friends?! And do not do that again." She is seething mad, but manages to keep her voice cool and even. Does she ever shout?

"I plan on doing more than just touching your leg Belle. And if I wanted, I could make you beg for my touch."

"I beg for nothing. What the hell are you doing?"

"Well I was doing a bit of shopping, but I got distracted by a beautiful woman." I stroke a finger down her cheek.

"You need to stop." She demands.

"Why? Do you not like tenderness? Do you not like being treated the way you deserve?" I take her hand, "I want to treat you the way you deserve to be treated. And I want you to let me."

"I can shop on my own if you two want to sneak off." A voice says from behind us.

Belle snatches her hand away and looks at her Nan, "No Nan I have already been rude to you once, I am not doing it again."

Her Nan strokes her cheek, "Oh darling you are forgiven for that. I'll forgive you for anything." She then looks at me, then back at Belle, "So you are not a couple then?"

"I am trying to be." I declare, "I would like to date your granddaughter."

"I think you would be the best decision my granddaughter has ever made."

"Hello I am right here you know." She sputters.

"And hopefully you are listening." Her Nan replies.

I walk ahead with her Nan, Belle hangs back, this really is a family meet and greet, it went very well...for me, I have Evelyn's approval, and I am not even dating Belle...yet.

"Would you object to me sharing your trolley Evelyn? My items will fit in the smaller compartment of the trolley."

"Of course you can. Belle stop dawdling." I look back to see her walking with arms crossed, with a look of awe on her face, she is surprised her Nan has taken to me so quickly.

I walk to her and speak in a hushed tone, "Look I get this isn't an ideal situation for you, but it is for me. I want to know you, to date you. I meant it when I said that."

"Would you like to have dinner with us at some point Parker?" Her Nan asks.

I look at Belle, she is pleading with her eyes that I say no. "Of course Evelyn, I can think of nothing else I would rather do, than have a meal with two beautiful women."

Belle

I am officially in hell. Are you serious? He has agreed to have dinner with me and Nan? He hardly knows Nan, he hardly knows me and I hardly know him. And Nan should know a damn sight better at her age, inviting a stranger for dinner. Is she insane?

I just stare blankly at the shelf before me, "You're shaking." His hot breath on the back of my neck, makes me swoon mentally, I am so glad I have enough will power to not do it for real.

"Trying not to kill you. Of all the things to agree to, it had to be dinner with Nan." I am seething mad.

"Correction, you and your Nan. How many more time Belle? I want to know you, so if that means dinner with your Nan then I will do it." He puts his hands on my hips, "Anything to be close to you."

"You don't know me Parker." I try and stay calm.

"But I am planning on knowing you Belle, everything about you. That is a promise."

"You might not like what you uncover."

"What I don't like, I will accept, but I know enough, you affairs are the worst thing you have done, unless there is something else the papers, magazines and tabloids haven't documented, but that is something I highly doubt."

Dammit the affairs are the worst thing I have done, there is nothing else, and he still wants to know me.

"The silence speaks volumes."

"You don't know my reason for them. That could change your mind about me." I hope it does, "You have not heard how I justify having them. That could also change your mind about me."

"I will be the judge of that, just give me a chance."

"You're not going to stop are you?"

"You want the truth? No Belle I'm not, not until you give me a fair chance."

He is going to wear me down, until I have no choice but to let him in. Do I tell him about Fox Mason? Will he even care about him being in the picture? I don't even notice his hand on my back, because of my daydream. But yet when I do, I don't flinch away, his gentle touch baffles me, no man has ever been so gentle with me, not even my own father.

"You do want me Belle, you want to date me, you want to get to know me, you just don't want to want to. Sometimes you just have to give yourself what you don't want to want."

"You aren't going to let me have the deprivation and that is what you think I am doing, depriving myself of what you offer." The fucking bighead really thinks he is something special.

"I know I confuse you, you have slept with rough men that much I can tell, you had bruises on your wrists Friday night, rough bastard you were with, I don't like the thought of you seeing him again." He says.

"We're not even going out, and yet you are ordering me around."

"Not ordering, I said I don't like the idea, I know you are going to because you want to try and get whatever you feel for me out of your system. But when you are with me, and I do mean when, you will get rid of the rough bastard."

"Depends on how good you are in bed." I say cockily.

"I will be like no one you have ever had." He matches my cocky tone.

"I will hold you to that."

"So does this mean you are going to sleep with me at some point?"

"Look Parker contrary to popular belief, I am not easy, you have made it perfectly obvious you want to date me, I am not going to lie, you are attractive, and baffling, I have to give you props for effort and persistence. So if it goes well, then a relationship requires a good physical connection. So yes if it goes well, I will sleep with you, but it will take time." And a goodbye fucking from Fox.

"Good I like a challenge." He kisses my cheek, how I wish it was my lips.

"So is everything official then?" Nan asks.

"Nothing is official as of yet Nan, I have agreed to what Parker has asked, and that is to give him a chance, there is still a long way to go."

We then carry on shopping, I fail to relax the entire time Parker is around me, he makes me buzz with awkwardness and anticipation I have no idea what to make of the way he makes me feel, it is so hard for me, I am not used to feeling anything especially towards me. Fucking that is what I am good at, that is what I know, and the mindless care free nothingness that comes with it.

Parker Wilson is a shock to my system, and if everything goes well with him, then he will rock it to its core.

Chapter Four

S O I AM ON MY way to see Fox Mason, I have had a tough
morning and usually an encounter with him helps, so after
calling ahead to make sure he is home and up for it, I am at his
house, in a tight black pencil dress, I knock on his door, and he
wastes no time grabbing me roughly and kissing the life out of me.

He guides me back into the kitchen, where he roughly turns me
round and bends me over his kitchen table, I hear him undo his
trousers, and feel him roughly pull my lace panties down.

As soon as they are down far enough, he drives into me hard,
causing me to scream, he barks like a man possessed as he keeps up
the merciless pounds, "Oh fuck!" I scream, as he pounds into me
again, "Jesus!" His grip on my hips and thighs is a fierce one.

After a few more merciless, ruthless and possessive pounds, I
scream as I climax.

He still keeps up the pounds until he climaxes, and when he
does he roars, "Fuck!" He drives himself deeper and deeper, until he
has nothing left to give, then he collapses on top of me.

As soon as I catch my breath, I push him off me, pull up my
panties and go to leave, "Are you not even going to stay for a coffee
or something?"

"Do you ever stay for a drink? You know how this works, we call
to see when one of us is free and meet up for a fuck, then we go our
separate ways. Or have you forgotten that?"

"How could I forget? You make it so obvious that is what you
want."

I don't want what he has to offer anymore, seeing him has only made my day tougher, "Well then maybe I had better stop being so damn predictable, pull up your pants Fox you look pathetic."

I then walk out of his house and go back to work, M.K and Bailey are both in my office when I get there.

M.K has on a pair of black trousers, with a white long sleeve blouse.

Bailey has on a light blue denim dress.

"There is a fucking limp this time. Fuck Belle he is getting worse with you. Pull up your dress." M.K orders.

"M.K I am not going to pull up my dress."

"Belle we have seen you in your underwear for Christ sake, just pull your dress up." Bailey says softly.

"Or do we have to do it for you?" M.K threatens.

Knowing that she will in fact do that, I just do as she asks and lift up my dress, I then also see that my hips and thighs are badly bruised.

M.K is riled up further, "Fuck sake Belle, it looks like you have been raped!"

"It does look bad Belle, if Nan sees she is going to flip." Bailey adds.

"Don't either of you tell her."

"She will not hear it from either of us, if you bin him." M.K demands threateningly.

"Oh so you don't like him, so you resort to blackmail. That is real smooth M.K."

"Yeah, yeah I am blackmailing you Belle, but this I am doing for your own good. Bailey get her a hot water bottle and a coffee." She then walks out.

"Where the hell is she going?"

"Don't ask me, you know what M.K is like, she is either going to stew or smack Fox. And as much as I would love for someone to smack that bastard, I don't want M.K to be the one to do it, because knowing M.K, she will not stop at one hit, not after seeing the state you came back in." Even Bailey is mad and it takes a hell of a lot to make Bailey mad.

Parker

So I am at the studio, doing a shoot I have on a tuxedo, doing various poses that make me look official.

Scarlet Hawthorn is the one taking the pictures, she has had a thing for me for a while, she is pretty, but people who rely on their Mummy for support are not my type, with strawberry blonde frizzy hair that sits below her shoulders, deep set light brown eyes, oblong jawline, big full lips, upturned nose, she is skinny and borderline anorexic, she is wearing a royal blue low cut dress, that sits just above her knees, she is giving me the eye like always.

We all hear a door open, M.K is striding towards me, in a pair of tight black trousers, and a white long sleeve blouse, "What the hell are you doing here?" Scarlet scowls at M.K.

"Oh keep your knickers on." M.K barks with the same contempt. "Parker a word please."

That is the nicest she has ever spoken to me, almost pleading, her tone alone has me saying, "Yeah sure thing." We walk a safe distance away.

"Look Belle's told me what you said about wanting to date her. Does that still stand?"

"Yeah, yeah it does."

"Please make it soon."

"Why? Has something happened?" I put my hands on her arms and notice she is shaking, "M.K you're trembling. Tell me. What's happened?" I'm almost pleading now.

"He's hurting her, Fox I mean. She's acting like it is normal, but you didn't see the bruises he gave her today. Parker, if you care about her, then help her, show her a different way, because I am close to killing the bastard."

I feel myself go rigid with anger, but I keep my cool, I take out my card from inside my jacket pocket, "Here is my card. What time does Belle finish work today?"

"Four."

"I will be there, don't tell her."

"Here is my card." She pulls it out of her pocket, and gets a pen out of her other pocket, for a pissed off woman, she thinks of everything, she takes hold of my hand, "Belle's number, do not let her see it." She looks over at Scarlet, "Someone has the hots for you." She smiles.

"Has done for years, not my type, I am a one woman man, and I am hoping to make Belle that woman."

"I hope she lets you." M.K then leaves.

Belle's Nan and both of her friends like me and think I would be good for Belle, now she just has to believe it.

Right I am not fucking about now, if that bastard is hurting Belle then I am getting her away from him, otherwise it is not M.K that needs to worry about killing him. I just might.

I have on my best suit, it is a charcoal black Armani suit, I have a black tie with it. Belle is finishing at 4:00, and it is 3:30, her office is about fifteen minutes from my apartment block, I am making my way to her now, I want to get there early in case Belle leaves earlier than M.K anticipated. Or in case M.K's loyalty to her friend makes her change her mind, and she tells Belle what she has done.

I'm not a slow walker, I am used to being hounded by people so I used my quick stride, to get to the places I need to be, I am not one to stroll or meander. I am also eager to get to Belle, just in case she plans on seeing that bastard Fox after work. Also I did think the next time I was going to see her, would be across a dinner table with her Nan, so I am glad to be seeing her sooner, I quickly call M.K, "I'm on my way." Is all I say, I don't give her a chance to speak. She will only be telling me I am too early. I already know that.

I don't care, she could be hurt right now, and not for the first time because of that bastard, I AM going to show her a better way.

I walk into her building M.K is already there, she looks pissed, "Are you trying to make my life difficult? She will know that she has been set up."

"Now she will not, because you are not going to tell her, you did not see me at work today, and you seem clever enough to be able to think of a reason for you absence. Now just get me to her office."

"Alright this way Mr Wilson, I will talk you through you options."

We get into the lift, M.K pushes the button for her floor and for Belle's, "The lift goes straight up to her office."

"Did you come straight back here after speaking with me?"

"Yeah why?"

"Only you seemed mighty angry, and you are prone to hitting people that hurt Belle."

"I saw you, came back here. I didn't seek out Fox, or try to." She then huffs, "Alright a lie, I did try and hunt Fox down, but I didn't find him, then I came back here."

"I have no intention of hurting Belle, I don't know what it is about her, but you don't have to worry."

"You are the first man to say that and me actually believe them, this is my floor. Good luck." She almost smiles at me, as she gives my arm a friendly pat.

The lift then shuts, I hate lifts they are too congested even when no one is in them.

After an eternity the lift opens, I step out of it and into Belle's office, her head snaps from her work to me, "What the hell are you doing here?" Her tone is sharp but it is more from shock I think.

She looks lovely in her tight black pencil dress that shows off a bit of cleavage. I hope she didn't wear that for the scumbag that fucks her so viciously he marks her.

"I have come to take you on a date." I declare.

"A bit short notice."

"Why do you have plans?" I challenge.

"No." Her honesty shocks me, "But I am not dressed for a date."

"Belle a bin liner would look amazing on you. What you have on is fine, I will wait for you to finish."

She then hits me with suspicious eyes, "How did you know what time I finish Parker?"

"I didn't. Why is it soon? Because I don't mind waiting if I have to, I have nothing pressing on."

Again with the suspicious eyes, "As a matter of fact, for today I am done. So I am all yours."

How I wish that were true. She shuts down her computer, switches off her lights, gets her bag and makes her way towards me, we both turn to leave.

"So busy day?"

"A little bit. I saw Fox this afternoon." Now I am really surprised by her honesty, but it does explain M.K's urgency when she came to see me earlier, she is hurt right now.

"We were not officially dating this afternoon, this is a date Belle." I quickly remind.

"I know you told me to expect one, I am not going to lie, affairs, fucking married men is all I know, so I have no clue what I am doing." Wow she is being quite open.

"What you're doing is fine. And the rest of your day?"

"Busy, I had to oversee a wedding this morning, a politicians daughter married a marine, the event was held at Westminster Abbey, so they had money to burn and even more money to line the business and my pockets, the staff can expect a hefty bonus this year for the money this event brought in alone."

I would not have pegged her for the type to give out bonuses.

"And how was your day?" She asks.

"Good, I did a shoot, I am doing an interview for Cosmopolitan magazine in a few weeks so Imelda wanted a few shots of me doing what I do best."

"Scarlet still her photographer?"

"Yeah she is good at what she does, so is Dylan."

"Shame about their mother."

M.K then comes into the lift, "Oh I didn't know you had an appointment Parker."

"He didn't. He is taking me on a date." She acknowledges it is a date, progress already.

"Oh right cool, just so you know, if you hurt her, I will make your life a living nightmare." She jabs a finger into my chest, but I know she is doing it for show.

"I wouldn't dream of it, I plan on treating Belle the way she deserves to be treated." I put my left hand on the centre of her back, and she trembles. Damn! There goes that curiosity again. Is it want or nerves? I would love to find out.

The lift door opens and we step out, "Alright kids have fun." M.K says as she approaches Bailey, who has on a light blue denim dress, "Belle has a date with Parker."

"Oh I hope it goes well." She chirps.

We then go on our way. "So where are we going?" She enquires.

"We are going to a place called Clarks, it is a quaint little restaurant, you will like it."

I take hold of her hand and interlink our fingers, at first she is tense, but she doesn't try to let go. Soon she just relaxes.

Belle

This is nice, walking hand in hand with someone, his hand is soft, warm and gentle, which considering he is quite muscular, I am shocked by his tenderness, and we walk in a comfortable silence.

We walk into the restaurant, Parker is right it is a quaint but very nice place, "My family come here quite a lot, my Dad is the editor of the Daily Mirror, my Mum is a new reporter for the BBC, but she had to take a little break."

"Oh nothing health related I hope." I say with concern.

"Oh no not exactly, we had an unexpected little sister, let's just sat my Mum wasn't expecting to be pregnant at forty four."

"Oh, how did your father react to that?"

"He was ecstatic, of course it came a bit of a shock to him, but with three children all grown up and moved out, one child on his way to university in a couple of years, I honestly struggled to imagine that house without a child in it, if I struggled to imagine that, I have no idea how my parents felt."

We go to an empty table, Parker pulls out my chair and I sit down, Parker sits opposite me, and puts his right hand at the centre of the table, "Tell me about your family please." I ask putting my elbows on the table, and placing my chin on the back of my hands.

"Hold my hand Belle, it is why it is there." I do as he asks with no hesitation. Why does he have to be so easy to be with? I don't want to want him, but I can't help but want him, he obliges me and tells me about his family, "There is my Dad Joel, he is an older version of me, the men look like the men, the women look like the women, well that is with exception to Jack, he is Ashley's twin, so he favours my Mum in looks, my Mum is called Catherine, but people call her Caty, she's forty six, erm rusty brown hair, these light blue eyes that are big and kind, she is the best woman I know, then there is Ashley, she's twenty six, she trained to be an interior and exterior designer, and a carpenter, she is multi-talented, but she's a cop, the protector of the family so to speak, she is always there in time of need, then there is Jack, he is two minutes younger than Ashley, he's been away for five years training to be a doctor, his training finishes in a couple of months, then there is Julian, he's fourteen, computer nerd, he is going to be an amazing Computer Forensic Scientist one day, but last but most certainly not least, there is Skyla, she is the life and soul of the party now she is in her terrible two's, she is driving my poor Mum mad."

He speaks of his family with such a fondness, you can tell they are close, I would have loved to have had that growing up.

"Are you ready to order?" A young waitress asks.

"Oh we haven't even looked at the menu yet." I respond shocked, usually I talk and look at the menu, but Parker had my full attention.

"How about a bottle of champagne? By the time you come back we will be ready to order." Parker suggests.

"Sorry sir, I have to ask. Do you have any ID on you?"

"Yes of course." He takes out his wallet, and shows the waitress.

"Very good sir." She hands it back to him.

"I feel a little insulted." I say when she is gone, "Surely I don't look that old."

"Not old enough to be twenty five, but old enough to look over eighteen, plus the last time you were on the news, they gave away your age. Regardless you look beautiful, I say again photographs don't do you any justice. I prefer the real thing."

What a charmer. "Thank you. So what do you recommend to have off the menu?" I ask Parker, "I have never been here before."

"Ok brutal honesty, I only come here because the braised lamb with roasted vegetables is to die for, it is my favourite meal. What's your favourite?"

"Oh now there is a question, now see I love to cook, I have even started writing down new recipes."

"No kidding, I thought you would have your own cook." He is genuinely shocked.

"You're not the first person to be shocked, but I did have a cook growing up, and it was so annoying, not being able to go into my own kitchen, my house has no boundaries, people can go where they like, M.K and Bailey even go into my bedroom while I am asleep, because the balcony outside my room leads to the kitchen."

"Wow that is trust."

The champagne then comes, "Have you decided on your meals?"

"Yes I would like the braised lamb with roasted vegetables."

"I will have the same please." Parker pours out the champagne, "Just the one for me, I'm driving."

"That's fair enough. You never did tell me what your favourite meal is."

"No I didn't sorry it's a French dish, Tartiflette, all it is, is French bacon, potato and reblochon all put into a casserole, Nan showed me the recipe, it is the first meal I ever learnt to cook."

Parker suddenly goes seriously, "Oh no, I am so sorry, I had no idea."

"What?" Now I'm nervous.

The reason for his sudden change in demeanour becomes clear, a woman with rusty brown pony tail that sits just above the centre of her back, big round blue eyes, more intense than kind, with a tight triangle jawline, slightly pointed nose, her lower lip is thing than her upper lip, her figure is hard to tell with her uniform on, but she is about five foot eight.

"Brother dearest, long time no see. Care to introduce?" Her voice is a bit husky, but her tone cool.

"Three days is not a long time. I am on a date, a first date so don't scare her off. Belle this is my sister Ashley. Ashley, Belle O Neil."

"As in old police commissioner's daughter?" I nod, "Oh belated condolences for your loss, your father is the reason I became a cop."

"Thank you that means a lot." I hold out my hand in a friendly gesture, which she takes, "I am happy to meet Parker's older sister, he has just been telling me about his family, you are the protector."

"That I am. Parker you need to bring Belle to dinner, before Mum and Dad find out about your girlfriend through other sources, you know what the press can be like."

She then walks off, "Girlfriend? Is that what I am?"

"I would say so yeah, you have held my hand twice, we are drinking champagne, going to enjoy a nice meal, have a good talk. Would you like to call this what it is? Would you like to be my girlfriend?" Oh wow never in a million years did I ever think I would have to consider this question.

"Yes and yes. This is a date, and I would like to be your girlfriend very much."

He takes hold of my right hand, and puts it to his lips, "You have just made my day."

"Here is your food guys." The waitress declares.

We both thank her and begin our meal, "So tell me about your family." Parker suggests.

"There is not much to tell, it is just Nan, M.K and Bailey. You have not only met them, but you have seen how close we are."

"What about life growing up?"

"Again not much to tell. My Mum took care of me until I was old enough to go to boarding school, which is where I met M.K and Bailey, we roomed together, my Mum carried on doing her acting, but she got ill when I was thirteen, so she had me come back home, she wanted me close, so she had me home schooled, after Nan taught me my first dish, I said fine I will come home, but on the condition I learnt how to cook, she agreed. We grew closer, I took care of her until her death."

Parker

She is so used to having a poker face, everything she is telling me is with no emotion at all, she speaks about the way she took care of her mother until her death, as if she is describing a bad day at work. It is only until I look in her eyes and see that in them she has so much emotion, that I realise she is so used to hiding emotion, she has forgotten how to express it. I need to show her.

"Where was your father?"

"Work, someone had to bring in the money, even though I took majority care of my Mum, we still had nurses to pay, my Dad hired privately. When my Mum died though my Dad quit policing after thirty five years, and then he became the best event planner in London it only took him five years, people expected it to take him longer, but he was only in event planning seven years then he died. But in the process of doing that he found a second family, your boss and her kids."

There is nothing but utter contempt in her eyes, "You really hate them don't you?" I ask.

"Believe me or not, I did try and be friendly, but after four years of being made to unwelcome and unwanted in your own home, it got real old real quick."

There is more but she is not going into it, "That must have hurt your feelings."

She scoffs, "Not after I stopped giving a shit, if I cried they laughed, if I pleaded or even begged, they'd think it was hilarious, Imelda's contempt for me grew, when my father left everything to me, so Imelda tries to ruin me. Her snivelling brats help her, but soon come crawling to me for handouts when Mummy doesn't pay out." They made her this cold hearted person, part of me hates them for that.

"Do you ever give in to them?"

Now she actually laughs, it is a fake and sarcastic laugh, I would love to hear the real thing, "Yeah right, they spend their whole lives abusing me, if I give them money, they will be nice, because effectively I have bought them, give people like them handouts, they will keep coming back for more."

"You really don't like them." I state.

"The version of them you see, and the version I LIVED with are two totally different things, who knows maybe I do really bring out the worst in people. Parker you have their respect because you are their best worker, but if they were to hear you were on a date with me, your life would be made really difficult."

"Why come then? And why agree to be my girlfriend?"

"Curiosity got the better of me. As for the girlfriend thing, I urge you Parker reconsider. If you value your career stay away from me. I don't want to be the reason for your ruin."

She is genuinely scared. But is it for me or herself?

"And if I think you are worth the ruin?"

"Then you are stupid, I hurt people, I wreck families, and even knowing all of this. You still want me?"

"Yes Belle I do, I have no idea why, but I do."

"Then I pity you Parker, because nothing can save you if you make this decision. But me and that is what I am doing."

She then gets up to leave, oh no it is not ending like that, I never had Belle down as a women who runs. Emotionally yes, physically no.

Belle

It was going too well, I not only enjoyed his company, I opened up to him a little too much. Why? I hardly know him, Fox never generated these feelings, and we were having sex, Parker has barely touched me, and my mind is fucked right up. Well at least I had a taste of a normal relationship even if that is all it was, just a little taste.

I am half expecting the hands when they touch my shoulders, of course he was not going to make this easy.

I wasn't even surprised when his hand ventured down my arm to claim my hand. But what I wasn't expecting was him to pull me into an alley, and kiss me, with his right hand on my cheek,

and his left hand on the small of my back, it is a new but telling kiss, he makes sure it burns with passion, by biting down on my bottom lip and grazing his teeth along, then after giving a satisfied murmur, he changes the gear to soft and gentle, fuck he makes me feel, horny, wanted, safe and loved all at the same time.

Parker

I didn't intend to kiss her, but I am so glad I did, she didn't fight me off, she fell into the kiss, wait no it was more like she floated into it actually, she tastes like honey, she even puts her hands on my sides and presses her body onto mine, "Do I look like I care about my career?" I challenge when I pull out of the kiss.

"You lied." She says plainly.

"What?"

"When we first met and you cornered me in the toilets, you said that I would know you were going to kiss me, I had no idea that was coming."

I chuckle my hands are still are on her cheek and back, "You will know the next time I kiss you, I promise."

"Do you want a lift home? It has been a long old day."

Her offer shocks me, "If you don't mind."

"I asked didn't I?" She chuckles, "Where do you live?"

"The new apartment blocks that overlook the river."

"Oh wow expensive, come on then, I know where that is."

I take hold of her hand, this time she doesn't even tense up, she is just content.

When we get to her car, I sputter with shock, "This is yours?"

"Yeah I can afford it." She shrugs.

"Clearly." I state.

"You just going to stand and admire it, or get in it?" She jokes as she approaches the door.

I climb into her car, "Please tell me you have reconsidered, your reconsideration about being my girlfriend."

"You really don't care about my step mother do you?" I still can't put my finger on if she is worried for me or for herself. Time to be blunt with her.

"No Belle I don't give a shit, I knew who you were when I asked you out. She will not sack me, even if she does I have enough money to begin my own business venture, which I told you about." I put my hand on her leg.

"Modelling has been your life Parker." She states as she starts driving me home.

"It was always going to be temporary Belle, in four years it is done anyway. I am rich now, I will be richer then. And hopefully I will have someone I can think of as home."

"That would be nice." She muses.

We could have that, I think to myself.

Too soon she pulls up outside my apartment block.

"Here we are." She chirps.

"Walk me to my door and kiss me goodnight Belle." I say softly.

She doesn't even give it any consideration, "Alright." She doesn't even hesitate getting out of her car.

She waits for me to join her and we walk hand in hand, as we walk to my door. She leans back on the wall, looks in my eyes, they are glowing, so shiny, so happy, I hope I am the reason, her gaze drops to my lips, and she bites her own. My blood boils. She is truly amazing.

She reaches out and takes hold of my tie, and pulls me to her for a long, passionate kiss, she keeps her hand on my shirt collar, I suddenly get why papers have deemed her the 'Queen of Seduction.' She knows exactly what to do with her tongue, she gently bites down on my bottom lip and even purrs her satisfaction into my mouth.

Fuck I want her right now, but I can't have her, not when there is evidence of that bastard Fox on her body.

Not wanting to break the contact yet, I put my hand on her hips. She winces and jerks away, I hurt her. How have I? I barely touched her. I kneel down to take a look, "No Parker don't." She says panicked.

"It's alright Belle." I reassure and lift up her dress her hips and thighs are badly bruised. "Fox did this to you?"

"He didn't rape me." She is quick to defend him, "He just likes it rough, that's all."

"You can have it rough and not leave marks on someone Belle." I straighten out her dress, and stand up, I am boiling mad, but I cannot show it, I cannot let her see it, I don't want to scare her away when this, whatever this is has barely begun.

I put my forehead on hers, "Please Belle I beg you, don't see him again. That is not normal, it might not be rape, but it is still abuse. Let me take you out again."

"Alright, when?"

"It will be soon, and where we go will be a surprise. In the meantime." I get my phone out of my pocket and call her number, her phone rings in her dress pocket, "You have my number, if you want to unwind call me, my apartment number is four one zero, so if you need to see me swing by."

"How did you get my number?"

"It is logged into Scarlet's phone." I lie, "Don't worry I deleted it after I stole it for myself."

"Good, thanks."

"No problem, now bid me goodnight and kiss me."

"Wow you are bossy." She jokes.

This time she wraps her arms around my shoulders, the kiss is tender, her mouth is warm, our tongues float by each other like two clouds in the sky, she reluctantly withdraws, and I mentally curse her for it.

"Goodnight Parker, I hope to see you soon."

"You will I promise, you know what to do in the meantime."

I then walk up to my empty apartment, in a sense it is big enough to be a bungalow as you walk in, you see a light brown floor and red walls, it is the same floor and walls in every room, on my walls there are pictures me with my family, or just of my family either individually or together. As soon as you walk in you are in a big fancy lounge, which is equipped with a grey velvet box sofa, which if two want to lounge and watch a movie then they can, but it is big enough for five people, with speakers and a stereo built into the stereo, it makes it good for listening to music, and also there is a control panel, if you flick a switch it exposes fifty inch Panasonic TV mounted on the wall, there is also a coffee table a foot in front of the sofa.

On the wall behind the sofa is a book shelf with all kinds of books on law and business, especially to do with the hotel industry. Two feet left of the shelf is a door that leads to my bedroom and bathroom.

Straight ahead from the sofa is a huge doorway that leads to the kitchen, which holds all of the top of the range equipment.

I go into the my bedroom, with a big walk in wardrobe a black faux leather king size bed, with a bedside cabinet, there is a huge window that overlooks the river, something is missing, oh I know I should get a love seat just before the window, it would be nice to sit with someone I love looking over the river and watching the sunset, sharing a kiss or two.

I bought this place as soon as I could, I love it at first, now it is too empty, I need someone to share this with…Belle.

She kissed me, she wants me, she is my girlfriend, it is early days, but she is happy with the label, girlfriend I get my phone out of my pocket and text her, 'Thanks for the date, thinking of you. Goodnight Belle x.'

I then call my brother Jack, "Hey bro."

"Hey bro how is everything going?"

"Everything is going fine thanks mate, how is everything your end?"

"Everything is great, I have just been on a date."

"Oh yeah, who with?"

"Belle O Neil."

"As in had countless affairs, broke up countless marriages and families, that Belle O Neil?"

"Yes bro that Belle O Neil."

"Well fuck bro, you sure as hell know to pick them."

"I am going to marry her." I smile.

"Well Jesus, I will have to be there for that."

Belle

I have just got home, oh wow what a huge day this has been, I have gone from being someone's rough fuck, to being someone's girlfriend, and he is younger than me, but he is so mature, he has so much ambition and he is so gentle, so tender, so easy to be with, even seeing me hurt, also hurt him. And boy he tastes heavenly and smells just as good.

I wish he had of invited me up to his apartment, but he has promised to take me out again. He asked me out, to be his girlfriend.

As I walk in my phone goes off, it is him, 'Thank you for the date, thinking of you. Goodnight x.'

I walk into the lounge, there is two of the finest King Louis loungers with floral patterns and gold frames, there are coffee tables a foot in front of each lounger, there is a fire place on the back wall again King Louis with a gold frame, there are pictures of M.K, Bailey, Nan and I, either all of us together or of each of us with Nan.

Both M.K and Bailey are in their lounge clothes.

M.K has on a grey vest top with shorts of a darker shade.

Bailey is in a pink nighty, which has a cat yawning on the front with the word, 'A yawn is a silent scream for coffee.'

M.K is curled up on the sofa reading a book.

Bailey has her feet up on the sofa and is working on her laptop.

M.K looks up from her book, "Hey how was the date?"

Even Bailey looks up from her laptop and after seeing the grin on my face, she puts it on the coffee table in front of her.

Because I feel all happy and light, I go and sit with Bailey lift her legs up so I can sit down, and put her legs on my legs.

"This is certainly no encounter with Fox." M.K muses, "Come on tell us."

"It was so nice, we spoke of family, he bought champagne, we had a lovely meal, I agreed to be his girlfriend, I had a wobble, tried to run, he caught me, he kissed me, I drove him home, he asked me to walk him to his door and kiss him goodnight, I didn't want it to end, but he touched my hips, saw the bruises, I am not seeing Fox again. I am with Parker, he even text to say he is thinking of me."

"So you have a boyfriend?" M.K muses, "Thank fuck for that, I am happy for you Belle, really he is a good guy."

"Yeah he really is, I want to see him again." I admit.

"I am happy for you, but Fox is going to be pissed off." Bailey says.

"I will handle him, he will not get near." M.K puts in.

"No it is alright we had a row before I left, so I am not expecting to hear from him."

"Let's hope you are right. Now as for Parker, do not let him do all of the hard work, he took you out on a date, next you take him on one." M.K advises.

"Alright I will."

Chapter Five

Parker

I WAKE UP AFTER DREAMING of Belle, as I have done every night since our first date, I have not seen her in a few days. I am worried she has gone back to that bastard Fox, but then I remember, I have heard nothing from M.K, I am sure she would have texted or called if Belle had of gone back to him.

It feels like forever since we touched and kissed.

I can't think about that now, I have to model a new suit for Armani in a couple of hours on a big catwalk in Chelsea, I wonder what the companies are thinking paying shitloads of money to wear a suit for a few minutes, but you know more money for me. With a bank account approaching the five million mark, I could have afforded to turn it down, but I would have gotten too much hassle from Imelda.

The good thing is a lot of the top modelling gigs are held in London, my career has taken me to Wales, Scotland, New York, California, Miami, Spain, Italy, France and Australia.

All of that is done now, I look around my big empty apartment. I wish I had someone to share all of this with, which if everything goes alright with Belle then I will have her, granted she is rich in her own right.

I just want someone to hold at night, to tell them I love them, and for them to say it back, I want to have kids with someone one day, it is too early to say I see that kind of future with Belle, but I do want to see that future with her.

She turned my life upside down when I saw her, there has to be a reason she has been all I can think about since I saw her.

I just meander through my day, get up, showered and dressed, going for smart/casual as usual going for a pair of dark blue jeans and a white t-shirt, I will go and look after Skyla for a bit, and do a bit of shopping.

Then I will head to the studio knowing that Imelda will be there to meet me and we will take a limo to my shoot.

I am beginning to hate routine.

Well no tell a lie I am beginning to hate my routine, I want to add, wake up to someone I love to my routine, I want to add, spend time with someone I love to my routine, I want to add love to my routine.

Belle

Taking on board what M.K said to me about making as much effort for Parker as he does for me, I decide to check my diary and find that my day finishes at 5:00, my last client is at 4:00.

I also check the studio website to find that ironically Parker finishes work at 5:30, he is doing a shoot in Chelsea, if I go straight to the studio from work. It is walking distance and I will be discreet, I hope to keep our relationship as low key as possible, for now anyway, I don't want my step mother and her brats finding out about us yet, it will only make his life hard. I don't want that. He is the first decent man I have met.

I have booked a reservation at Medlar for 6:00, it is my favourite place to eat, I have been thinking about it since our first date.

I have gone for a long royal blue dress that shows off a little cleavage and hugs my figure nicely.

My phone rings, it is Nan, "Hey Nan what's up?"

"Hello dear, I was wondering if you wanted to grab something to eat later." She chirps in her constantly cool tone.

"Oh I can't tonight, how about tomorrow?"

"Of course, although I do hope the reason for you not meeting me tonight, is because you are resting and not working from home, or seeing a certain undesirable gentleman."

"I am seeing Parker." Shit I forgot to tell Nan I had a date with him a few nights ago, "Nan I am really sorry. But it is the second time I am seeing him. He took me out a few nights ago."

"Oh don't apologise, however I must now ask. When are you going to bring that dashing young man to dinner?" God I love her, I smile to myself.

"Nan we have barely been seeing each other a week. What's the rush?"

"You're right, take your time, I would prefer it to be before I am dead."

"Nan!" I laugh, "You will outlive me."

"I will let you go dear, enjoy your date." She then hangs up and I get back to work.

Parker

Putting on suits, walking the runway, it is all child's play to me now, I can do it in my sleep, it has been my life for the last eight years, walk the walk, look confident, do as they tell you beforehand, smile, don't smile, look confident, look vulnerable, strike a pose at the end of the runway, or just keep it slow and poised as you move, wait for everyone else to do it, if they want to see the what you were modelling again, then go out there again. And when people say I am done, then I can go home.

Dylan comes along for this one, his scrawny, but looks just like his Mum and sister, he keeps his hair short and straight.

I no longer see them in the same light, I did have a fondness for them, but since my date with Belle, I now see them, all of them as three people who inflicted so much pain on a child no less that the little girl turned into a cold hearted woman. I can't forgive them for that.

"So a bunch of us are going out for drinks." Sam chirps half naked as we are getting changed from suits to casual, or in Wayne's case suit to suit.

"Dylan and Scarlet going to be there?" I ask.

"Yeah they usually do."

"No then." I do not hide my distain as well as I should have.

"Whoa, do you have a problem with them or something?" Wayne asks.

"No I just don't feel like being drooled on by Scarlet tonight, that's all."

"Fair enough. Maybe it is best you don't go, gives me a chance at her, she's hot." Wayne muses.

No she is vain and nasty, Belle has told me enough, "Go for it brother." I finish getting dressed, "See you around guys." I then leave.

Belle

I wait on the street opposite the studio Parker is going to be coming out of, the limo is already waiting, the models are usually out before the top dogs. I get my phone out and get ready to call him.

In no time there he is, he looks drained I can't help but wonder why. I hit call. It barely rings, "Belle hey how are you?"

"Don't get in that limo. Look across the street."

He does that, clocks me, I wave, he quickly strides over, "How did you know where I was?"

"First things first." Sensing that he needs it, I grab hold of his shirt with my right hand, I put my left hand on the back of his neck and kiss him the same way I did a few nights ago. His right hand travels to the back of my neck, his left to the centre of my back.

Our tongues go to war, we are nipping each other's lips, we are quickly running out of oxygen, we both pull out of the kiss breathless, "Oh wow, I have missed you." Parker gasps.

"It has only been a few days." I mutter, "Parker are you alright? A moment ago you looked really drained."

"I'm alright, just sick and tired of routine, so I am glad to see you. But I repeat, how did you know where I was?"

"Your studio website, I wanted to take you on a date, so I found out where you were today, so here I am, all yours." I lightly kiss him, "How was your day Parker?"

"Same old, same old, cat walks, run ways. Yadda, yadda. You are the highlight of it. You look very nice. And how was your day?"

"Pretty quick, a few consultations and paperwork."

"So where are you taking me?"

"It is not far, a French restaurant called Medlar, me and Nan like to go there once a week."

"I don't think I am dressed for a fancy restaurant."

"I know the owner, so it will be alright, I just have to give him the sweet eye."

I take hold of his hand, "I am very underdressed."

"Oh Parker shut up, it will be fine."

"How are your hips?" He asks.

I suck in a breath through my teeth, "Tender but getting better, I haven't seen him since. I am not going to see him again."

"I believe you. I trust you Belle."

"A phone call a day, so we can talk about how our days have been. I'm sorry I would call you, I will start calling you, I am only just learning how this works."

"Well you have the dating thing down to a T."

We get to the restaurant, walk over to the counter to check in, I know the guy at the counter, he is in his thirties, black short combed back hair, dark blue eyes, square jawline, bulb nose, uneven straight lips, he has on a pair of black trousers and scarlet red long sleeve polo shirt.

"Hey David, it is not often the man in charge is front of house, reservation for O Neil."

"Ma'am we have a dress code here." He informs.

"David." I lean on the counter, "This is all my fault, I took my date by surprise, otherwise he would be following the dress code. Tell you what, if you over look it just this once, I will leave a top big enough for the whole staff to get a bonus."

"Oh Miss O Neil, you play hard ball."

"Always. So what do you say?"

"I say please follow me to your table." David leads us to our table, "Is there anything I can get you Miss O Neil?"

"We will peruse the menu, the wine must fit the meal."

"Very good Miss O Neil."

Parker looks at me, "Well played. So what would you recommend Belle?"

"The chicken in red wine vinegar is to die for, and with that I would recommend, a bottle of the finest merlot."

"I will have that then."

"They also have some lamb dishes which is your favourite."

"They also have your favourite dish on the menu. Why aren't you having that?" He enquires.

"Because it is nowhere near as good as Nan's. Speaking of which she called me today, wanting to meet me for dinner. And when I told her I was going on my second date with you, she wanted to know when you were going to be coming to her for dinner."

"And you said?"

"I said it is early days, and there is no need to rush. Is there? It is only a second date it is not like we have known each other very long." I say casually.

"That makes sense. We hardly know each other, but yet we have gotten pretty intense pretty quickly." He points out, "We have held hands, and kissed only in ways lovers do."

Oh fuck he is right, now I am getting scared, "Oh fuck you have met my family already, whether you meant to or not. You have been shopping with Nan."

"Belle, Belle, calm down." He moves to sit beside me and puts his arm around my shoulders, "Sometimes it is just the way it goes, look let's just go with it Belle. See where things go. No pressure. I don't want to be blunt, but us sleeping together will never be on the cards, while you still have the bruises on your hips. And going by the state of them, it is going to be a couple of weeks. And even when they are healed, it doesn't mean we will be anywhere near ready."

I then relax, "How has no one managed to snap you up yet?" I ask.

"The right woman hasn't come along yet."

"And you think that is what I am?" I challenge.

"I think you have the potential to make someone very happy Belle. And I like the idea of making you happy."

David then comes over to take our orders, "What would you like to order?"

"We will have two of the chicken in red wine vinegar, along with your finest bottle of Merlot."

"Never thought I would see a sight like this." David muses.

"A sight like what?" I ask.

"You settled down, man on your arm."

"It is early days, we are seeing how it goes." Parker answers.

How is he so perfect? He makes me feel so at ease. He doesn't even have to try, he just does.

"How is M.K and Bailey?" He asks me.

"Oh they are good, M.K is the one that told me to do this, a relationship is two people making the effort, not just one, that is what she told me."

"Sound advice." He praises.

"I thought so. How is your family?"

"They are good, Skyla is a nightmare, we all try to pitch in where we can, she stays at mine one night a week, and I have her on days off."

"I hope Ashley didn't give you a lot of flack."

"Oh she is desperate to play the role of big sister, you know protector of the household and all in it, she will probably get worse when Jack comes back from uni, he is her twin brother after all, they have a bond that no one can fathom, they missed each other like mad when he first left."

"So basically she wants to do what I call, 'An M.K.' on me." I joke.

"She and M.K might actually get along." Parker laughs.

"Two people out to protect their family, it could either be common ground or a complete disaster."

"Ashley is laid back all the time she knows her family is alright."

"No relationship?"

"She sees them as adding another person to worry about, her family is her life, that is all she needs apparently."

"Yeah, M.K is the same, but she has a different reason to be."

"Alright tell me about your friends. You met them a boarding school." Parker begins for me.

"Yeah erm, we were kind of thrown together, Bailey and I became fast friends, I couldn't help but love her. M.K on the other hand, she was standoffish, she settled in quickly, too quickly, she never spoke of her family, or of her home. After the beginning of our fourth term we learnt M.K didn't go home for her break, and that she never did." Why am I telling him all of this? "I can't go into why, not my burden."

"Family thing I get it."

"It took M.K a while to even speak to us, but about a month of us being there, Bailey was being picked on by a couple of girls, one of them went to hit Bailey, I went to step up, but M.K beat me to it, by that time Bailey and I were a package, M.K accepted that. Then it became the three of us through boarding school. M.K would go home with Bailey on half terms, Bailey's parents both died when she was young. Her adoptive Mum Irene was cool enough. She died when Bailey was thirteen, so I would bring them home with me. For a long time it has been, M.K, Bailey, Nan and I. Nan became our Nan. She classes us as her three grandchildren."

"So it has been the three of you for a long time?" He asks.

Our meals then come, "Yeah it has. When we were separated because I was looking after my Mum, we missed each other something terrible. Alone we are good. Together we are great. Family."

"I can't imagine my life without my family." He means it.

"We had a very different upbringing Parker, your family clearly loved you. After my father died Nan was the only blood relative I had left, I learned to cope without family."

I have never been so open with someone who is not Nan, M.K or Bailey, so all of this is new to me, I have no idea why I am telling Parker so much, but it is just so easy to talk to him, he shows no judgment only understanding.

I'm not used to people who are not my family being so nice and understanding towards me, I am not going to lie, it is a little bit of a shock to my system.

Parker

I can't help but pity her in a sense, we finish our meal, and I put my arm around her again, she doesn't seem bothered by it, she is getting used to contact from me.

"That must have been hard for you."

"Not really, I have a family, Nan and two sisters who I would do anything for, they are all I need."

She says that with absolute certainty, those three people are not only all she has had, they really are all she has needed.

"You can rely on them."

"Absolutely one hundred percent."

"You love them." I state.

"More than anything in the world, they are my life." She is capable of love, she just doesn't like to show it.

Why does she sleep with married men? And men that treat her like shit?

Why does she allow everyone in England to think that she is some kind of cold hearted temptress?

"You have so much love in your heart, why not show it?" I ask her.

"Because Parker, I got used to only having three people to love. I have forgotten how to let anyone else in. Hence why I keep telling you to leave me alone."

"Belle if you tell me to leave you alone through anything other than fear, then I will never come near you again, until that happens I am going nowhere."

"Shall we go for a walk?" She suggests.

"Yeah sure."

She signals for the check, and she is true to the word, she gives the manager £500, clearly has money to burn.

"You have more money than sense."

"You can't take it with you."

We leave the restaurant, I take her hand and interlock our fingers, "Why do you insist on walking like this?" She asks.

"Interlocking fingers is a sign of unity that you are proud to be together."

"Oh. It's nice, I like it." She muses.

"So do I." I smile. "So where do you see your future going Belle?"

"I thought I had it all planned out. But something changed."

"What changed Belle?"

"I was on a night out with friends, and I met you." She glances up at me, "And you keep scaring the hell out of me."

I stop walking, pull her to a stop and caress her cheek, "Why do I scare you Belle?"

"Because I want you Parker, I want what you have to offer me, I don't even know what that is, but I want to find out." She puts her hands on my chest, "I want something Parker."

"I will give you that Belle, I will give you something. Belle I have no idea what it is about you, but the moment I saw you, something in me clicked Belle, I have no idea what or why, but something in you did as well."

"There is still a lot we don't know about each other." She points out.

"We will learn Belle, we will learn, we need to learn about each other. Just give this, give us a chance." I put my hand on her cheek and kiss her tenderly our tongues float by each other nicely.

Her right hand slips down to my waist, her left hand moves to the back of my shoulder, as she sighs into my mouth.

I will never get tired of her lips on mine, she has a constant taste of honey.

We pull out of the kiss and carry on walking hand in hand, Belle has a lot of depth, she is not only scared of hurting me, she is scared of getting hurt herself. I scare her, I have concluded, it is not me that scares her, it is the way I make her feel that scares her.

All in all today has been pretty good, only this morning I was thinking of how boring my life is, and here was this amazing woman, wanting to take me to dinner, that is one thing ticked off my relationship bucket list, and Belle doesn't even know about it.

Belle

Never in my life have I been so scared, this is so new to me, Parker is so open and honest about what he wants from me, he has not mentioned love yet, but I know at some point that is going to be his goal.

"What are you thinking?" He asks me.

"Just how a few days ago I went from being mercilessly fucked, to being on a date with a guy that wants a relationship with me. I never imagined dating anyone, I never thought I would be walking hand in hand on a stroll. What are you thinking?"

"How you will never be mercilessly fucked again." He glares at me but continues, "Just this morning I was thinking of how boring my life is, how I have the same old routine. And then all of a sudden, just as I am about to go home to nothing and brood and then eventually go to my parents until they go to bed, my girlfriend decides to take me on a surprise date."

He's lonely, I can't help but notice, lacking the one thing he really wants, "Well in that case I am glad to pull you out of your routine. I felt like making a change myself. What is your home like?"

"Big. I thought I would like a big apartment that overlooks the river, but it is too big, too empty. It is not a home yet, I know what it is missing, and it won't be a home until I have it. Tell me about your home."

"Oh it is huge, six bedroom, it is big enough to avoid people if you want to avoid people, but small enough to know where people are. Would you like to see it?"

"From the outside, if I go in, I would want to spend the night with you."

"And it is too soon."

"Yeah." He sighs.

"Tell me about your childhood home."

"I grew up in a busy house, Julian will never know the struggle of needing to get to the bathroom, but having to wait and then having to run to school because you are going to be late, because your two older siblings have hogged it because they are bigger than you. And also Jack and Ashley would hit anyone that upset me, I was a weedy kid."

"Fighting for the honour of their family." I muse. "Who can blame them? I can't picture you being a weedy kid. Time has clearly been kind to you."

"I'll tell you who could blame them, the head master when he stuck them in isolation or excluded them, and my parents when they were excluded or in isolation."

I chuckle, "Maybe you're right, M.K and Ashley might get on alright after all."

"Probably, we have always been a close knit kind of family, something happened with Ashley while Jack was away at uni, I stepped up and was there for her, and that made us closer."

We get outside my house, "This is mine."

"Wow it is amazing."

"Three bedrooms have en-suites, so there is never a cue for the bathroom." I gloat on a smile.

"Lucky cow." He smiles back.

I laugh, "Yeah I am I admit."

"I guess this is goodnight." He sighs.

"Kiss me and wish me good night Parker." Belle orders gently.

He doesn't hesitate, he puts his right hand on the back of my neck, I can't help but notice he loves kissing me slowly, I put my hands on his waist and pull him to me, he murmurs with want, he has this constant taste of wine, kissing him makes me feel drunk.

"You're going to make me wait aren't you?" I ask as we kiss.

He pulls out of the kiss, "I can't have you if you are marked Belle, so yes I am, but mark my words, when your body has healed, I will take you then, and I will keep taking you until your body is quivering beneath mine, and the only way you can express pleasure is a mere whimper."

Oh fucking hell, just the way he said that, has made my blood boil, he really means it, "Let's just hope they heal soon."

He smiles, "I will see you soon Belle."

"Text me or call me to let me know you have got home or wherever it is you are going alright please."

"I am going home. And I will do."

He kisses me again and then leaves, "Oh boy I am in trouble." I say to myself.

Chapter Six

Belle

I AM SAT IN MY office just doing some paperwork, some final agreements for an upcoming event, when Dylan saunters into my office.

In his skinny jeans, and baggy grey shirt. He is an up himself, scrawny jackass that thinks I have nothing better to do with my time, than sit and listen to his pathetic excuses as to why I should give him money.

"This should be good." I throw down my pen, lean back in my chair and fold my arms, "Go on what do you want now? The latest hover board?"

"Oh how droll." He drawls, "Can I not check up on my step sister?"

"Funny how I am only your step sister when you want something. So come on then what do you want? What is Mummy refusing to get her purse out for this time?"

"I want a new camera for work."

"Things like that come out of the studio budget, IF it is important. What do you really need the money for Dylan?" I sigh trying to keep my patience.

"Alright I have gotten behind on my rent."

"Finally some honesty. How?"

"I went out and spent too much."

"And you want me to bail you out?" I snort, "Oh Dylan, you really are hilarious. Fuck off."

"You really are a stone hearted bitch!" He spits.

"Oh dear and who made me like that? Huh Dylan? I was never a part of your family, and you dare ask me for handouts. Get the fuck out of my office, before I get security to escort you out."

"Get fucked Belle!"

"Oh I will just not by you Dylan, I like men, not scrawny little shits who think going out on the piss is more important than paying their rent!"

He goes red in the face, "Fuck this!" He then storms off.

Fuck this is right, I then storm out of my office, I am going to the studio, I am done with this. I wonder how Imelda will feel knowing that her children come to me for handouts when she is too tight to put her hands in her own pockets.

"Where are you going?" M.K asks as she is getting into the lift when it reaches her floor.

"Could ask you the same thing." I retort.

"I have a meeting with the Metcalf's." She answers, "We were going to go to lunch when I was done."

"Don't worry I will be back by then, I promise."

I walk to the studio, in the hope it will give me time to cool off, and better yet so I can actually think about what I am going to say.

I get there to see Parker is here, he looks really handsome in his medium blue ripped jeans, and black paid shirt, they are going for the country look, it suits him, he notices me, he thinks I am there for him, I give him a subtle wave and slight smile.

"What are you doing here?" Scarlet spits her whole image screams desperate to be noticed, in her skinny jeans that are too tight, only revealing that she has no curves, her black top is also too tight, and she has gone way to heavy on the make-up, she has had work done on her lips to make them look fuller, she has on too much eye shadow, mascara and eye liner, and so much foundation it looks like she has six extra layers of skin.

"I want to see Imelda now." I say with the same distaste as Scarlet.

"Oh we always know when you are in the building Belle, you swan in and bark orders like you own the place." Imelda's strawberry blond hair is frizzy and bob styled, her almond eyes are thin, her jawline is square, her lips are big and full, her nose is upturned, making her look as snobby as she is, she has a lovely hourglass figure, she never seems to age, and always seems to look flawless, she dresses too young though, in her low cut scarlet dress, with a belt around her mid-section, she is all leg. She always has a dead tone with me, there is nothing there.

"Step mother." I roll my shoulders to stop the hackles from rising, "Do you see me as part of your family?"

"Well of course I do." She doesn't even attempt to warm her tone, not even by a degree.

"You don't have to lie in front of your minions to save face, you can tell the truth, we both know it, so I repeat. Do you see me as part of your family?"

Now she is honest, "No Belle, your ties to this family died with your father."

"Good I feel the same way. Why is it then your children think they can only treat me like family when they want money?"

"I didn't know...."

"No of course you didn't. Because it is every time you fail to open your purse to them, they suddenly remember they had a step sister that you helped them bully and victimise." I ruffle my hair, "Now I have been patient, but not anymore, I want you, all of you to stay away from me. Am I understood?!"

She is embarrassed. GOOD! Knowing I caused it makes me glad, "Yes you are understood, you have always been difficult, even when you were young."

"ENOUGH! Difficult?! I was difficult?! You and your children made it obvious I was not welcome in my own house, I was still grieving for my mother and you waltzed in and took over, you ensured no memory of my mother laid in your sight. Your children and you called me vile and horrible things. And I was difficult?! You abused me and victimised me, so if I was difficult it was because you were a vile unfeeling bitch that made me feel like a burden. But don't worry you never have to see me again, and I expect the same thing from you."

I walk out, I need to, I can't breathe, I can't think, my head is spinning, it is hurting, every encounter with Imelda ends like this, I feel sick, drained, tired, so tired.

Parker

Belle has just been publically humiliated by Imelda, but that doesn't bother me, what bothers me was the real hurt, the real pain that was in her voice. It is too much, I run after her.

"Parker where are you going?" Scarlet calls after me.

"Someone has to check she is alright." I say as I run out.

I turn right knowing she is probably going to go to her office, I catch sight of her and run after her.

When I get close enough, I take hold of her hand, "Belle wait."

She turns to face me, "What?" She looks drained, more drained than I have seen her, wow I argue with my family, but they have never left me looking half dead, her face is pale she almost looks ill.

I say nothing I just wrap my arms around her, and hold her tight against me, I hear her sigh, she nuzzles into the crevice of my neck, and wraps her arms around my mid-section.

I have learnt so much about Belle from that little encounter, she does hurt and she does get hurt, Imelda has just hurt her and I hate her for that, Belle didn't deserve that, she didn't deserve any of it.

"Are you alright?" I whisper in her ear.

"I am now." She sighs.

Belle

How could I not be alright in Parker's arms, never before have I ever been held by a man that was not my father, he makes me feel safe, like I am the most precious thing in the world, I am so content, I even nuzzle into his neck and wrap my arms around his mid-section.

I could stay like this forever, but Parker has other ideas he pushes me out of his embrace, and places a tender on my lips our tongues floating by each other nicely.

"What are you doing now?" He asks when we stop kissing.

I check the time, "I am supposed to be meeting M.K and Bailey for lunch."

"I will walk with you."

"Honestly Parker, I'm…"

"Don't you dare tell me you are fine Belle, I am going to walk with you." He takes hold of my hand and interlinks our fingers, and we begin walking to Starbucks. "So do you want to talk about what happened back there?"

I scoff, "Don't act like you didn't get an eyeful of my little display, it is obvious what happened back there."

"That it is not what I meant, I know I saw you publically embarrass Imelda, because you got sick of being used by her children, and to make it public information that you are not her daughter."

"I have never been her daughter!" I snap.

Parker drags me into a nearby alleyway and smashes his mouth onto mine, he takes total possession of my mouth, all of my focus is on trying to control my already raging hormones.

"That's better, I don't like seeing you upset Belle. I'm sorry you had to go through that, I'm sorry she hurt you so publically, I'm sorry that the whole experience made you so drained, you looked ill when I got to you."

"Why did you come after me?" I sigh.

"Because you left upset, she hurt your feelings."

"Parker I have told you, in order for my feelings to be hurt, I need to have them in the first place." I state.

"I know you have them, you cannot fool me Belle, I have seen them, you showed them in that studio, you were hurt, you were angry, and the way you held on to me, you needed comfort."

"And you provided it, look let's just forget that whole sorry mess happened, that brats know where they stand, as so I. Now I need to meet M.K and Bailey. Come on if you are coming."

He takes hold of my hand and makes sure our fingers are interlinked, we make our way towards Starbucks, by the time we get there, M.K and Bailey are already approaching.

M.K clocks Parker and I holding hands, she isn't shocked she knows how much I like him, she pulls Bailey to a stop so they can wait for us.

"How did your meeting with the Metcalf's go?" I enquire.

"It went alright, except they kept arguing about the damn flower arrangements, but I managed to help them come to a compromise. You know me. Why did you take off earlier?"

"I had something to take care of." I shrug.

"Dylan was in your office again." Bailey puts in, "No prizes for guessing what he wanted."

"No prizes for guessing what he didn't get." M.K smiles she's proud I don't give in to them, "Still where did you go?"

"I thought it was high time Imelda knew what her darlings were doing, so I went to go and tell her, that if she had no intention of me being a part of her family, then I don't have an intention of being a part of it either, and I would be thankful if Scarlet, Dylan and Imelda could stay away from me."

"Let me guess she went into the good old, 'You have always been difficult' speech." Bailey rubs my arm.

"Yeah I blew my top, and then stormed out, Parker came to check that I was alright, and offered to walk me to meet you guys for lunch."

"Oh how chivalrous of him." Bailey chirps, "Would you like to join us for some dinner?"

"If that is alright with Belle." Wow I actually get a choice, when I was with Nan I didn't, but that was before I agreed to go out with him.

"Call it a thank you for caring enough to check up on me, you are more than welcome to join us." I turn to Bailey and M.K, "I believe you two have already met my boyfriend."

"Oh she is going with labels." M.K laughs, "How very formal and official."

"Shut up M.K." I laugh.

We go into Starbucks, order our food and then sit on the second floor to drink and eat, Parker sits close to me, he claims that if he wanted he could make me beg for contact, so far I'm not begging for contact, he being very hand on, and I am not complaining.

"So what did brother dearest want this time?" M.K hates my step family with a passion, she never attempts to hide it, she just says it how she sees it.

"He put going out and getting hammered before paying his rent, he went to dear old Mummy, who clearly isn't a soft touch like I thought, he then came to me, pulled the good old, 'need a new camera for work' trick."

"When has that ever worked?" Bailey snorts, "What is it Scarlet uses? Oh yeah I need a new dress for the charity ball."

"Yeah I am not being funny, I am a lot of things. But even a lot of those things are coming to an end if all goes well here."

I feel Parker's hand on my leg, I look at him and he looks at me with nothing but compassion and empathy, he knows I am referring to my relationship with him.

"So Parker, when you are done with modelling, then what?" Oh no intervention M.K style.

"I would like to own my own hotel, I figured it would be a good venture, something to hand down to my children, if I have any."

"Do you see yourself married with kids?" Oh fucking hell stop!

"Depends on if I am with the right woman, I mean when you meet the right one that is the preliminary goal, to eventually marry this person, and have children with said person. But I am also aware that some people do not share the same views, so I will happily be with someone who shows me that they are one hundred percent committed to me and our relationship."

"But to get to that stage, it takes time." M.K states.

"Yes I am aware of that." Sensing that this is some kind of interrogation, Parker puts his arm around my shoulders. "I takes time to truly love the person you are with, too many people are just jumping into bed with their partner and then call it love because they find the sex good, a relationship is not just about having a good physical connection, but an emotional one as well. A relationship is based on empathy, compromise, respect, honesty and trust that is how bonds are made."

"What is your biggest dream for right now Parker?"

He takes a deep breath and tenses, which makes me go tense, "I love the idea of coming home from work and either having someone waiting for me because they have finished work before me, or knowing that they are going to be coming home soon, I like the idea of not just having sex with a partner, but making love with them, connecting while we do this, I like the idea of having rough sex, but not so rough we hurt each other, but rough enough to pound out our frustrations after an argument, same for after we have had a rough day. I want to fall asleep holding someone I love in my arms, and wake up to either still find them in my arms, or even if they are not there, knowing they are somewhere in the apartment waiting for me to find them is enough. Or if they wake up to find I am not beside them, to get up either wrapped in a sheet or completely naked to come and find me, where I will most likely be in the kitchen preparing them breakfast in bed."

Not one mention of making them beg for contact, Parker is every woman's dream, and yet here he is with me. Someone who does not deserve him, I don't know at what point during Parker's speech I laid my head on his shoulder but it feels so nice, and he smells divine.

Parker

I meant everything I said, nothing was a lie, and just lately I have been picturing that life with Belle. Is it love? I have no idea, but I do know one thing, seeing her confront Imelda, and seeing the way she looked so defeated afterward killed me, I hated it.

M.K right now is just being a good friend, I am certain I'm going to get a similar grilling from Belle's Nan at some point, Belle's head on my shoulder feels so right.

All of a sudden her phone rings, "I am going to deal with this." She the runs off.

"Well that wasn't a client, she never answers calls from clients when she is on lunch." M.K looks at Bailey.

"It wasn't Nan either, she was quite angst." Bailey purses her lips, "What we both know who that leaves."

"Who does it leave?" I demand.

"I am not going to tell him." Bailey throws her hands up in a peace gesture, "Nothing against you, but Belle is dealing with it."

"M.K who was on the phone?"

"Before I tell you, hear this, she has been ignoring and avoiding him."

"M.K who was it?" I am trying to keep her cool.

She thinks for a moment and then gives up the information I want, "It's Fox Mason."

That name alone is enough to have me spring from my seat and storm outside. I look for her, and she is not in the street, she must be heading up to her office, her lunch is nearly over, I also head there.

I storm past reception, get into the lift, I am too riled to even think about how cramped the space is, when I get to Belle's office she is still on the phone, she has her back to me, "Yeah alright, I will see you later then."

She is arranging to meet him, I am boiling mad, she hasn't even given me a chance, and she is arranging to meet with that monster. I'm heaving, I storm towards her.

Belle

I get outside and answer my call, "I told you not to call me again! It's over Fox! I want nothing more to do with you!"

"You cannot end things without an explanation, and before you use that bullshit about me being married, I have already told you I'm not."

"There is someone else." I admit.

"Is this one married? Have I been left for a married fucking man?" He spits.

"No I haven't left you for a married man, I have left you for a single man, he has taken me out on dates, and has not jumped on me for sex right away. And he is gentle with me Fox. I actually like him."

"I don't believe you. I will be in touch Belle!"

He then hangs up, I block his number, "Like hell you will be in touch." I smile to myself.

I get into my lift, and call Nan.

"Hello dear, how is your day going?"

"It is going good thanks. And yours?"

"It is going good, I did some shopping, went home and cleaned, and just got out of the bath. Are you alright?"

I sigh, "Dylan came to see me for money, I told him where to go, then Fox called me."

"Well those Hawthorn kids are nothing but trouble, you did right staying away from them. And as for Fox, you are better off without him."

"I didn't stay away from the Hawthorn kids, they didn't want me. And as for Fox, someone better came along."

"Their loss."

"Yeah it is. So anyway Nan, I was wondering if you are free for dinner tonight. I really want to see you."

"Had a tough day so you want your old Nan huh?"

"Yeah something like that." I sigh.

"Tell you what, come to mine tonight and you can help me whip up your favourite, I know you love doing that. Oh and bring Parker if you can."

"Yeah alright I will see you later then."

I hang up, and no sooner do I hang up, vicious hands grab my shoulders, at first I think it's Fox and a fear spikes in me, but then when I'm spun round and I see Parker's face, I'm shocked.

"I TOLD YOU NOT TO SEE HIM AGAIN!!!" He bellows.

"AND I'M NOT!!" I shove him off me, "Yes it was him on the phone when I left Starbucks. But it was Nan on the phone just now!" I shove my phone at him, "Check if you don't believe me!"

He does check, and then he looks at me, the anger in his eyes has dissolved only guilt remains, "Belle I am so sorry."

"So much for trust!" I spit, "When I have had a bad day I call Nan, she helps me feel better. I have blocked Fox's number, he cannot contact me through mobile again, so there you go."

"I shouldn't have doubted you. I'm so sorry, give me another chance. Belle please." He steps towards me, and I slap him around the face, tears are stinging my eyes.

"One thing I can handle is being called a liar by people who don't know me. Being called a liar by someone who is supposed to care about me. Who I care about! That is totally different."

He then stares at me shocked, I am also awestruck at the words that have come out of my mouth, he takes hold of my arms gently this time, and tugs me to him for a tender, almost pleading kiss. "Belle I'm so, so sorry, please, please forgive me." He kisses my cheek and my neck, "I am so, so sorry baby. I will never doubt you again. Please say you forgive me."

I can't take much more, tender kisses, or hard possessive ones, every kiss makes me want him, "I will give you one more chance. Never do it again." I demand.

"I promise baby."

"Alright I believe you." I really do believe him, we share a tender kiss, "Nan wants you over for dinner tonight, we are having my favourite meal."

"I will be there. It's a date. How are your hips?"

"All better." I show him to prove it.

"Well then the evening doesn't have to end with us separating. I can make up for my terrible behaviour properly."

"Play your cards right, and I might let you." I smile.

Chapter Seven

Parker

G OSH I AM SO NERVOUS, I have no idea why though, I mean
Belle's Nan is alright, and I had her won the moment she met
me. Which only made Belle's hackles rise higher.

I am kicking myself for the way I treated her, she's right, I had
no right not to trust her. But soon I smile to myself, she forgave me.

I get back to work. Scarlet is quick to be hot on my heels, I find
how vain Scarlet is so annoying all of sudden, she spends way too
much time trying to look good, and she just doesn't it is just sad, she
is not a patch on Belle.

"Parker why did you run after Belle? We still have work to do."

"I ran after Belle, because what your mother said hurt her
feelings, and I wanted to check she was alright."

"But you don't know her or what she is like." She's quick to
defend her mother, oh but of course she is they are both as hateful
towards Belle as each other.

"Yes you're right I don't, which is why I don't know if what was
said to her was warranted or not, hence why I ran after her, because
I didn't see what the papers and you make her out to be, I saw her a
woman who had just got her feelings hurt."

"Do you fancy her or something?" Scarlet grimaces.

I have to be careful how I answer this, Scarlet has a thing for me,
she is also my bosses daughter, "Look my parents raised me to be the
kind of man that runs after a woman if they are upset, regardless

of the reputation, or if I know them or not. Is it my fault that they raised a gentleman?" I smile.

"No I guess not. You have the full package, good looking, fit, smart, funny, a gentleman. You are one big fuck me package. Which I would not say no to by the way."

Scarlet Hawthorn, usually men would love for a woman to throw themselves at their feet, but me on the other hand, it just screams desperation, we work together and occasionally have the odd drink, where we go out as a group, I am never alone with her, if I wanted to date her, I would date her, if I wanted to fuck her, as she so eloquently put it, then I would have fucked her. You would have thought she would have got the message by now.

Obviously some people are slow on the uptake.

So I carry on working, it is fun doing a modelling shoot with your oldest friends, we all rose up together, I love them like brothers, I would eventually love to tell them about Belle, but I have no idea how they would react to the news, I hope they would be happy, but they also love Imelda like a mother, so probably not.

They think the sun shines out of the Hawthorn's arses, and they buy all of the stories they spin about Belle, even slag her off, I used to do that, then I saw her in person, then I talked to her, and then I realised she is not bad, she is sad. She is actually really sweet, kind and willing to do anything for the little family she has.

Belle

He wants to sleep with me, and he wants to do it tonight, I know there is no pressure, and I know that he won't do anything to add any, he is not that kind of person.

One thing that does scare me, is the way he reacted to the thought of me arranging a meet with Fox, I wonder if that happens often, he did calm down quickly and he was sorry, but still the way he snapped, and the look of pure murder in his eyes, it was scary to witness.

I don't think he makes a habit of it, he is so laid back usually, so I am willing to give him the benefit of the doubt.

M.K and Bailey then come into my office, "So what did that bastard want?" I know M.K is talking about Fox.

"He wanted to fuck me, which is all Fox ever wants to do to me."

"So lunch with friends, things really seem to be going well with Parker."

"Yeah." I say unenthusiastically.

"Aw what happened? Did you two have a row?" Bailey asks holding my hand.

"Not a row as such, after Fox called me, I called Nan, I arranged to meet with her, Parker heard the end of the conversation, where I was telling Nan I that I will see her later, and he grabbed me and shouted in my face."

"Oh shit Belle, I'm so sorry it is my fault that happened, I told him it must have been Fox you were on the phone to, I did also tell him that you have been avoiding and ignoring his calls, since you and he became a thing. I am so sorry." M.K repeats.

"It's alright, how he found out doesn't concern me, his reaction on the other hand did."

"The man cares about you, he wants to protect you."

"You didn't see his face M.K, he looked like he wanted to kill me, or at least like he wanted to kill someone."

"And his reaction when he realised he was wrong?"

"He was sorry, but still what about the next time he gets the wrong end of the stick? I slapped him M.K, I actually slapped him."

"Oh Belle." Because I am getting distressed Bailey wraps her arms around my shoulders, she keeps her hands on my shoulders when she pulls away, "Look I am sure this was just a one-time thing, Parker knows Fox hurt you. I thinks his reaction was one of a man terrified about losing someone he cares about to the likes of Fox Mason. And Parker does care about you Belle."

My lift opens again, both M.K and Bailey move in front of me thinking it is Fox, when we all see it is who I know to be Parker's older sister Ashley, who has on a tight leather skirt, a black blouse, with black high heels, I also notice she wears a little bit of make-up when she is not working.

Both Bailey and I breathe a sigh of relief, M.K lowers her hackles, a bit but not much, "Who are you?" M.K demands.

"Well no prizes for guessing who you are, I have seen the pictures of you protecting Belle from the paparazzi, I don't believe you have ever been named though." She coolly rolls her shoulders.

"I'm M.K and this is Bailey, we're Belle's family, I didn't hear you answer my question."

Ashley meets M.K's challenging stare with one of her own, "I'm Ashley, Parker's sister. Although you were expecting someone else when the lift opened, I can't help but wonder who."

"Yes we were." M.K admits, "Who doesn't matter. What do you want?"

"I want to speak to Belle, she is seeing my little brother, I am the oldest, it is my job to protect my siblings, even the one that is only two minutes younger than me, so here I am, to make sure she has no intention of hurting Parker."

"It's alright M.K you can leave us." I say, "Go on I have faced worse things today, I can handle an interrogation from my boyfriends sister."

M.K and Bailey then go to leave, but not before M.K and Ashley give each other another challenging stare, I have no idea if it because they are being protective or what.

When my sister's leave I just say, "I apologise for M.K, it has been the three of us and Nan for a long time, and she has always been the protective one."

"Yes I can see that. What are your intentions with my brother?"

I go around my desk and sit down, gesturing for her to do the same, as if she was a client, she is hesitant, but she does it.

"You don't beat about the bush. I like that." I fold my arms in an attempt to shield myself, although from what I don't quite know. "I like your brother, I am quite fond of him. I don't have any intention of hurting him, I am hoping to have some kind of a future with him, we have gone out a few times as you know. He is going to have dinner with Nan and I tonight, I am also going to tell him that seeing as he has met my family, it is time I met his. I like him Ashley, he is like no other man I have been with he actually wants to know me."

"Please tell me you are not with another man." She chides.

"No, no I have not been with another man since Parker and I's first date, I have not seen the other guy since that day, and he has been calling me, I blocked his number, he can't get in touch with me again."

She is shocked that I have been so honest, "Ashley he called me today this other guy, after he called me, I called Nan, Parker caught the end of the conversation, he thought I was talking to said other man, and he grabbed me and shouted in my face. Is that normal?"

Now she looks shocked, "No Parker is as laid back as they come, I have never known him do anything like that. However he did tell me that you were mixed up with a man that bruised you, and that M.K was so concerned that she turned to him for help. Fox Mason, it didn't take long to piece together, he is a rough bastard and does not like the word no, for confidentiality reasons, I can't go into how I know that." Now it is me looking shocked, "Look Belle, the only thing I can think is, Parker has genuine feelings for you, and he was worried that he was going to lose you to that monster."

"That what M.K said, well not in so many words, but those were lines. She likes him, otherwise on telling her about Parker's reaction, she would have wanted to break his neck."

"I don't doubt that, she seems very protective."

"Oh she kicks my ass when I deserve it. So does Bailey."

"Alright well you have told me all I want to know, you like my brother and don't have any intention of hurting him, not only do I accept that, I believe it. So I will leave you to your day." She then gets up to leave, "One more thing, when Parker falls, he falls hard, but he has a heart of gold, and will worship the ground you walk on. And if you break his heart, it will take him ages to get over it. So be damn sure of your intentions, because he is already sure of his, he might not have told you what they are, but he is sure of his.

She then leaves.

Parker

I'm still so nervous, I have no idea why though, her nan likes me, she had made that perfectly clear, but still I'm so nervous, I manage to get through my day. "So drinks after work?" Scarlet asks in general.

"Yeah I'm in." Wayne answers swiftly. How Scarlet can't see that Wayne has a thing for her is beyond me, he is always giving her doe eyes, she is always too busy eyeing me up to notice.

"Yeah I'm in too." Sam replies then turns to me, "Parker."

"Oh no I can't, I promised my Mum I would have dinner with the family, we have all been busy, so I promised the tonight."

"So family orientated, I like it." Scarlet muses.

"I had better go, I don't want to be late."

I then leave, I feel bad for lying to my friends, but the truth at this very moment in time, is just simply not an option. I don't want my relationship with Belle to become public knowledge just yet, and I know for a fact that Belle will not want that either, granted me holding her hand, kissing her and going on dates with her so publicly and openly is probably not the best the idea, but I can't help it, she is so hard to resist. Anyway the point is, the people that are meant to know, which is the people closest to is know, ALMOST all of them do, I have met her family, she just has to meet mine.

Remembering that, I get my phone out of my pocket and call my Mum, "Hello my baby boy. How are you?"

She always manages to make me blush by calling me her baby boy, "Hello Mum, I'm alright thanks. How are you?"

"Exhausted, it's been a long day. When are you going to come to dinner again? We miss you."

She always gets straight to the point, "That's why I'm calling actually, there's someone I want you to meet."

"Girlfriend?" She asks hopefully.

"Yes but Mum, you might not like her right from the off."

"Oh don't be silly, I'm sure I will."

"It's Belle O Neil." I inform.

"Belle O Neil, as in the woman who has left a string of heartbreaks and divorces in the wake of every man she has ever touched? That Belle O Neil?"

"Told you, you might not like her."

"Parker." She groans, "Are you crazy? She is going to rip your heart out, chew it up, and hand it back to you a mangled and useless mess."

"She's different to what people think Mum, she's not the heartless bitch everyone thinks she is, she is actually really nice, she gives her employee's bonuses at Christmas, she took in her friends in when they had nowhere to go, she is actually very open and honest, your mind will be changed."

"You really like her don't you?"

"Mum I honestly think she is the one. She is all I can think about, I've met her Nan, I bumped into Belle and her Nan while I was out shopping. She loves her Nan very dearly. She is nothing like the papers portray."

"But there's a reason she is portrayed like that, but fine if she is important to you, then of course I am willing to meet her, we're all free Wednesday."

"Thank you Mum. I love you."

She then hangs up, knowing the conversation is over, I then make my way home, I tremble with anticipation at the knowledge that by the end of the night, Belle could be here in my apartment and in my bed, I'm terrified, I'm half in love with her already, this could make me fall all the way.

I do a quick tidy around, well that is the intention, but I find myself looking in my fridge, throwing out all of the food that's out of date, I hoover the rugs in every room, I change my bedding, I even check to make sure I have condoms, we don't have to sleep together tonight, but if we do then at least I know I'm prepared for it.

I look at my watch, I'm due to meet Belle in an hour. I go to get showered and changed. What do I wear? Do I go smart or casual? I don't want to appear a try hard, but I don't want to look like a slob either.

I will go in between, which to me is a pair of black jeans and a white polo shirt.

I make my way to Belle.

Belle

In a word today has been bizarre, it has gone from bad, to worse, to better, back to bad, and then back to better and then back to bad, then back to better, and hopefully it is only going to keep getting better.

Bailey and M.K come into my office, I've been expecting them since the visit from Ashley, "So what did Parker's sister want?" M.K demands, she doesn't mess around, I have to love her for that.

"She wanted to warn me, not to hurt her brother, which is understandable, especially given my track record."

"How did you reassure her?" Bailey asks, sitting down and gesturing for M.K to do the same thing."

"I told her about Fox, not mentioning his name, I just told her I was seeing a man who was a bit rough."

"Understatement." M.K states.

"She didn't need to know the gory details, I just told her that since meeting Parker, I ended things with him. Girls I am going to level with you, I really like him. We are having dinner with Nan tonight."

"Are we going to expect you home?" M.K enquires.

"If all goes well then no." I say honestly, "It's a mutual decision it's not vital that happens tonight, but after all of the shit day I've had, I think it would be a good way to end it."

"Well let's hope he's nothing like Fox, look coming home with a limp, that is one thing, but coming home with bruises that makes it look like you have been viciously raped, that is a totally different matter entirely."

"Parker didn't like the idea of having me, while I was bruised by Fox, I don't know if it's a male pride, that he didn't want evidence of another man on me, while we were having sex."

"It could be either or both, he might not want to see you hurt, he might not want to have you when evidence of another man is on you. It's understandable, now it can be a clean slate."

"I think he plans on taking you a different way to what the others did. I don't think he plans on being rough with you. Well not all the time at least." Bailey puts in, "I mean think about it, he said at lunch, you can have rough sex and not mark your partner, and he openly admitted he likes to connect with his partner, the best way to connect during sex, is to be slow and gentle and savour each other. I think that's what he plans on doing."

"Which would certainly make a change to the rest of the creeps you have fucked." M.K states matter of factly.

"I know it will. Why am I so nervous?"

"Because for once you want you want a relationship with all the trimmings, and he wants to have something with you. You want to have something, and sooner or later you're going to push him away, because you're going to start falling for him." M.K predicts.

"Thank you Mystic M.K, is that a solid prediction, or is it susceptible to change?" I ask sarcastically.

"Be sarcastic all you like Belle, it doesn't change the fact I'm right, and you're used to people letting you walk away, with Parker it isn't going to be that easy."

"I'm with M.K on this." Bailey puts in, "Parker isn't going to let you go easily, if what he said at dinner is correct, when he loves he loves hard."

"I smell intense then, I mean when he loves, he loves hard, and how many girlfriends has he had exactly? That is a good question there."

"That is a good thing to ask him." M.K suggests.

"Then he might want to know how many men I have slept with."

"Oh fucking hell! Even we have lost count of that one. You have had a lot of skeletons in your closet." M.K blurts.

"Thanks guys, just make me sound like a proper slag."

"No offence Belle, but you kind of were."

"Yeah sorry babe." Bailey agrees.

"Well he knows about all of that. And he still wants me. I can't help but wonder why."

"Uh oh. It's starting."

Parker

It's time to pick up Belle so we can have dinner with her Nan, I am still so nervous, and I hope I am doing a good job hiding it, probably not. I walk into Belle's buildings just as M.K and Bailey are leaving.

"Oh you're going for the smart/casual look I see, that's cool Nan likes the idea of people being relaxed around her." Bailey states.

"You all call her Nan?"

"Yeah she has done a lot for us, the minute she saw how close we all were, she just said, 'You're family to Belle, so you are family to me.' She's hard not to love to be honest."

I make my way up in the lift, and on the journey I notice the confined space more than I want to, it's suffocating and horrible, I'm trying to keep calm, I really hate confined spaces.

But the time I get to the office my breathing is under control, but as Belle looks up to smile, she can see something is wrong, "What is it?" She looks concerned almost worried. Why?

"Oh nothing, I'm not really a fan of confined spaces, and the only way to get to you is to get into a lift. I got a little panicked."

"Come and sit down." She says getting up, circling around her desk, so she is closer to me, she perches on her desk, and this is the first time I notice, she has some damn fine legs on her.

"Sorry that the only way up here is by lift, but you didn't have to come up, you could have called me and waited."

"No I like coming up here and seeing you work, knowing that you are in charge, it makes you even sexier."

She leans down so she can kiss my cheek, but I surprise her by turning my head and capturing her luscious lips, and taking her mouth hungrily, she mimics the kiss perfectly, placing her hands on my sides. I have my right hand on the small of her back and my left hand on the back of her neck.

"If we didn't have plans with your Nan, I would be having you right here and now." I inform.

She looks at me bewildered, "If we didn't have plans with Nan, I might just have let you." I stand back so she can straighten herself out, "You know you didn't have to bring flowers."

I forgot I had them, "I could hardly show up empty handed, it is hardly gentle manly."

"I hope you are only a gentleman over dinner."

"I plan on being a gentleman when I take you home tonight as well, that is if you still want me to."

"I would be the perfect way to end the day." She smiles.

Belle

One thing is for certain about tonight, I don't think Parker is going to leave any room for questions or doubts. Although I'm going to try and ask questions, it's not so that I raise any doubts, it's to eradicate any of my doubts, if along the way I make Parker question his feelings for me and why he has them, maybe it's for the best.

As we leave the office and step into the lift, I ensure that I put my arm around Parker's waist, to keep him calm on the trip down to the lobby.

"Are you alright?" I ask him.

"With you holding onto me like that. It's hard not to be alright." He says putting his arm around my shoulders.

We leave the building in our embrace, for a couple hoping to keep our relationship under wraps, we're not doing a lot to keep it under wraps.

Arm in arm we walk to my car, separating so that we can get in my car, we get in and I start driving to Nan's.

"I told my Mum about us."

"Oh." I don't know why I am surprised, his sister already knows, so it was only a matter of time before the rest of his family finds out.

"Did I do the wrong thing?"

"No, no." I say swiftly, "My family know already, so why would I mind?"

"We've been invited to dinner next Wednesday."

"Oh, I've never been introduced to family before." I shift nervously.

"There's no need to be nervous."

"Parker there's every need to be nervous, I'm the woman that has wrecked marriages, ruined families, and broken hearts, your family isn't going to be my biggest fans."

"What matters is what I think of you, and I think you're amazing." He puts his hand on my leg.

"You don't know me Parker, not really."

"I know enough to know you're nothing like the papers portray you to be. And I know that you have been totally honest with me, when I've asked you questions. And that you will continue to be."

"Alright I will meet your family, but they won't like me."

"Maybe not at first, but when they get to know the real you, they will love you."

I pull up outside Nan's house, "Your Nan lives in a bungalow?" Parker asks shocked.

"Yeah trust me, I'm not happy about it. But this is one of the finest establishments in Kensington, I made sure of it before I bought it."

"I bet you did."

We get out of the car and I walk to the boot and get out a bag, "What's in there?" Parker asks.

"Oh some wine and some bits and pieces Nan asked me to get for her."

We walk to the front door and I knock briskly, Nan answers the door in a royal blue dress, with a necklace I got her for her birthday.

"Oh there you are, and you got my shopping, please come on in, I will get you the money for the shopping."

"Nan we go through this every time I get some shopping, there is no need to give me money for shopping for you."

"Worth a shot." She turns to Parker, "Oh Parker you look dashing. You didn't have to bring me flowers."

"To show up empty handed would just be rude." Parker bends down to kiss Nan.

"Something smells divine." I declare.

"It's your favourite." She touches my cheek, "But I have saved the part you like to do. Only because she hasn't told me what she does to make the gravy taste so good."

I now bend down to kiss her cheek, "And I don't plan on tell you either. No one is allowed in the kitchen for a moment. This is top secret."

I then go into the kitchen to make the gravy.

I don't know if Parker can sense how nervous I am, but I am so nervous, he is the first man I have brought to meet Nan, but it is not like he is one of my affairs, so I should be relieved the first man I have bought home for Nan to meet is one without baggage, maybe that is what makes me nervous.

Or it could just be Parker in general.

Parker

Now it's just Belle's Nan and me, "She takes her recipes seriously I see."

"Cooking is one of her passions, if I didn't have a guest I would in the kitchen with her, she's mesmerising to watch.

"I shall have to see for myself one day."

"Oh how rude am I being, come and sit down, dinner is nearly ready, so if we got and sit at the table."

She leads me into the dining room, where there is a table and four chairs, "I am used to Belle, M.K and Bailey coming over here for dinner, they make a habit of coming round together once a week, sometimes more, they also come by individually, I think they worry about me being lonely."

"They all love you very dearly, it's nice to see."

"I hate the way the papers portray Belle, but to her it's just keeping up appearances, when her mother died she went off the rails a little bit, and now it's like she finds it hard to break the cycle."

"Yes the papers can be brutal, I think if the papers were to see her a different way, then it would a shock to all of their systems. She let her guard down with me almost right away, whether she meant to or not."

"You really like her don't you?"

"I really, really like her yes."

"Maybe you could be the one to break the cycle."

"I sincerely hope so, I'm willing to try."

Belle then comes out of the kitchen, wraps her arms around her Nans neck and kisses her Nans cheek, "I have done the gravy, is there anything else you need help with?"

"Sit down near Parker, when I start bringing the dishes in, come through to help me."

Belle holds onto her Nan for a couple more seconds, she is longing for love, and she holds on to those that do love her.

"Alright." She says letting go of her Nan and then fulfilling her order of coming to sit near me.

For a moment I just look at her, when she notices the close scrutiny she under, she chuckles nervously and says, "What?"

I just say nothing, I put my hand on the back of her neck and kiss her lightly and tenderly, she mirrors the kiss.

Then her Nan comes in, we both pull away like we have been caught doing something we shouldn't, "Aww I never thought I would see the day a man treats my granddaughter nicely."

"Well get used to it, I plan on treating Belle the way she deserves to be treated."

"I am glad to hear it."

Both Belle and her Nan leave the table, I then come to the realisation, I love her, well I love the side of her that's rarely seen, the loving, loyal and vulnerable side to her. I know when I started to love her, it happened when we stood outside The River, when she was telling me it is best to leave her alone, I can't tell her this yet, I want her to need me first.

Both Belle and her Nan come through with plates and glasses of water, "Nan sit down, I will get the rest." Belle suggests.

"You fuss over me too much. If you looked after yourself as well as you look after me, I would have no reason to worry about you."

"I like fussing over you Nan." Belle declares. Fuck my heart could burst with love for this woman.

Belle then disappears in the kitchen, "She clearly loves you." I say to her Nan.

"And you love her." Her Nan says matter of factly, "Don't worry she won't hear it from me."

I smile at her lightly, "Thank you, that means a lot to me."

"What means a lot to you?" Belle asks coming back into the dining room with a plate that holds her plate, a pot of gravy and a glass of water.

"This evening with you and your Nan means a lot to me, I have never had dinner with the family of a girl I am dating before."

"How many girls have you dated exactly just out of interest?" Her Nan asks, I couldn't help but wonder how long it would be before that was asked.

"Only one for eighteen months, but it wasn't meant to be, at first everything was great, she was my age, sweet and lovely. But that soon changed, she was only after one thing, and that was my money, my career was just taking off, and because I was blind with love, I didn't see she was using me, Ashley and my brother Jack both gave me a slap of reality and I ended things with her. To find she had another sucker lined up, she moved on a week later." I have no idea why I am so nervous telling Belle about my ex, it is not like I have a lot of baggage, well not the amount she does.

Belle

Oh wow Parker has only had one girlfriend, but it was a long term thing and he was treated abominably, "That is a terrible way to treat a person, I know the way I treat men is questionable a lot of the time, but at least I don't use them for money, I have plenty of my own. How long ago was that?"

"A couple of years ago, I guess I was just so clouded with wanting to settle down, to share everything I have with someone, I let her fool me for a while."

"I'm sorry that happened to you." I say honestly.

"I'm over it, she never really loved me, so I didn't waste time pining over her, I have had six casual flings since her. All of them lasted a few weeks at most, then we went our separate ways."

We finished our meal and let the food settle for a bit, Parker's hand lands on my leg. He seems content in his environment.

"So Parker." Nan begins, "What's different about my grand-daughter" I tense up at the question.

"You know I have no idea, but I look at her and I picture being content and happy with her, when she has finally realised I am not going to be like the rest of her endeavours and she lets me in."

His hand creeps higher and higher up my leg, I jump up, Nan looks at me like I am deranged, "I will get on with the dishes, and bring dessert."

I rush into the kitchen with a tray full pots.

I enter a little dream world, I find Parker very endearing his experience with this girl, did for a while warp his idea of love, because he went after something that didn't require emotion, now he wants a life with me. What if I can't be what he wants?

I jump as a pair of strong arms snake around my mid-section, "That gravy was divine. What was in it?" Parker asks kissing my neck and shoulders. Fuck he causes reactions in my body no man has ever caused in me before, I tilt my neck to give him better access.

"If I told you, I would have to kill you." I remark weakly.

"I could fuck it out of you." He replies cockily.

"I doubt you would even try."

"I want to so things to you Belle that no man has ever done to you before. Fuck the things I want to do to you."

"I think you are already succeeding there." I shudder.

"I don't know whether to be elated or saddened by that statement baby." He gives me one last kiss, "Is there anything you need help with?"

"You could get the lemon swirl cheesecake out of the fridge, it's a homemade specialty. You will love it."

"Alright." He smiles that smile that makes my heart skip a beat.

Parker

After having a lovely dessert with Belle's Nan, we are now exchanging goodbye kisses and hugs with her at the door.

"See you two later, and behave yourselves."

We both laugh at her Nan's comment and leave hand in hand, "So your place or mine?" Belle asks.

"Mine there are less people there."

"Alright, but you won't get my world famous breakfast in the morning."

"You know I have a kitchen." I say cockily.

"I perform better in my own."

She starts driving, she doesn't seem nervous, but I'm surprised to say that I'm not nervous either.

It doesn't take long to drive to my place.

We get out of the car and walk hand in hand to my apartment block, "Oh wow." Belle muses in awe, "Now I wouldn't mind Nan living in a place like this."

"It's nice, but I live in the pent house, I usually take the stairs, which go right up to my apartment."

"What and you think I can't handle it?"

"Its twelve flights of stairs, you're fit but I don't want to tire you our before the real exercise starts."

I push the call button for the elevator, "The last time I was called fit, I was twenty one, and the guy calling me it was nineteen." Belle says half to me, half to herself.

"What else to men call you?" I ask.

"A good fuck mainly." She's not even used to a basic compliment, the elevator comes down, we step in and I use my key card to activate it, "Why do you have to use a card to activate the lift?"

"Because the lift goes all the way to my apartment, so the only person that can get into my apartment is the people that have a key card, which is just me, if I want someone to have a key card, then I have to ask Malcom at the front desk for another to be made."

"Impressive." She muses. She moves to me wraps her arms around my mid-section, her eyes are cloudy with want, "That was a very dirty game you played over dinner. What would you have done if I hadn't have stood up?"

I run my hands up and down her back, "You would have given me no choice but to finish the job, then you would have had some explaining to do to your Nan."

She gets up on her toes and bites my bites my bottom lips, before she has the chance to pull away, I capture her lips with mine, she pulls me closer, God she's amazing, she knows how to make men want her, and fuck I do so badly.

She takes off my jacket, as the lift opens we both stumble our blind to our surroundings, I pick up Belle and carry her to the bedroom, I place her on her feet, "We had a fight, and I was wrong."

"Forget it, you've already apologised, there's no need to keep apologising."

I get on my knees, "The apology isn't over yet. Has a man ever got down on his knees for you Belle?"

"No I can't say that they have."

I run my hands up her legs to remove her panties, "Silk." I chuckle studying the material, "I must say that has to be my new favourite material. Especially if you're wearing it." I hitch up her dress, "Enjoy this baby."

I take her in my mouth, she reacts instantly, making pleasure filled noises, she moves her left leg so that it is over my shoulder, so that my mouth has easier access, "Oh fuck." She gasps out.

But that only eggs me on, making me take her that little bit harder, making her cry out with pure pleasure, she's getting close, I slow down and she punches the wardrobe in a mixture of pleasure and despair, I am not in any hurry to end this, it feels too good, it feels like it has been too long coming.

Her breath is heaving, her knees are buckling from the pleasure my mouth is providing her with.

"Oh Parker." She gasps as she climaxes, I'm sure she knows I slowed down her climax on purpose, but right now, she's too sated from pleasure to even care.

I don't give her time to recover, she watches me, her eyes cloudy with sex as I ascend her body, I keep her pinned to the wardrobe, I kiss her hungrily, I remove her dress with ease, "I'm not used to undressing before sex."

I'm not shocked by her declaration, "You're going to get used to me savouring you Belle." I say surely, "Put you hands on mine." She does as I say as I unbutton my shirt and undo my trousers, "Take off my shirt."

She does that and runs her hands over my stomach, she isn't used to touching and savouring the men she sleeps with.

I back away so I can take off my trousers and pants, I walk over to her, take her mouth hungrily with mine, I put my hands on her breasts and tweak her nipples, she gasps into my mouth, I take off her bra.

I pick her up and carry her to bed, I'm inside her before we even get to the bed, she gasps at the slow penetration, "You're used to screaming during sex?" I half ask half state.

"Yes." She gasps the word out.

I keep the movement going as I speak, "That's all well and good, but you need to connect, to feel, to savour, rough sex is all well and good, but it's a quick fix, it doesn't build a foundation. Say you understand."

"I understand." She gasps out as I push into her again, "Oh fuck Parker."

I capture her lips, when I move on to kiss her neck she nibbles on my ear, her hands are running over my sides, and my back, she is savouring the feel of me, like I am teaching her to do.

My hands are lingering over her bum and her breasts, both are firm and pert and fit into my hands nicely, very nicely actually.

One of her hands finds my hair, and she threads it through her fingers, fuck that feels amazing, her legs curl over the back of my thighs, we're both gasping with pleasure, Belle has closed her eyes so she can focus more on the feeling, when we both get close to climax I say, "Open your eyes Belle, I want us to look at each other when we fly over the edge."

She peels her eyes open and after one more thrust from me, we both climax, "Oh Parker." She gasps breathlessly.

"That was amazing." I say when I have eased us both down, I stay on top of her and sniff her hair, "How was that for you?"

"I've been longing for a man to take me like that for the longest time, it was everything I hoped it would be, no it's more, thank you."

Fuck I love her more and more, all she has ever wanted was to be loved, I kiss the top of her head. "There is more where that came from, both inside and outside the bedroom." I promise.

Chapter Eight

Belle

THERE REALLY WAS MORE WHERE that came from, he didn't stop, Parker certainly does have a lot of energy, none of my endeavours have ever lasted as long or have had sex with me as often as Parker did, I'm exhausted, but I can't stay here, I need to be in my own environment, in my own home, I leave him a note, and try to find the stairs that lead out of his apartment, I take some time as I'm looking for the door to take in my surroundings, Parker is very clean, very house proud, he likes to colour match his possessions, I manage to find the door that is near the book shelf, that too is activated by a key card, which is on a hook right by the door, I take the key card off the hook and swipe it down, I open the door, and then I replace the key card, I shut the door and make my way downstairs, I'm halfway down the stairs when I hear, "And where are you going?"

I look up to see Parker leaning on the banister, he's put on a pair of black joggers, "Erm I've never actually stayed over at a man's house before, I prefer to sleep in my own bed."

He sighs and shakes his head, "For a woman who has had a lot of boyfriends, you have no idea what having one really entails." He backs me into the wall, placing his hands either side of my head, and gives me a hot kiss, "You wouldn't have gotten anywhere fast, where my floor starts, there is another door, that needs my key card, which you kindly returned to me."

I can't help but smile at him, he kisses me again this time when he deepens the kiss, I know what he wants, "Parker, you really tired me out last night, I'm not sure I have the energy."

He gives me a sick smile as he lifts me up, I squeal at his actions, "Tough because it's four in the morning, and I deserve a reward for waking up to find the woman I slept with last night has left me in bed, with nothing but a measly note."

"I put a kiss at the end." I attempt to justify.

"Oh you put a kiss at the end, but now I'm getting more than that."

He walks back up the stairs, and kicks the door shut behind him, he carries me back to bed, and places me on my feet, "Let's get rid of this." He removes my dress, "And this." The bra is gone, "And these." He gets down on his knees and pulls down my panties, he shoves me onto the bed playfully, and takes my panties off the rest of the way.

He takes off his joggers and scrambles on top of me, he's quick to push into me, I'm quivering beneath him, he's devouring my neck, his hands are roaming my body, all I can do is whimper with every one of his strokes, I have nothing left to give him, but he is still finding something to take.

"I can't get enough of you." He whispers, "You're so irresistible, everything about you screams, take me." All I can do is whimper beneath him, "I want to take you to places you have never been before Belle."

"You are." I gasp, "You already are."

He kisses me and carries on with his strokes, he carries me to climax, all I can do is whimper as I do, Parker gives a long groan as he climaxes.

This time he keeps a tight hold of me, I now have no choice but to sleep, his hold won't let me move, never in my life has a man treated me so tenderly, and now he wants to hold me as I sleep, I think I love him.

This time when I wake up its Parker that's not in bed, but I can smell coffee, I get up and look for my clothes, I manage to find my underwear, but not my dress.

I just shrug and make my way towards the smell of coffee, I find Parker in the kitchen, he's cooking breakfast, he looks at me and smiles, "Now there is a sight I have been wanting to see for a long time, a woman leaving my room in her underwear, and finding me in the kitchen cooking breakfast."

"Where have you put my dress?" I ask him.

"First things first, get that sexy body over here and kiss me."

I chuckle at his demand, but I fulfil it, I walk over to him, hook my arms around his waist, and kiss him tenderly the way he likes to kiss his women. I didn't dream falling in love with him, it really did happen, the evidence is in how my heart throbs when I see him.

"You didn't answer my question." I say when I pull away.

"It's in a safe place, where it will stay, until we have had more time together and talked for a bit."

"Oh Parker." I groan, "I don't like games."

"This isn't a game, when I am in my apartment I often walk around like this, and I want you to be comfortable enough to do the same. You have a nice body. Indulge me."

I smile, "Alright fine, I'll indulge you." I gently bite his shoulder.

"You do that again, I won't be accountable for my actions." He kisses the top of my head.

"I'll be good." I promise, "Only because what you're cooking smells so incredible."

"Have you ever had eggy bread?"

"I can't say I have no."

"Well then you've been missing out."

He gets out a couple of plates and glasses for water, he dishes the eggy bread up on to a couple of plates, and takes my hand so we can go around the counter to eat, he sits down and lifts me up on his knee, he puts his left hand on my hip and eats one handed.

"I can sit in a chair."

"I like holding you." He kisses my neck.

I sample his food, "Oh my God you can cook."

"My Mum taught me, and my Dad told me a gentleman always cooks for a woman after he has slept with her, it shows the utmost respect."

"I like your parents regardless of whether they like me or not." I put my head on his shoulder, "Thank you for last night. No man has ever treated me so tenderly."

"So are you going to sleep with me again?" He asks nibbling on my ear.

I cackle at his actions, "You have food on that plate, and you're trying to eat me."

"You didn't answer my question." He says softly.

"Yes Parker, you're all I want now, as long as you want me, I'll never go back to the way I used to be."

It's too soon to tell him I love him, but if things keep progressing the way they are, then it will be soon.

Parker

I'm all she wants, it's not the same as need but it's close enough, it's too soon to tell her I love her, but fuck I do, I do love her. She's amazing, she is so fucking amazing, how all those men could have treated her so badly is beyond me, she deserves to be treated like the amazing woman she is.

I kiss her shoulder, "You're so amazing Belle, I hate that men treated you like anything less than the way you deserve."

"Thankfully I have you now, so all of that will change."

She nuzzles into my neck. Fuck she breaks my heart, all she has wanted is for someone to love her, to show her love and tenderness, and none of her endeavours have done that, now she is relying on me to provide her with love and tenderness. She may not have said the words she needs me, but she has implied that is the case. It's only a matter of time before she says it.

"So what are your plans for today?" I ask her.

"I have some appointments, and an event to oversee, a christening."

"And the odds of you being on your own with men?" I ask her.

She looks at me with challenge in her eyes, "Are you showing me your possessive side Parker?"

"I'm not possessive, just protective, there is a difference, after last night and this morning, I don't think you can blame me."

"And will you be taking your shirt off for modelling today?" She asks me.

"That's different."

"How?"

"That's my job."

"So is me maybe talking to men, on my own in my office, doesn't mean I am going to fuck them, or even want to."

"Damn right you won't, not now you have me."

"Now that's settled." She gets off my lap, "I need my dress, I have to go home and get ready for work."

"I might want more time with you."

"And I have to work, come on Parker, don't play games. Please."

I roll my eyes, "Oh alright." I go and get her dress from the airing cupboard, "When will I see you again?"

"Erm I'll call you." She says putting her dress on.

"That doesn't answer my question."

"Soon, a day, two days max."

"If it is too long, then I am coming to get you."

"Alright, fine." She walks over to me, "Do I get a kiss?" She smiles.

I pull her to me for a long passionate kiss, when I pull away she's flushed, "Is that what you wanted?"

"That will do. I will see you later."

It takes everything to not tell her I love her, but I manage it. It nearly kills me though, I miss her already.

Belle

I have just got home, I go to find M.K and Bailey, they would be up by now, I know they are home, because Bailey's car is in the driveway, I go into the lounge, they're not there, so I go into the kitchen, they're both in there giggling about something, and they're both in their lounge clothes, M.K is in a pair of grey lounge shorts and a pink vest top, and Bailey has on a tiger onesie.

"Oh look whose home the dirty stop out." M.K beams a dirty smile at me, "And no limp." She walks over to me, and hitches up my dress, which has me rolling my eyes, "And no bruises, go on tell us about it, I can tell by that stupid grin on your face that you're dying to."

"Oh my God, last night was so amazing, he was so gentle and considerate, he is a light sleeper though, I tried to leave at four this morning, and he caught up with me, and carried me back to bed, where we had sex again, I didn't have the energy to do anything, but he has the stamina of an ox."

"Oh really?" Bailey laughs, "Go on then how many time did you do it?"

I think for a moment, count it out in my head, "Twelve times."

"In one night?" Bailey says in pure shock.

"Yeah we went straight to bed when we got to his place, he recovers quick, but the way he has sex is slow, and fuck he knows exactly what he's doing, and then we did it again at four this morning, where he kept hold of me, so I couldn't leave him alone in bed again, we then had sex another two times before breakfast."

"Wait, wait. Back up a moment." M.K puts her hand up to stop me in my tracks, "I'm still at the part where you left him at four this morning. Why'd you do that?"

"Oh erm, I've never slept over at a man's house before have I? So it felt weird, I wanted to be in my own bed, but it turns out if he didn't wake up to get me, I would've been stuck between his door and the door that divide his floor from the others."

"Oh, oh what did he cook you for breakfast?" Bailey asks excitedly, she's really happy for me.

"Eggy bread, he cooked it, he had me sit on his lap while we ate breakfast, I've never known anything like it." I sigh dreamily.

"And at what point last night did you fall in love with him?" M.K asks matter of factly.

"How did you know?" I didn't think it was that obvious.

"It's in your eyes, and the fact you haven't stopped smiling since you came home is a dead giveaway."

"I had no idea it was that obvious, it happened last night, I can't pinpoint exactly when, but it happened." Now I start to panic, "Oh fuck, I've only been with him a couple of weeks, and I'm in love with him. What am I going to do?"

M.K grabs my arms, "First off, you have to calm the fuck down. Belle surely you knew that one day this was going to happen."

"I didn't think it was going to happen with a guy I have only known a couple of weeks, and he's younger than me. People are going to call me a cougar, a cradle snatcher."

"Oh so people are allowed to call you a slag, a cheat and a home wrecker. But heaven forbid people call you a cougar, and a cradle snatcher, he isn't that young, I happen to think he's very mature for his age." M.K retorts.

"And Belle he's crazy about you." Bailey puts in, "Look Parker loved you the moment he saw you, it's too soon for either of you to have these feelings, but fact of the matter is they're there. Neither of you are going to admit to having these feelings, out of fear that the other isn't going to say it back."

My phone then goes off, it's Parker, 'Missing you already xx'.

M.K looks over my shoulder, "See the guy is crazy about you, you have literally only been home an hour, and he's missing you already. He loves you."

Parker

I have just got to work, "Parker we weren't expecting you in today." Scarlet says in a pink crop top and black skinny jeans.

Both Wayne and Sam are in suits they have been doing a shoot.

"I wanted to see how the pictures from the last shoot came out." I suggest, the truth is the apartment is too big without Belle, I want her with me all the time now, I want her to come home and stay with me.

"Oh sure, we can all review them if we want, take a break for a bit." Scarlet turns to the guy.

"Yeah I can have a break." Wayne says, "Sam?"

"Yeah that's cool with me."

We stand around the laptop Scarlet starts scrolling through the pictures, she's really good at her job, I think her mother is holding her back, Scarlet could be working for a major company round about now, if her Mum loosened the reins a little.

"These are really good." I muse, "You're really talented Scarlet."

She blushes, "Thanks Parker."

"You're welcome."

"You seem different today brother." Sam notices, "You seem in a really good mood."

"That's because I have an amazing girlfriend."

"Really? Since when?" Scarlet blurts.

"A few weeks, we've been on a few dates, I've met her family, she's going to meet mine, and last night was the night, she came back to mine after we had dinner with her Nan, she's all round amazing."

"Oh go on mate, so what's her name?" Wayne asks.

"I prefer not to say, it's not fair for my friends to know before my family get to meet her, but she is the reason for my good mood."

"It's good to see you happy." Sam says.

"I honestly think she is the one." I admit.

"We should go out for drinks to celebrate."

"Yeah sounds good." I respond.

"Parker while you're here, why not do some poses for me?" Scarlet suggest.

"Yeah why not, we can go out for drinks after."

When we are done with the shoot, Wayne is suited and booted in a sky blue suit with a black shirt.

Sam is in a pair of beige pants, and a black t-shirt.

And I have on a pair of black jeans, with a white t-shirt.

Wayne has just got a round in, "There we are." He holds up his glass, "To a job we love."

"The job we love." We toast.

"So Parker we can't help but notice you gave a lot more during the shoot today, so whoever this mystery woman is, she is having a very good effect on you."

"Oh yeah she is amazing, I can't wait to see her again, when we aren't around each other we talk on the phone and text, she's meeting my family on Wednesday, I really want to see her again before then."

"Is she nervous?" Sam asks.

"She has never actually met a partners family before, she has never been in a serious relationship, she is used to casual flings."

"How old is she?" Wayne asks.

"Twenty five."

"An older lady." Sam muses.

"Not that much older." I retort.

"Used to casual flings, so in other words she used to be a slut." Wayne blurts.

"Don't talk about her like that. She didn't used to be a slut, she's used to men treating her badly, so she didn't know what to do when I came along and treated her the way she deserved."

"Alright bro, chill out, I was only kidding."

He wasn't 'only kidding', and he knows it, but I am not going to start a row, because he is a thoughtless prick.

I know it has only been a few hours since I have last seen Belle, but the distance is killing me, I want her in my apartment to live, I know how crazy I sound, I have only slept with her once, she has only spent one night in my bed, and I want her to live with me.

As if by magic she walks in, she is dressed all official, in a pair of black trousers, and a white designer blouse, she hasn't seen me, but she's looking for someone. Who?

The then mystery person makes an appearance, it's a man, she smiles at him, it's a business smile, he kisses both of her cheeks, and for some reason this little move from him makes me want to launch myself over the bar, and kick seven shades of shit out of him, she's not his to kiss.

What's wrong with me? I'm not a possessive person, well I didn't used to be. Is this what love does to people.

She goes upstairs with this man, who I still have no clue what he looks like.

"Was that Belle O Neil going upstairs with a man?" Wayne asks.

"Certainly looks that way." Sam answers.

"She does know this isn't a knocking shop right? This isn't somewhere she can fuck men. Although I have heard she is a really good fuck, I wouldn't mind having a go, just to see what all the fuss is about."

I stand up at that comment a little too abruptly, "I will get this round in."

I go to the bar. Do I go upstairs and make sure it is solely business she's conducting? She hasn't given me any reason not to trust her, so I'm not going to spy on her. I get the drinks in and keep a look out for her coming downstairs.

Belle

God this is painful, never in my career have I had such a demanding client, and he insisted it's me he deals with, his name is Daniel McDowd, he is handsome, with his upturned lips, grey protruding eyes, short pointed nose and triangle jawline, and his charcoal suit with a crisp white shirt, is tight enough to show off some well-defined muscles. I know he has worn that suit for me.

Although he is good looking, he's a pompous arsehole, he is arranging a promotion part for himself, and there is to be a large picture of him on the stage and an ice sculpture of himself, I'm making a note of everything he wants, but it is so draining.

"So you want an ice sculpture, a blown up picture of you on the stage, you also want a live band. Mr McDowd, I can't help but wonder why you're organising your own promotion party."

"If I'm honest, I wanted to arrange my own promotion party, because I wanted to meet the most successful event organiser of her generation."

I read right through that line, "I'm not the most successful event organiser of my generation, I own the most successful event planning COMPANY this generation has seen. What you meant to say was, you wanted to meet the event planner that has a reputation for having affairs, so that you can see if I am really as beautiful as people make out. So what's your verdict?" Why am I indulging him?

"I think you're more beautiful than what they say." He puts his hand on my knee, I should shift away, but it's not what I do.

"Thank you I get that a lot." I need to wrap this up now. "Alright so I am going to finalise everything you have asked for, I will be in touch to let you know on the progress when I have done all of that, I'll be in touch."

"Do you want to have a drink?" He asks.

"I shouldn't really, technically I'm still at work."

"You're the boss, if the boss can't break the rules then who can."

"I actually have a boyfriend. I'm trying to change."

"Belle, I'm asking you for a drink, not for you to fuck me."

I then relent realising it will be easier to just give him what he wants, "Alright fine, one drink."

We go downstairs, "What will you have?"

"A glass of vino."

"A large glass of vino, and a pint of Carling please."

Parker

Belle is now downstairs with that man, they are both at the bar, I'm tensing at the sight of them together. Who is he? And what the fuck is he doing putting his hand on her back? Incensed I stand up and make my way over to them.

When I get to her I say, "There you are."

She jumps and turns to face me, I put my hands on her cheeks and kiss her deeply and passionately, she's trying to pull away, but I'm not letting her, "We're supposed to be having drinks with my friends." She's confused, I pay no attention.

I grab her drink and her hand, I practically drag her to my table, when I get there I simply say, "Fella's this is Belle, my girlfriend. Belle these are my friends Sam and Wayne."

I sit down and pull her to me, I then put my hand on her hip, "No kidding, you're going out with the old commissioner's daughter." Sam muses.

"He is also going out with your bosses evil step daughter. And the woman who has been fucked by over a hundred men, but thanks for not mentioning that I guess." What the hell is she doing?

I tighten my hold on her, she's being silly, there's no need for her to be so crass in front of my friends.

She downs her drink, and then winces, she knows she's in trouble with me, "I'm sorry there was no call for that, that meeting was intense, the guy wants the world, and fancied me, I even told him I had a boyfriend, but that didn't stop him hounding me for a drink with him, I only said yes in the hope he wouldn't ask me again, then you showed up and saved me."

She puts her head on my shoulder, she needs comfort and is seeking it from me, I run my hand up and down her back and kiss her head.

Sam and Wayne look on baffled, "So this is a recent thing for you two then? Belle you settling down now?" Wayne asks.

"I wasn't expecting to, but it looks like it, yes."

"Looks like you can tame the wild."

Belle then sighs, "I had better get back to work."

She kisses my cheek, when I don't let her go, she lightly kisses my lips, "Please let me go." She says so quietly only I can hear her. I let her go and she leaves.

I follow her.

Belle

I walk out of the bar, I'm not expecting Parker to follow me. So when his hand lands on my arm, he makes me jump, "Hey are you alright?"

"Yeah I'm fine, I just need to get back to work, I thought I was meeting your family before your friends."

"That was before Mr Fancy put his hand on your back."

Now the reason for him looking fit for murder is clear, "Mr Fancy as you so call him, is a client and he is arranging a promotion party. There was no need to get possessive."

"And there was no need to be crass in front of my friends."

"Oh please Wayne hated me from the moment he saw me, you could see it on his face. You know what? I get people love to judge people they don't know, and I know I haven't done much for my reputation, but most of what you and your friends know about me, is what a twisted old bitch has told you."

"He will learn and get to know you."

"Get your head out of the clouds Parker, mud sticks, reputations hardly ever change, they become part of you."

He captures my mouth and kisses me deeply and passionately, it takes my breath away, "God I've missed you so much, please say you have missed me."

"I've missed you. I have missed you Parker."

"Move in with me." He blurts.

"What?" I reply shocked.

"Now I know you heard me."

"I heard what you said, I just can't believe it."

"Believe it, move in with me."

"Parker we've only been together a couple of weeks, we only slept together last night."

"And I hate the idea of waking up without you now, I want you in my apartment, I want you to call it your home, I want you to move in with me." He kisses me again, "Come back to mine with me now, and we'll talk."

"In other words have sex." I retort matter of factly.

"It would be good if that's how it ended up. Please come back to mine, let's talk about this."

"Parker you have a very young way of looking at things, it's not as simple as moving in with you, I have people to think of."

"People who know we are together, it's only a matter of time before it happens." He kisses my neck and wraps his arms around my mid-section, "Come back to mine and let's talk baby, please."

"Alright fine." I relent, "Let's talk."

Parker slips his arm around my shoulders, I instinctively wrap my arm around his waist, it feels nice, comforting even, when I get into my car and drive to his apartment block, we spend the journey in a comfortable silence, it's nice.

When we walk into his apartment block, he nods to Malcom and I give him a little smile, he swipes his card and we step into the lift, I begin to feel nervous, I have never been in the position of someone I care about wanting me to move in with them before, but then again I have never cared about a man in this way before either, this is all new to me.

As soon as the lift shuts, and Parker swipes his card down, he doesn't waste any time, his hands are on my hips, his mouth is over mine, I don't know what to do with myself, his hands move to my breasts, I shudder and grant him full access to my mouth.

"Parker I thought we were going to talk." I battle to say through the kiss.

"Well I'm trying a new tactic." He says and carries on kissing me, "Just think if you were living here, we could do this all the time."

"We both work." I point out.

The lift beeps and the doors open, he lifts me up and carries me inside, as soon as we're inside, he takes off my top, and starts undoing my trousers, I manage to unbutton his shirt and pull it off.

He pushes my trousers down as far as he can reach, and he places me on the kitchen counter, I wince as the cold surface hits my skin.

"Lay down Belle." Parker orders softly, I do as he says, as he removes my trousers fully, "Almost perfect." He muses, he circles around the counter and ruffles my hair until all of the pins fall out, "Now you're perfect. But now here's a dilemma. How do I take you?"

"Are you kidding?" I gasp. I'm sprawled on his kitchen counter and now he's questioning how he is going to have sex with me? This man is unreal, "Parker I really don't give a shit. Please just get on with it."

"Hmmm bossy." He muses, as he takes possession of my mouth, "I'm going to do it a new way." He runs his hand down my midsection, "Move in with me." He says nibbling on my ear lobe.

"No." Is my simple response.

He bites my bottom lip, moves his hand under the material of my panties, he pushes his fingers into me, his other hand is roaming my body lingering over my sensitive spots, I'm gasping and moaning at his actions, his mouth travels from my lips, to my neck and to my chest, he's trailing his hot tongue all over, I arch my back at the raw pleasure he's filling me with, he looks down at me, "Move in with me."

I take a moment to catch my breath, and then I manage to respond, "No Parker."

He takes my mouth again and carries on working me with his amazing fingers, one of his hands finds my hair, I can't help but love the fact he hasn't stopped, he's still working to pleasure me, most partners would have stopped worrying about their partner's pleasure and only focused on their own, if their partner wasn't giving them their own way.

"Oh fuck Parker." I gasp. He's taking me to new unexplored heights and I'm loving every second of it.

"You could have this any time you wanted, if you move in with me."

Oh he's playing just plain dirty. I can't help but admire his tactic, Parker has now totally enthralled me, turns out, he's got a mean streak, sometimes it's hard to believe he's younger than me.

He carries to climax, "Oh Parker." I gasp out his name.

"Move in with me."

It takes everything I have to say, "No."

Oh fuck, it was so, so hard to say no after that, I do want that more often, I want him to do that to me more often, I want sex with him in general often, he isn't going to stop wearing me down, part of me wants him to, I won't agree easily, I'm too practical for that.

Parker

She's a tough cookie, but I could tell it took all she had to say no the last time I asked her to move in with me, I ease her down, she's panting and sweating, I don't give her time to recover, I remove her panties, and fuck there is something about her in silk that drives me mad, seeing her in that underwear turns me on so much, I remove my own pants, lift her into sitting position and simply glide into her.

"Oh Parker." She groans her voice full of sex.

"I love hearing you say my name like that, and you could say it more often if you…"

"Parker I'm not going to move in with you yet." She interrupts tiredly, "Please let's just focus on this, on us. For now."

She puts her hands in my hair and kisses me, and it works, Belle could distract me from anything with a simple kiss, or by walking into a room with silk underwear, or better yet naked.

"God I love you in silk." I say laying my hands on her breasts, "Please tell me that silk is the only material of underwear you have, and every time I undress you, there is going to be silk underneath."

"If that's what you want, then that's the way it will be baby." She nibbles on my ear.

Oh fucking hell I love her so much, how anyone has gone this long without seeing this side to her is beyond me, she is capable of being a lover, of sharing sweet words, she can be vulnerable, and yet I have been the only man to see it, I feel honoured in a way.

"Move in with me." I say and promise myself it will be the last time today.

Is it my fault that just as she goes to answer we both climax?

"Parker." She groans rolling her head back and riding the wave. I kiss and nibble on her neck as I empty into her.

By the time she's done, she's trembling in my arms, I have to put my hand on the counter to hold myself steady, when I've eased us both down, she kisses me lightly, looks me in the eyes and says, "No, and you brought me here under false pretenses, I thought you wanted to talk."

"We did talk." I retort, wrapping the ends of her hair around my index finger, "I love your hair when it's down, it's so wild and unpredictable, and it's silky smooth just like the rest of you."

"Slick move changing the subject like that, but no Parker we didn't talk, you tried to use my ecstasy against me, and you also failed." She kisses my nose and gives me a sweet smile.

"I miss you like mad when you're not here and fact is I don't need to, if you move in with me, we can see each other a lot more."

"You're relentless." She kisses me lightly, "If I promise to come by more often will that appease you?"

She wants a compromise, "It might for a while at least. But you are going to be moving in with me Belle."

"It's early days, I didn't even know I was ready for a relationship, you made me ready. Just slow down a bit, you have me, I'm not going to see another man, I'm with you, I really like you. Believe me, trust me."

Really like me? It's not the same as love, but it's a good start I guess, "Alright fine, I really like you too, I do trust you. I just miss you when you're not around here."

"I promise to come by more often." She kisses me again, "And if I am going to be spending more time here, I need to know where everything is."

"Alright." I sigh.

If she thinks it's going to be that easy, then she's mistaken, Belle O Neil will have moved in with me, within two weeks that much I can count on, I know I can lean on her friends and her Nan for support, and I have a trick up my own sleeve, she is not going to like it, and she is going to resist, I am more or less banking on that, but she will succumb to my wishes.

What doesn't make sense to her makes perfect sense to me, and what makes perfect sense to me, is her moving in with me.

Sooner or later it will make sense to her, she just needs a little bit of gentle persuasion, and if that doesn't work, then a hard shove to my way of thinking.

Chapter Nine

Parker

I T's been a couple of days since Belle agreed to come by my apartment more often, and so far it's not working for me, and I'm not even planning on giving it a chance, I know what I want, and I'm going to get it.

I have spent the last couple of days investing in a wardrobe and a bedside cabinet for Belle, as well as getting her a key card of her own.

I am just getting some things for dinner, I am going to cook for Belle tonight, and try and convince her to move in with me again, it didn't work with sex, even though I am going to try that method again, I'm also going to shower her with romance.

"Good morning Parker."

I turn to see her Nan, in a long red dress, she always looks so elegant, and moves gracefully, I can see where Belle gets it from, "Good morning." I smile, "How are you?"

"I'm alright thank you, how are you? And how is my grand-daughter?"

"We're both good thank you. I've asked her to move in with me."

"Oh have you? That's wonderful news, I know how much you love her, and I also know how happy she is with you."

"She said no." I try not to let on I'm disappointed.

Her Nan doesn't seem surprised, "She trying to be practical, right now she is going through the motions, a new relationship, something she's never had before, you're also a younger man."

"What does that have to do with anything?" I ask confused.

"Parker it may not seem like it, but Belle does care about what people say about her, and we both know the papers are not overly nice about her. And while she's accepted that she hasn't done much to help herself there. She isn't just thinking about herself now, she has someone who could get caught in the crossfire, and that someone is you, she is trying to protect you."

"I don't want protecting, I want her to move in with me, screw what the papers have to say about her going out with me. Screw what people think, I love her. That's all that matters to me."

"I'll talk to her, she just needs a little push." She starts fishing around in her bag, when she finds what she looking for she hands it to me, "It's the keys to her gate and her house, the gate is Bluetooth so just push the button to get it to open. If you pack some of her clothes, if she plans on staying at your home more often, then it makes sense to have some of her things there, like clothes, a tooth brush, shower gel, shampoo, conditioner, toiletries. You know what I mean, you're a clever boy."

"Yeah, yeah, I'm with you, it makes sense." I bend down and kiss her cheek, "Thank you, this means a lot to me, I'll get the key back to you as soon as I'm done."

After finishing my shopping, going home and unpacking it. I'm now outside Belle's house, with a duffel bag in tow, her car isn't in the drive, so she isn't home, part of me is glad, the other part is disappointed.

I push the button to open her gate, and make my way up her drive, her driveway is so colourful with aqua blue, yellow and sky blue slate, when I get outside her house, I notice that the slate continues to a nice patio, where I can picture Belle and her friends eating, laughing, talking and drinking.

I unlock her door, walking into her house, she likes the beach theme, it's a very nice floor, it's like sand, and the walls are like the ocean and the sky, I'm quite shocked that she likes this kind of design.

Right I have to focus on my mission, Belle's bedroom is the only one with a balcony, I go upstairs and look for her room, I look to the left and there are three doors, I open one, the bathroom, I open the second door, a bedroom, but no balcony, I open the third door and the same.

I then realise it's the only door on the other side of the corridor, Belle is so used to isolation, even living with her friends she picks the room the furthest away from them.

I feel a little choked, but I approach her room, I open her door, I notice that she likes the theme to be the same in every room, M.K and Bailey respect that. Why the need for so much order?

I look at her bed and picture her sleeping, the way her arm extends, the way her leg slightly bends, it's like she has been waiting a long time to have someone to hold.

I go into her en-suite and every piece of furniture is King Louise, I can picture her bathing, her hair all wet, her being so relaxed she's nearly snoozing. Or is she the sort to listen to music and sing? I would have to learn, I make a note of all of her shower gel.

I now move into her bedroom, and look through her clothes, I pick the things I have never seen her in before.

"You picked the wrong house fucker." I hear a voice I know to be M.K say from behind me.

I quickly turn and duck, as a cricket bat come towards my head, "Whoa, whoa M.K, it's me Parker."

"Parker! What the fuck are you doing here?!" She snarls, she looks quite fetching in her three quarter length jeans and black long sleeve crop top, she looks around, "Belle didn't mention she's moving out."

"She isn't yet, I've asked her to move in with me. She's turned me down for now, and we have made a compromise, well she thinks we have, me on the other hand, I'm slowly moving her in with her even noticing."

M.K laughs, "And you think Belle will fall for that? Really? She isn't stupid."

"I know and she's agreed to spend more time at my apartment, so surely it makes sense that she has some stuff at mine, if she plans on being true to her word."

"Did she say the words I promise?"

I frown, "Yes she said I promise."

"Right when she says those words, she will never break what she's promised, those words mean gold both when she says, and when she hears them, I can't tell you why, but you can ask her."

"Alright then I will."

I just have to find the ideal opportunity.

Belle

I'm at work in my office in a pair of grey trousers and a hot pink designer blouse, when I hear my lift ding, I look up to see Nan, in a long red dress, she never lost her glamourous streak, I'm quick to stand and approach her, "Nan do we have plans that I've forgotten about?"

"Oh no darling, I was in the neighbourhood and wondered if you had time for a quick chat."

"I always have time for you Nan." I kiss her cheek, "Sit down, I'll pour us some coffee."

She does as I say and takes a seat on the sofa, I pour us both some coffee and go and sit down beside her, "So I don't mean to be blunt." I start, "But what do you want to talk about?"

"I was out shopping this morning, and I saw Parker."

"Oh, how was he?"

"He was alright, he seems like the kind of person that is always alright, he really likes you."

"I know he does, I really like him."

"He likes you so much, he has asked you to move in with him."

"He told you that?" I ask her shocked.

"Yes he also said that you turned him down."

"Nan it isn't practical to move in with someone I have only been with a couple of weeks."

"But is it practical to love him?"

Of course if I couldn't hide it from my friends, I wouldn't be able to hide it from Nan. "No it isn't, and I have no idea what to do about it."

She puts her hand on my knee, "You just go with it darling, love is a lovely thing to be in."

"Until you're not in it anymore." I look her in the eyes, "Nan I've only been with him a couple of weeks and I'm terrified of losing him."

"Oh darling you won't lose him, that boy knows all of your flaws and still wants you despite all of them. You need to speak to him and seriously think about moving in with him."

"Alright I'll talk to him. Thank you Nan. Would you like to have lunch?"

"I have nothing else on, so I would love to."

I have text Parker to ask him if I can see him, I get to his apartment block, and he's there waiting for me in the lobby, he kisses me lightly when I get to him, he keeps his arm around me when as we walk to the lift, when we walk into it, and it starts moving he nuzzles into my neck, "I've missed you." He kisses me tenderly. Fuck I never get tired of the emotions he fills me with.

"You told Nan, you asked me to move in."

"It might have come up in conversation." He moves his hands to my breasts, my breath shakes, "She told me you might be worried about the kind of trouble the news of us being together might bring me. If that is the only thing bothering you, then you need to stop worrying and just move in with me."

The lift opens, we both walk out, "Parker it's not just that, it's not practical, not yet."

"And when will it be practical Belle?" He asks.

"I don't know, Parker please."

He puts his hands on my cheeks, "It's alright, it's alright. I want you to do something with me."

"What?"

"Have a bath with me, please, I've already ran one."

I blink at him a little bit baffled by his request, and the fact he's given in so easily.

"Alright, let's have a bath."

He takes hold of my hand and we walk into the bathroom, and fucking hell, his bathroom is huge, everything is marble white, his toilet is near the sink, on the right wall, above the since is a five foot high, two foot wide cabinet, on the back wall there is a round shower cubicle, on the back left corner there is a cupboard, and slap bang in the centre of the bathroom, going into the floor, is the biggest bath I have ever seen.

"Fuck this bath is bigger than mine."

We both undress, when he's undressed he slips into the bath, "Have you ever bathed with a man Belle?"

I slide in opposite him, "No I haven't."

"Come here." He orders softly.

I move towards him, he turns me round, wraps his arms around me, and kisses the side of my head, "There's nothing like having a bath with your partner and holding them while you bathe."

I look around the room, and notice some shower gel that I use, "You have a feminine side Parker."

"No silly, I got it for you. I can't expect you to use mine can I?"

"I can always shower and bathe at home."

"If you stay here more often, then you're going to want to shower and bathe here too. And when you move in."

Without warning he spins me round and guides me onto him, "Oh fuck." I groan, I should have seen this coming.

"When you move in." He kisses my neck, "Ride me baby. Go on, enjoy it." I do just that, I keep the pace the way he has taught me, the gentle, loving pace.

"Belle." He murmurs, never has a man called out my name, whether it be quietly or shouting during sex, "When you move in we can do things like this all the time, we can have sex everywhere in the apartment, we can hold each other as we sleep, wake up beside each other, cook each other meals, look forward to coming home, because we are dying to see each other. This place is empty without you Belle. Move in with me."

Oh fucking hell, when he has me like this, he's so hard to say no to, and he must know it, hence why he gets me like this, and then he asks me to move in with him when I'm like this, drowning in the ecstasy he's providing me with, all I can think is how often he could get me like this, if I did move in with him.

"Parker." I kiss his neck and nibble his ear, "Fuck I love what you do to me. But no."

"Belle you're so stubborn."

"Takes one to know one." I climax, "Oh Parker." I roll my head back and ride the wave.

He puts his hands on my hips and guides me in and out of him, so that he can find his release, I put my hands on his shoulders and cooperate with his movements, "Oh fuck Belle." He climaxes and kisses me hard, "Belle you know this is right, this is so right, everything we do together is so right."

"How are you only twenty?" I ask baffled, "Twenty year olds want to fuck, they want to drink alcohol until they throw up, and then drink some more. They don't want to settle down, especially with a woman like me. Parker I've hurt so many people."

"I don't care Belle, I wanted you the moment I saw you in The River with your friends, I see the true side to you, the loving, tender side to you that no other man you have been with has seen."

"You give me the kind of loving I've been craving for years, I do want a relationship with you, but I want to do it right, take it slow."

"Belle I've done everything I've wanted to do, travel, although that was with work, to me it counts, I have money and lots of it, so I'm in a good financial position to settle down, it was just a case of finding someone to settle down with, and I have found you, I want to settle down with you."

"So do I, it's just I want to make sure this is the real deal."

"I promise you it is, to me it is."

He has no idea how important those two words are to me, if he did then he wouldn't have said them.

I just simply say, "Alright then. Can I get out now? I don't want to go all wrinkly. It's not an attractive look."

"Alright, oh I bought you a robe, if you open the cupboard in the corner, it should be nice and warm."

I get out of the bath and pad over to the cupboard, it's a heating cupboard, wow he really does living in luxury, even I don't live like this.

He reaches over my head to grab it, he passes me mine and puts on his own, his has his name embedded on the left breast, I look at mine which also has my name on it.

I look at him tiredly, he gives me a sheepish grin, "I couldn't resist, it fits you nicely, although it won't be on for long."

I roll my eyes at him and begin to walk to the bedroom, if he wants me to treat this place like it's my own then I will, usually when I'm at home, I rest my eyes or nap as I dry off.

I stop in my tracks when I see the new wardrobe and cabinet.

"Why have we stopped?" He whispers in my ear. Saying nothing I walk over to the wardrobe, I open the doors, then I go to the cabinet and I open that.

"Who packed my clothes?" I ask him.

"Well I did." He says plainly.

"Whoa, whoa, how did you get into my house?"

"Your Nan gave me her keys."

I silently curse Nan, then quickly retract it, "And you packed my clothes. And went through my underwear drawer."

"If it's any consolation, M.K nearly took my head off with a cricket bat."

"Usually her aim is better. And she let you pack my clothes?" Now I am angry with HER, "Parker why are my clothes and underwear in a wardrobe and cabinet that weren't here the last time I was here?" I put my thumb and my forefinger to the bridge of my nose in an attempt to fend off a threatening headache.

"I thought it would make sense to have clothes here, if you plan on being here more often."

"So you thought you would do it for me? Without asking?"

"Yes." He isn't even sorry. I could swing for him.

"Great." I say shortly.

"Belle. There is one more thing." He leaves the bedroom.

"I dread to think." I sit on the end of the bed. This man is proving to be totally unbelievable.

He comes back into the bedroom and passes me a card, "And what's this?"

"It's a swipe card to get you up here, if you want to see me and I'm not here, then you can let yourself in and wait."

"So I say no to moving in, and you're answer is move me in anyway." I'm shocked by how calm my voice is, I'm fuming.

"No you promised you would spend more time here. So it makes sense to have a card, a wardrobe, a cabinet and some clothes here." He moves towards me and kneels in front of me, "You will be moving in with me Belle and soon, I know I'm being selfish, but with you I can't help it."

He kisses me possessively, "Unbelievable man." I murmur as we kiss.

"Impossible woman." He groans, "I can't promise life will be easy, but I can promise I will make you happy Belle."

He has no idea how happy he is making me already.

Chapter Ten

Parker

I AM AT MY PARENT'S house, my Mum is doing some tidying, even though the place is already tidy, with a cream wall, laminate flooring, there is a set of stair going along the back wall, as soon as you walk in you are in the lounge, with two three seater sofas, one by the window, the other in the centre of the room, and there is a two seater sofa along the right wall, and an arm chair beside it, there are coffee tables beside each piece of furniture there is a door along the right wall which leads to the dining room, and another door beyond that that leads to the kitchen.

My Mum is in her lounge clothes, as she always is when she has no plans with her morning, I can't say I blame her, she used to work a lot of hours before she had Skyla, she barely had a moment to herself, even though Skyla can be a pain, I think she has been a Godsend to mum, she makes my Mum stop and take a breath from time to time, which is a relief to my Dad, he was also starting to worry about her, but he does nothing but worry about my Mum.

Right now she is a pair of grey jogging bottoms and a white long sleeve top.

I have a naughty Skyla in my arms, she seems happily babbling away, wearing nothing but a pair of sky blue pants and a pink vest top, today of all days she's refusing to wear trousers and it's driving Mum mad.

I have on a pair of medium blue jeans and a red t-shirt.

"I hope you plan on wearing something smarter when you bring your girlfriend here today."

"Mum she has seen me looking casual before, and you don't need to dress up, I'll tell Belle it's a casual get together, it might make a change from all of the formal do's she goes to."

"I can't believe of all the girls you could fall for, it has to be one of the most controversial girls in London." Mum scoffs, "At least she isn't Chelsea, which is a bonus."

"No she isn't which is probably why I love her, slept with her and have asked her to move in with me."

"You've asked her to move in with you? Parker my boy you really don't do things by halves do you?"

"Mum I love her. I haven't felt this way about anyone, not even Chelsea."

She sees in my eyes that I'm telling the truth, "All the more reason not to rush, and it's obvious you've impacted on her in a positive way, she hasn't been in the papers due to a scandalous affair in weeks. But Parker are you really comfortable knowing that that the next time she will be in the papers it will be because people have learnt she is in a relationship with you?"

"No it doesn't bother me, because people will see that there is another side to Belle that she doesn't show to a lot of people, Mum I promise you, you will be pleasantly surprised."

"To be honest with you, part of me is already. Alright Parker I am willing to give her a chance."

"Also tell Ashley to play nice, and the same with Julian too. And as for this one." I hold Skyla over my head to make her laugh, "Let's hope she keeps her trousers on tonight."

She gives me a cheeky smile and says, "Nope."

"Cheeky monkey." I smile at her and pass her back to my Mum, "I'm going to go and see Belle, she's on a day off today, "I will see if there is a chance we can have some lunch."

"Alright darling, see you later."

I kiss her cheek, "See you later."

Belle

I'm at home having a much needed day off, in a pair of black skinny jeans and a royal blue designer filly blouse, working with Daniel McDowd is proving to be a bit of a challenge, after fixing myself a pasta salad, I am about to make my way upstairs and have a bath, when M.K and Bailey come in, both of them chatting amongst themselves.

Bailey is dressed in a nice floral tea dress.

M.K is dressed in a pair of black three quarter length trousers and a black long sleeve designer blouse.

"Hey what are you two doing back here?"

"We came to have lunch with you." Bailey answers.

"Oh sorry I didn't know, I've already eaten. I'll drink a coffee with you though."

We all walk through to the kitchen, I pour the girls a coffee, as they get their lunch ready, "So how's work?"

"Mr McDowd called for you three times. What part of she is on a day off does he not fucking get?" M.K states.

Knowing what M.K is like, I turn to Bailey, "Please tell me she didn't say that to him."

"I have no idea." Bailey shrugs.

"I didn't, thanks for the vote of confidence, although the day isn't over yet, so there's still time, I don't like the guy, he gives me the creeps, and he makes it clear he has his eye on you."

"He knows I have a boyfriend, Parker made it perfectly clear on my first meeting with him, Daniel put his hand on my back, Parker was there, I didn't know this until he spun me round, kissed me like a mad man, and then dragged me off to meet his friends."

"How is everything going with him?" M.K asks.

"Amazing and intense." I smile.

"Why intense?" She asks.

"Just because I never thought I would ever feel this way about anyone well ever, all of a sudden here I am with all these feelings, I'm in love with a man I have only known a couple of weeks but it feels like I have known him forever, and he wants me to move in with him, I've never been so scared and so elated in my entire life."

"He's asked you to move in?" Bailey asks, "Well what the fuck are you doing here? Pack your bags and get the fuck out."

I laugh, I can always count on Bailey to make me laugh, "Am I the only person that can see how mad this is? We have only been together a couple of weeks."

"Sometimes that's the way it works." Bailey shrugs, "Sometimes love is something you build on, sometimes it hits you like a ten tonne truck."

"And you were smiling when you said the relationship can be intense, so you like it." M.K states.

"Oh God I love it, he's always touching me, holding me, kissing me, and the sex, oh fuck the sex is amazing, I never knew people actually talked while doing it."

"Yeah it's possible, sometimes it makes it better. But what do you actually talk about?"

"He asked me to move in with him during sex."

"Oh that is a dirty game." M.K gasps, "Really, really dirty."

"And you." I point to M.K, "Your aim used to be better." I turn to fill M.K in, "Parker was here the other day packing a few items of my clothing. And M.K only NEARLY took his head off."

"Only nearly, M.K you're losing your touch." M.K sneers at the pair of us and we giggle, "So he was packing some of your clothes?"

"I told him I would spend more time at his place, so he decided to pack some of my things, and place them in a wardrobe and bedside cabinet that he bought solely for me."

"Wow, wow the guy has some brass, you have to admire him." Bailey muses.

"If you say so." I respond, "Right I am going to go and run a bath, I will see you guys later." I kiss them both on the cheek and hug them.

"And seriously think about moving in with him." Bailey shouts after me.

"I am trust me."

I go upstairs and start running my bath.

Parker

I have just gotten to Belle's house, I can see another car in the drive, it must be one of the other's cars, so I call M.K.

"Hey Parker, what's up?"

"Are you at home?"

"Yeah. Why?"

"I'm outside, do me a favour and let me in will you?"

"One second." Soon the gate slowly opens, "Come on in."

"Thanks." I hang up and walk up the long drive, when I get to the door I knock briskly.

M.K answers, "Hey, Belle's probably in the bath right now, but you can wait for her if you like." I just make my way upstairs, "Or just go on up." I can just picture her shrugging, "Whatever."

I walk up the stairs, I go into her room, I hear her singing Emeli Sande Read All About It. I stand in the doorway and watch her a moment, she's rubbing soap into her arms her hair is hanging down, she can add singing to the list of talents no one knows about.

"I wondered if you ever sung in the bath."

She jumps when she hears me speak, "Who let you in?"

"M.K, she and Bailey were heading back to work." I walk and kneel by the bath, "I missed you." I kiss her tenderly.

"I would ask you to join me, but the bath isn't big enough."

"If you sit forward, I can do your back."

She sits forward, passes me her soap, I lather it onto my hands and begin a light massage, "Oh God." She groans in pleasure, I move my hands up to her shoulders, "You really are quite a man."

"Which is why you…"

"Which is why I, really like you, are dating you, sleeping with you, and letting you keep some of my things in you apartment."

I nibble on her ear, "You really are amazing Belle. I can't wait for you to meet my family, by the way we're keeping it a casual thing, you don't have to get all glammed up, my Mum likes to dress casual, now that she has had Skyla, my Dad will most likely be in jeans as shirt, as will Julian, Ashley always dresses a little classy, as for Skyla that little monster is going through a phase where she won't keep her pants on."

"Could be a good trend, I might do it myself." She muses.

I chuckle, I imagined her to be the sort to turn her nose up at things like that.

"So other than your little sister prancing around in her undies, are there any other surprises I am to be expecting?"

"I might wind up getting Julian in a head lock for being a little shit, and I might have to play aeroplane with Skyla, you might have to deal with a lot of questions."

"I might have guessed that." She tenses up, "I am going to get out now."

I release her shoulders, she gets out, wraps a towel around herself and dries off her arms and legs, I go and wrap my arms around her, "You don't have to be nervous baby, they will like you, maybe even love you, once they get to know you."

"I'll take your word for it."

"What do you normally do when you get out of the bather wrap up and dry off?" I ask her.

"Go and lay on the bed to rest my eyes, or have a nap."

"Lead the way."

She walks into her room, I stay a couple of paces behind her, she really does have nice legs.

She lays down on the bed, "Oh and take off your shoes, M.K should have told you to leave your shoes at the door."

I take off my shoes, lay down on the bed, prop up on my elbow, and run my free hand op Belle's legs, "I really love your legs." I murmur.

"I really love your arms." She gives them a testing squeeze, "I feel safe in your arms."

When was the last time she felt safe? I wonder.

She strokes my face, runs her hand up to my hair, and pulls me to her for a kiss, when I pull out of the kiss, I ask her, "Are you ticklish Belle?"

"As if I would be stupid enough to tell you that." She laughs.

"Alright let's find out." I start at her feet, she kicks me off on a giggle, I do the same to her knees, she has a smug look on her face and doesn't react, I move to her sides, "Oh no Parker! Please, please stop."

"Make me stop." I chuckle, "Have you ever play wrestled Belle?"

"Only M.K for the remote."

In one smooth move she uses my weight against me and manages to flip me over so she's straddling me, she holds my hands over my head, "Do I win?"

"Kiss me." She smiles and does as I say, she drops her guard and I roll her over, "Nope we're still going."

"Dirty game." She brings her knee up, and stops just short of my groin, to defend it I bend one of my legs, again she manages to flip me over.

She's a lot tougher than she looks, but her eyes are smiling, she's never done this with a man before, she has never had fun with a man before, she has never played silly, loving games with a man before, I might not be the first to sleep with her, but I am the first to show her what a real relationship looks like.

Belle

This is super fun, I have never done this with a man before, it is really fun, he makes me bring out the child in me, I straddle him and land a hard kiss on him, he runs his hands up my sides, I put my hands on his shoulders, "Belle." He murmurs, I take off his shirt, as he undoes his trousers, I run my hands up his chest, God he feels so amazing everything about him is strong and masculine.

And just like that everything has changed, we have gone from wrestling to having sex, it must be an aphrodisiac or something, because it is a major turn on, I am not going to lie.

Parker must feel it too, he flips me round so I am once again beneath him, he removes his trousers and his pants, and runs his hands up my towel, "Let's get this off shall we?"

I arch my back so he can remove my towel fully, he rains kisses over my exposed breasts and the centre of my chest, I cry out, he trails his lips up to my neck, as soon as he gets to my neck, he sinks into me, I gasp, he takes my mouth with his. My hands find his hair, I lose touch of my sense with Parker, every time he has me like this, I can't think straight.

"Belle." He groans, one of his hands runs up from my thigh to my breast, "I love the way your breasts feel in my hand, perfect fit. I love the way our mouths move together, it is like my mouth has been waiting for yours, I love the way our bodies mould together when we hold each other, and when we have sex, it's like our bodies were made for each other."

Fuck he says the sweetest most amazing things, I nibble on his ear, "Fuck Belle, I love what you do to me. I love the way you make me feel, I love the way we have sex."

"Fuck Parker." I gasp, "I love how amazing you are in bed."

We've never actually said we love each other, but the indication is there that we clearly do, we just have to say it.

Both Parker and I climax together, I give a throaty moan for mine, he groans into my neck for his.

When he's eased us both down, he holds onto me tightly, "I've wondered what it would be like to have sex with you in this bed."

I scoff, "I have never had sex in this bed before."

"Really? Why not?"

"Because I sleep in this bed, the men I have been with were never interested in SLEEPING with me only fucking me, so I used either the guys house, a hotel room, my office or their office, fuck them and leave, it always suited both parties, and if they were happy to fuck me in the marital bed, then that's their look out, I kept mine pure."

"Now here I am." Parker says smugly.

"Yeah now here you are."

He rolls onto his back beside me, places my left arm on his chest, my left leg between his legs, "Rest you head on my shoulder."

He takes hold of my hand and runs his free hand up and down my back.

I could stay like this forever.

After what does feel like forever, I get up and put on some sky blue matching silk underwear, Parker soon sits up and takes notice, I narrow my eyes and point at him, "Mr Wilson, when I get dressed, I plan on keeping my clothes on." I inform.

"Come here and call me Mr Wilson, we'll soon see how keeping your clothes on works for you then."

"Babe it's nearly it's nearly five, we've been in bed for the last two hours, we're due to be at your parents place for six."

I go and open my wardrobe to look for something to wear, "So it's a casual thing?" I poke around to find something casual, "What about jeans and a blouse?" I ask him.

"Yeah that should be fine." He comes to stand behind me, and looks in my wardrobe.

"You have no boundaries." I muse.

"Not when it comes to you." He replies dryly.

"So when I find my mail opened, then I know who to yell at."

"I do have some boundaries, I would never open you mail or go through your phone."

"But to go through my wardrobe and my underwear drawer, is totally acceptable." I retort.

"I am going to know what is in your wardrobe and underwear drawer, when we move in together. I also know when you move in, your underwear will be all silk. So what does it matter?"

"Oh Parker. For tonight can you not bring that up?"

He gives me an unapologetic smile and nuzzles my neck, "Baby you're about to have dinner with my parents, it's safe to say you moving in with me will get brought up."

"You're an unbelievable man." I moan.

"But you…"

"But I can't imagine being this happy without you." I know what he is fishing for, I can't say it yet.

He finds a pair of jeans, and a red Laura Ashley top, "This will look nice on you, but before you put it on, I just want to…" He runs his hands up to my breast and gives them a squeeze, he then spins me round his hands travel down to my bum, when he pulls away and says, "That should tide me over until I can get you naked again."

I roll my eyes, "You have a one track mind."

"As you pointed out the other day in the bath, I'm a twenty year old man, my mind isn't on much else, especially when you look constantly sexy."

"At least you're honest. And I don't think about much else when I'm around you. So the feelings mutual."

Parker

We have just arrived at my parents' house, Belle insisted we get a bottle of Champagne, Belle takes a deep breath, "Come here." She stands beside me and clings to me, I wrap my arms around her shoulders, "Stick with me baby, you'll be alright." I kiss the top of her head.

We just walk right in, the only person missing is Jack who is still at University, but everyone is here now, my Mum, my Dad, Julian and little Skyla, who must have been bribed into a pair of pink trousers to go with her pink top. She comes running to me away from Ashley, who is playing monster.

Ashley has on a black leather skirt and a black polo blouse.

I lift her up and hold her over my head on a squeal, "Alright you little monster." I settle her on my hip, "Getting her nice and excited before tea."

"Mum wanted her out of the kitchen." Ashley shrugs.

My Dad comes downstairs in a pair of medium blue jeans and a grey polo shirt, he looks good for a man in his forties, "The only way to get her out of the kitchen id to play monster and chase her out."

"And I make the best monster." Ashley declares proudly, "Hey Belle."

"Hey." Belle says sheepishly.

"Dad this is Belle. Belle this is my Dad Joel."

My Dad walks over to shake Belle's hand, "Pleasure to meet you Belle. My wife is in the kitchen, I hope you like Salmon omelette."

"I love it."

"This is Skyla." I turn so Belle can get a look at her.

"Oh well isn't she the cutest." Skyla reaches out and grabs Belle's necklace.

"She has a thing for shiny things at the moment, Skyla let it go."

"No it's fine." Belle takes off her necklace and dangles it in front of her.

"She can be a bit rough, I don't want her to break the chain."

"As long as the charm doesn't get lost, I'm not bothered about the chain, I've had stronger ones made."

She carries on entertaining Skyla, even gets comfortable enough to coo to her.

"Would you like to hold her?" I ask.

She gets a look in her eyes that is a mixture of fear and excitement, "Sure but erm, will you stay with me?"

"Belle I'm not leaving your side tonight."

I pass her Skyla and she sits down and places her on her knee, "So this is the little monster you keep telling me about. She doesn't look scary to me."

"Seems to me like you tamed the beast."

Skyla puts her hands in Belle's hair and pulls a pin out, "She doesn't like my hair up either. I'll take them out."

She does just that and ruffles her hair, Skyla throws her hands in it marvelling at how soft it is, just like I do.

I look at Belle in awe, she is actually good with children, and looks good while doing it.

My Mum then comes in, in a pink tea dress, I stand up to kiss my Mums cheek, "Belle this is my Mum Catherine, Caty for short."

"That is your father's fault."

Mum approaches Belle and shakes her hand, "It's lovely to meet you Belle. I see you and Skyla have become acquainted."

"She's lovely." Belle beams.

"Say that when you've spent the whole day wrestling her into pants." Mum jokes, Julian comes downstairs in a pair of black jeans, and a white vest top, "Julian I said casual, not slobbish." Mum jibes.

"Julian this is Belle, Belle that's Julian."

"Oh you're the one that wants to go into internet security."

Oh wow she not only paid attention, she remembered, Julian's face lights up, "Yeah that's right."

"I know some people, if you need some help setting up an apprenticeship, then let me know."

"Alright I will thanks."

Mum goes and sits by my Dad on the two seater sofa, "How was work?" She asks him.

"Not as tiring as yours darling, looking after a small child."

Skyla starts squirming on Belle's knee, Belle sets her down on the floor and puts her necklace back on, I reach for her to cuddle up to me, which she does.

"Relax baby, you can be at home here." I say softly so only she can hear me, she slips off her shows and puts her feet up on the sofa.

Skyla starts running around, "Looks like trouble is at it again." Mum sweeps Skyla off her feet, "Julian can you take Skyla and wash her hands with her please. It's nearly time for tea."

"Is there anything I can help with?" I hear Belle ask.

"No thank you, Parker can help me, I need to speak to him anyway."

I kiss her cheek, "I'll be right back."

I go into the kitchen with Mum, "Well never in my life did I expect to see Belle O Neil holding and cooing a two year old in her lap."

"If I'm honest me neither, she was good with her though, calmed her down for a while, she took her hair down because it amused Skyla."

"You really love her don't you?"

I begin to feel a little choked, I'm a sensitive person, I'm not ashamed of crying, so I let my tears flow, "Until now I didn't think I realised just how much." My voice breaks, Mum is quick to come and wrap her arms around my shoulders.

I wrap my arms around her mid-section, "Oh my darling. Does she know?"

"Not yet, but she is going to find out, I plan on telling her soon."

We hold on to each other for a moment, then Mum says, "Dry your eyes, wash your face, and tell the others its times to eat."

I do just that silently thanking Mum for not making a huge deal out of this, I love how strong she is.

I go through to the others, Julian looks up at me, "Have you been crying?"

Belle looks at me instantly concerned, "I might have been." I answer.

"Julian." Dad says, "There is no shame in a man crying, it means he truly cares about something."

"Well said Dad, Mum says that dinner is ready, if we all want to go through."

Chapter Eleven

Belle

WHY HAD PARKER BEEN CRYING? I can't picture him crying, he always seems so happy, as everyone goes through to dinner I take hold of Parker's hand and pull him to me, "Why were you crying?" I ask him in a hushed tone

"I'll tell you when we're in private, it's nothing for you to worry about." He kisses me lightly, "Come on."

We walk through to the kitchen hand in hand, his Mum and Dad would be sat opposite each other if his Mum wasn't on Joel's lap, they're clearly used to embracing each other, Parker is clearly used to seeing this, it explains why he likes to hold me, his parents have the same connection, and they are still very much in love. Julian and Ashley are sat beside each other, with Skyla sat in a high chair between Ashley and her Dad, they all seem to be unscathed by their parents embrace, clearly used to it.

Parker and I sit down at the end of the table, "Certainly smells good. Oh I bought some champagne, it's the first time I have done this, so I figured the occasion called for it.

"Thank you Belle, I'll put it on ice, we can have it after dinner." His Mum says.

She does that and then gets the food out of the oven, drains the vegetables, and places them all in fancy dishes, Parker's Dad gets up to help her place them all on the table.

When they both sit down his Mum says, "Right then guest goes first, take what you want Belle."

I do as she says, and try to be as ladylike as possible, even Nan doesn't do spreads like this.

As soon as I have plated up what I want, I wait for everyone else to do the same, then I begin eating.

"So Belle, you own the O Neil Event Planning Agency? That must keep you busy?" Joel asks.

"It certainly isn't dull, depending on what people want, depends on how straight forward it is, right now there is a client planning his own promotion party, he had change location twice. And also top it off, it's me he wants to work with, I've had to enlist help, something I rarely have to do."

"I'm guessing the help comes in the form of Bailey and M.K?" Ashley asks.

"Yes the man can be ludicrous, M.K tells me he called three times today, on my day off, M.K was really quite annoyed about it."

"I would have been too, she's probably busy with her own projects."

"She's good at juggling, it's just paperwork I have to nag her about, I admit it's a tedious task, but it needs to be done."

"Do you see much of your Nan?" Caty asks me.

"As often as I can, she is my only living blood relative, M.K, Bailey and myself try to see her individually twice a week, and together once a week. Both M.K and Bailey don't really have family, only Nan and I. M.K is even more protective of Nan, then she is of me, there is a reason for that, which is not my burden to bear, but I will never forget this time when our Nan was mugged, M.K hunted the guy down, and well I let's just say, Bailey and I got to her before she could do any real damage."

"So she is not the sort of person to let the law deal with it?" Ashley jibes.

"Now when it comes to family, no she isn't." I feel the need to speak directly to Ashley, "M.K says Nan saved her life, she saved all of us in a sense. But M.K was a mess when Nan met her, she took M.K in, nurtured her until she learnt to love herself. M.K honestly believes she wouldn't be alive if it wasn't for Nan. If I'm honest neither would Bailey and myself, she gave us strength, life even. So we would die and kill for her."

Ashley backs down, she must see that my family is a touchy subject.

"We must say we were sorry to hear about your mother, and then your father." Joel changes the subject.

"Thank you, I don't think I would have got through it without Nan, M.K and Bailey. Look I am going to get this out now, I know I've had a controversial lifestyle, I'm well aware of what I've done in my past, I have made and I make no excuses, all I can say from the bottom of my heart, is that I care for Parker, a great deal in fact, I have no intention of hurting him, I might by accident, but never intentionally."

I feel his hand on my leg, I don't look at him because I know the moment I do, then I will melt with love.

His Mum then speaks, "Yes I can see you do."

Parker

She cares for me a great deal, it is not the same as love, but right now I know this is as close as I am going to get, I might just have to bite the bullet and tell her first.

My family have seen how passionate Belle is about her family, so passionate she squared up to Ashley, and made her back down, you have to admire my girl's spirit.

"So Belle." Dad starts, "You have no blood siblings, am I correct?"

"No I have no blood siblings, and I have no contact with my step-family, Imelda, Dylan and Scarlet, I never got on with them, I think Imelda was hoping that my father would push me out when they moved in, but that wasn't the case, I tried, I really tried to be nice, to be friendly but I think they thought if they treated me badly, made me uncomfortable, then I would leave, but my father wanted me to stay, his only daughter, the only thing left of my mother, his one true love, so I stayed for him, put up with what they threw at me for him, Imelda got rid of everything that could remind my father of my mother, except for this." She touches her necklace with a small smile, "I had to put a lock on my bedroom door, because one of them, no one said who, poured glue in my hair while I was asleep, I had to lie to my father about why I got it cut short. It was them that started rumours about my affairs, I only kissed the guy on the cheek and hugged him. But to be honest I couldn't be bothered to fight them so I just thought, if you can't beat them join them, so I became everything the accused me of being, and I never went back, until now."

So it is because of them she stared having scandalous affairs, she didn't make excuses, she provided an explanation, well to me she did. Her story breaks my heart.

We finish eating, "Julian you can help me with the dishes, and then go up to your room and do your homework please."

My Dad goes and stands behind my Mum, "Darling you cooked, let me do the dishes."

"You've been at work."

"And you've been looking after Skyla, I think I know who has worked harder, and it's not me."

Mum relents and kisses his cheek, "Alright, thank you darling. We have dessert in the lounge."

I stand and offer Belle my hand, "I'm so sorry."

"About what?" She asks me.

"Your story."

She strokes my cheek, "You're lovely, but I'm over it. I have a better life now. Most recently because of you."

We go through to the lounge, Skyla toddles over to Belle, and lifts her arms, sensing what she wants, Belle lifts her and puts Skyla on her knee, I sit beside her, Skyla gets hold of Belle's necklace again, Belle takes it off and lets her be entertained, "So Belle, what's the story with the necklace?" Ashley asks, she's not intending on picking a fight, she respects Belle now, Belle has earned her place in Ashley's eyes.

"Long nice version? Or short one?"

"Which ever one you want to tell."

"This isn't my story, it's Nan's story really. Nan grew up poor, she was born in 1937, so two years before World War Two. Nan's Mum gave birth to Nan young, she married at sixteen, he was eighteen, she gave birth to Nan at seventeen, he had only just turned nineteen, he was a miner, so they didn't have a lot of money, but they tried to give Nan everything they could, she never missed a meal, she never missed out on birthday and Christmas presents, her clothing might have had holes in and patches, but she made the most of it."

She clears her throat, she remembers the story well. She even places her cheek on Skyla's head, as Skyla has rested her head in her breast. Everyone is listening intently, "Then the war started, Nans Dad gets the telegram to say he has to enlist, so he went out and bought Nan's Mum something to hold on to while he was gone, and something to remember him by in case he didn't, he found this necklace, when he gave it to her he said, 'Because I can't give you my heart, I want to give you the best version I have of it, as long as you wear this, my heart will always be yours.' He left to fight the war, he didn't come back, Nan and her Mum spent a lot of time in and out of poor houses, Nan's Mum kept the necklace hidden away from debt collectors, she never moved on from her husband, her first and only love. When Nan moved out, her Mum gave her the necklace, and said the words, Nan then gave it to Mum when she married Dad, and then Mum gave it to me before she died, each time the necklace gets passed down the words are said. It's sad because it's almost like she knew she was going to die when she gave it to me." She then wipes away a tear, "God sorry I don't mean to cry."

I wrap my arms around her, "I love you." I whisper so only she can hear me, "You hear me? I love you."

She holds me closer on a little sob, and holds on tightly, that says more than words to me, it tells me I provide her with all the comfort she needs, "I'm alright now babe."

I loosen my hold but keep hold of her, "That was a really nice story Belle." Mum says wiping her eyes, even Ashley has shed a tear, and she never cries.

"Sorry I didn't mean to upset everyone."

"No you didn't, it was a lovely story." Skyla stretches on a yawn, "She's tired I'll take her to bed."

"No it's fine, I'll take her."

"Her pyjamas are on the bed, her room is the only room where the door is open." Mum yawns, "Oh she wears pull ups as well, they're under her bed."

Belle picks up Skyla and takes her upstairs.

Her story has pulled at the heartstrings of my family and me, I don't get how anyone could ever be cruel to Belle, it is obvious she never means any harm to anyone, she's actually a very vulnerable person.

Belle

I didn't imagine Parker telling me he loves me, he has no idea how much those three words from him means to me.

Never in my life have I ever held a two year old in my lap or carried one to bed, I amaze myself with how comfortable I feel.

It's easy to find Skyla's room, it's a little room, but she's a little thing, there's a toy box on the floor against the wall, her bed is only small with a duvet that is apparently Peppa Pig.

She had matching pyjamas, I remove her top, she's so sleepy she has no choice but to co-operate, but she's struggling to sit up bless her, so it's a good job that I do her top half first. I lay her down and take off her bottom half, I then grab the pull up her mother said was under the bed, I stand her up and place her little hands in my hair, that fascinates her, I lift her slightly pull up the pull up, I then do the same with her trousers.

With one arm I carry her to the head of the bed, pull the covers down, place her down and pull the covers up to her chin.

I start to walk out of the room, when I hear her say, "Story."

I turn back, sit on the bed, run my hand through her hair and think of a story.

"Once upon a time, there was a princess, now everyone thought that because she is a princess, she has a good life, but she hasn't had a good life, her life has been sad and hard, and it made her hard, because she got tired of being sad, only the people she loves that is her Nan and her sisters saw the good in her, the princess thought that was the way it would stay, until she came across a prince, who saw what she tried so hard to hide from people, and she felt relief, every time she was with him because he accepts her flaws and still wants to be with her, and she can be human with him. And she loves him."

I look down to see Skyla sleeping, I smile and kiss her forehead, "I'm going to let you in on a little secret, I love your big brother." I stand and turn to leave the room, where I see Caty crying, "You're not going to want me to come again, that's the second time I have made you cry. How much of that did you hear Caty?"

"All of it." She takes hold of my shoulders, kisses both of my cheeks and then pulls me in for a hug which I reciprocate, "I was wrong about you, you're good for my boy."

"Thank you, I mean it, I love him."

"I know."

We go back downstairs, "She wanted a story."

"Belle told a lovely story."

Parker stands up and wraps his arms around me, "What was it about?"

"A princess who has had a hard life, but everyone thinks that because she is a princess, she has had a good life, but her life has been hard and sad, which has made her solely hard, only three people have seen her true self, until a dashing prince came along and just simply made her show him, seemingly without even trying, as long as she is with him, she's human."

"Nice story." He muses, "Is the monster asleep?"

"Dosed off before I could tell her a secret."

"You're the princess and I'm the prince?"

"Good guess."

"The champagne should be chilled by now. I will just go and get it." Caty announces.

Parker and I sit on the sofa, Parker tugs me to him so I can rest my head on his shoulder, I put my feet up on the sofa, "Jack is an awesome story teller, he used to tell me stories to help me sleep." Ashley muses.

"You wouldn't believe he is the younger twin." Joel muses.

"So Belle what do you usually do with your evening?" Ashley asks.

"In the summer me and the girls like to eat on the patio and drink wine on my balcony. In winter we like to sit in my lounge. Where I lay before the fire, we either read or talk, depends on our mood."

"Sounds nice. You're really close to them."

"They're my family, I'm sure you get it."

"Believe me, I do now."

Parker's Mum then comes in with the champagne, pours it out and hands the glasses around, when I get mine, I lift my glass, "I would like to propose a toast. To me moving in with Parker."

He looks at me in awe, "Are you serious?"

I look him in the eyes, "Deadly."

"When?"

"Whenever you want me."

"Tomorrow?" He half asks half states hopefully.

"I finish work at…" I check my phone, "My last appointment is at two, so two thirty."

He kisses me soundly on the mouth, "I'll be there."

Parker

I didn't imagine Belle saying that she would move in with me. Is it her way of compromising because she isn't ready to tell me she loves me yet?

It's now knocking on for 10:00pm, my parents like to be in bed by 10:30, and Belle is dozing beside me, Ashley has gone to home because she has work tomorrow, I rub Belle's back, "We'd better go babe, it's getting late."

She sighs contentedly, "Alright then."

She puts her shoes on and stands up, my parents stand up to show us out, "Thank you so much for tonight."

Belle hugs my Mum, "The meal was lovely, everything was just lovely."

"You're very welcome, it was lovely to meet you."

We then leave, Belle threads her arm though mine. I just wrap my arm around her shoulders, she snakes her arm around my mid-section, and interlinks her fingers with mine.

"You've just survived your first family meal, congratulations baby."

"It was amazing, better than I thought it was going to be, your family is amazing Parker, the love your parents share is so real. They've been married for a long time, and they are still so in love."

"I want the kind of love they have."

"I hope I can provide you with that. I probably didn't give you the response you wanted when you said you loved me."

I hold her closer, "You were upset, it's fine, you holding me closer told me all I needed to know. I do have one question, did you agree to move in with me to compromise over the fact you're not ready to tell me you love me?"

"I agreed to move in with you because, something you said to me earlier has been echoing in my ear since you said it."

"What did I say?"

"That everything we do together seems so right, and after discussing it through with M.K and Bailey, and Bailey said some relationships take time to build a connection, and sometimes a connection hits you like a truck."

"And that's what happened with me, the first thing I noticed about you is the way you looked away when you realised I was watching you. You've had affairs with some rough looking bastards, and yet I intimidated you. The moment I realised that, I knew I wanted you."

"Alright, I'm going to level with you, I've had a thing for you since you did the Off The Leash photo shoot, you were so hot, I bought every magazine I knew you were going to be in. Not even Nan knows that."

I laugh and kiss the side of her head, "I'm trying to picture the great Belle O Neil perving over me."

She nudges me gently, "I don't perv, I just imagined all the things I would do to you if I ever got you in bed. Oh and look what happened."

I laugh again, "Fuck I love you. What's the plan for tomorrow?"

"Can we spend tonight at mine please?"

"Yeah of course, look Belle we can call off moving in with me, if it makes you feel better."

"No, no it's fine, I will explain it when we get to mine."

"Alright then if that's what you want."

Belle

Parker's right a lot of what we've done together has felt so right, we may have only been together a short amount of time, but it feels like it has been a lot longer.

We get to mine, I push the button to open the gate, we walk to the door, and I look around, I love this place, it's everything I ever wanted, we walk into the house, I look around again.

"My Dad liked everything dark, it was boring and dull, I came back home on the condition that I would decorate my room, I always loved the beach, so that was the way I decorated my room, it came out really well, so well I decided that when I moved out, I would decorate my house like it. So that's what I did, my father was a man of order, he liked everything to be in the rooms neatly and properly, he liked the rooms to be similar with design and furniture, it just looks orderly. When my father died, I didn't have time to grieve, not really, Imelda kept me around until the will was read, as soon as that was done and she heard I was left everything, she packed my bags the next day. I had to live with Nan for a while."

He puts his hands on my shoulders, "They really did try and fuck you over didn't they." He states with contempt, "I used to think they were decent people."

"They are decent people, just not with me, oh well all's fair in love and step family. Screw them. Let's go to bed, Bailey and M.K are probably in Bailey's room chatting. I won't disturb them."

We go upstairs and into my room, "This was my dream house, but that was before I found you. Seems like you have changed everything."

I strip off my clothes and dress in a pair of grey lounge shorts and a blue vest top, "You don't mind if we just talk tonight do you?"

"Why would I mind? Seriously babe, I might be young, but that doesn't mean sex is all I think about."

"No just most of your thought stream."

He approaches me and nuzzles into my neck, "Keep making comments like that, and I will soon get you in the mood."

"I'll be good." I push him off me and get into bed.

He strips off his clothes down to his boxers, and quickly joins me, "So now you're moving in, it might be wise for us to start telling people."

"I don't know Parker, I'm worried about the impact it will have on you, the wicked witch of London, snagging herself a young man, they will probably place bets on me cheating on you, or breaking your heart."

"I know you will never do anything to hurt me intentionally, Belle baby, I love you, we're moving in together tomorrow, it's time people knew we're together, it can be your chance to show people that leopards can change their spots."

I smile, "When and how are you thinking of informing the UK of our unity?"

"I have an interview with Cosmopolitan in a couple of days, you could come along we could do it then."

"You really don't do things by halves do you? First I agree to date, then I agree to move in, after only being with you a couple of weeks, and now, not two hours after agreeing to move in with you, you want me to agree to telling the UK that we're together as well."

"Because it makes sense, I'm telling you I love you after only being with you a couple of weeks. You admitted everything seems so right when we're together, so let's tell people we're together and we'll weather the storm that comes our way. And I know you love me Belle, it's in the way you look at me, hold me and kiss me, you just have to say the words, I can wait, I'm a patient man. Now let's get some sleep."

Parker

So today is the day that Belle decided to move in with me, I turn and reach for Belle, but she isn't there, I look and its daylight, I remember her telling me that her balcony leads to her kitchen, so I get up and make my way down to her.

And there she is still in her grey lounge shorts and light blue vest top, doing a little dance to some music playing in the background.

I quietly open the door and watch her, she moves fluidly around her kitchen, I hope she's as comfortable when she's in her new one. She see's me and jumps, "Fucking hell Parker, I didn't see you there."

"You should have woken me." I say accusingly.

"Then I wouldn't have got round to eating breakfast before my meeting. And you shouldn't be half naked in my kitchen, I wasn't the only one in the household that perved over your picture."

"Oh so M.K and Baily got an eyeful as well."

"Only Bailey. M.K isn't interested in muscles."

"What is her type?"

"Erm…" She isn't sure whether to tell me or not.

"Women." A voice says from behind me, I turn to see M.K still in her pyjama's which consist of a pair of plaid trousers and a black long sleeve top, "My type is women, I like a strong, independent woman, who have a vulnerable side, but don't let it show too often, I like my women to be smart, not book smart, but cultured smart, I need an understanding woman, who I can talk to and show my vulnerable side to."

Oh wow M.K has just told me that she is gay, which must be her way of telling me that she trusts me, "Thank you for telling me that."

"Not a lot of people know so…" She puts her finger to her lips.

"Oh I won't breathe a word I promise." I put my hands on Belle's hips, "Are you going to tell her the news?"

"I will when Bailey gets here, that's if she can remain standing after seeing you topless."

"I don't see the fascination myself."

"I don't see the fascination in Ruby Rose, but you still practically stalk her online." Belle accuses.

"I do not. She practically drooled over your picture." M.K fires back.

"I knew it." I whisper in Belle's ear and kiss her shoulder, "I used to drool over her picture in the paper, even the ones where she looked like crap."

"Thank you, but I prefer the term drained."

Now Bailey walks in, in a pink baggy nighty, she is certainly not a morning person, but as soon as she sees me, she springs to life, "Oh shit, I had no idea you two came home last night, we didn't hear you come in."

"Good job we have sound proofing in the rooms." M.K jibes.

"We didn't have sex last night." Belle states matter of factly, "Guys I have something to tell you, I'm moving in with Parker today."

"Alright cool." M.K shrugs, "Wait you're keeping this place right? We don't have to move out?"

"No, no you don't have to move out, I'm keeping the house, but I don't think Nan is going to be moving in here, as much as I've nagged, so if you get partners then the bedroom down here will be free, and I will let you and Bailey argue over who gets the room." She flips the last of the pancakes and places it on a plate, "Breakfast is ready. M.K and Bailey, you know where everything is, so you can get it out."

They do just that as Belle places the food on her marble dining table and sits on a stool.

M.K and Bailey place bowls of blueberries, strawberries, syrup and sugar.

"So when was it decided that you were moving out?" M.K asks.

"Last night, everything went well at Parker's families house, and I was thinking about what you guys told me, so I just thought why not."

"I also told Belle I love her." I say, "She didn't say it back, but I know that she will in her own time, I just couldn't wait any longer, and that was when she agreed to move in, she wanted to spend one last night in her home, before she moved out, hence why I'm topless in your kitchen."

"A fine thing to wake up to." Bailey toasts.

"Oi." Belle points a finger on a glare, "You can look but don't touch." She then smiles.

"Oh I wonder how many wives tell that to their husbands, every time they see you." Bailey jokes.

"Fat lot of good it did them, they were all fucking her by the end of the week. Didn't one of your affairs actually meet you with his wife?" M.K puts in, I'm not sure if I'm comfortable with this particular conversation, I know Belle had had affairs but to hear her talk about it, it's hard to stomach.

"He actually put his hand on my leg when his wife went to go and get more coffee, the second meeting he convinced his wife that he was able to meet me alone, because he had no interest in me, only to be fucking me on my desk an hour later. I shouldn't really gloat, but come on guys, that's the past."

"Oh yes look at her now, turning into a house wife." Bailey sighs.

"No one said anything about being a wife."

"It's on the cards." I put in. "As is children, you were good with Skyla last night, you're a natural mother."

"But not for a while, I haven't even moved in yet. One step at a time." Belle finishes her breakfast, "Right I'm going to have a shower, I have a meeting in forty five minutes, so I will love you and leave you." She says in general.

Belle

I really don't mind moving in with him, but talk of marriage and children is too much for me right now, Parker needs to remember a couple of weeks ago, being in love, well actually being in a relationship in general wasn't on my agenda, and not only am I moving in with him, I love him, and it has only been two weeks.

I switch on my shower and strip, I step in and let the water lap over my face, when I hear the curtain open behind me I jump, I didn't expect him to follow me.

"Mind?" He asks cockily.

"You have seen it all before." I match his tone.

He cups my breast, "I'm not sure how I felt about you talking about your affairs around me."

I wince, of course he's not going to like it, "I'm sorry I should have been more tactful. But Parker you're going to have to put up with worse that that when our relationship is out in the open."

"I know, I know. And I don't have to like it then either. You deserved better than them Belle." He kisses me hungrily, "I'm sorry I have to do this, please let me. Say you want it."

"I want it." I lift my leg to his hip, "I want you Parker."

He pushes into me slowly, and drowns me with an intoxicating kiss, I bite down on his bottom lip and graze my teeth along, he runs his hand down to my bum and gives it a good squeeze.

"Fuck Parker." I gasp, "Is there ever a time you don't give good sex?"

"No one has ever told me if I have, I always leave my women satisfied and wanting more."

He runs his hands up to my breasts, and starts devouring my neck, I nibble on his ear, "Oh Belle you're so perfect, so, so perfect. I don't care what people say about you, I see the real you, you have shown me the real you. So people can say what they like when we are out in the open. Because only I know the truth."

I kiss him hungrily now, and throw my hands in his hair "Oh Belle." He murmurs.

I climax, "Oh fuck Parker."

He keeps up the thrusts, until he does the same, when he does he simply kisses me like a man deranged.

When he has eased us both down he keeps holding me, "Babe as lovely as this is, I do have to go to work."

"Oh alright." He grumbles.

He lets me go and I'm quick to dry off, and get dressed in some black lace underwear and a long black dress.

He puts on the same clothes he had on last night, "Do you want a lift?"

"Yes please."

I go downstairs and kiss and hug Bailey and M.K as I'm leaving, "See you guys later."

We leave the house hand in hand, "So what does your morning consist of?" Parker asks.

"A meeting with the promotion client, and then overseeing a christening, today should be easy enough really."

"The promotion client. Is that the one you were in the bar with when you met my friends?"

"Yeah that's him." I say causally as I get in my car.

"He fancies you." Parker states.

"I know he does, he also knows that I have a boyfriend, I told him that when we had a drink, I only had the drink with him so that he might not ask me again, then you showed up and proved that I didn't spin the line about my boyfriend to ward him off."

"So you're glad I intervened the way I did?"

I start driving, "Let's just say I'm more intrigued, this will be the first time I have seen him since, M.K at my request has been handling meetings with him."

"Why did you do that?" Parker asks me.

"I don't trust him." I state, "Sorry where am I taking you?"

"Oh home, I want to get organised, my girlfriend is moving in with me today."

"Oh lucky girlfriend." I smile, "So tell me about her."

"She has a bit of a complicated past, and a lot of people only see her one way, for a long time so did I, until I met her in a bar, she was with her friends, she looked, so, so hot, I knew I wanted her, she was with a rough bastard, but I didn't care, I wanted her, I felt a connection, I knew she felt it too, and at first she tried to deny it, but she wanted me as much as I wanted her, eventually she agreed to date me, and then after three dates, we slept together, two days later I asked her to move in with me."

He then sighs and seems to enter into a daydream, "My girlfriend is sad, though she will deny it, and only three people have seen her soft side, she is showing it to me, she's amazing to sleep with, amazing to hold and to kiss, she speaks openly about her time growing up, and her mother's death, she's so used to having a poker face, she's not used to being vulnerable. She has no idea what having a boyfriend entails, but she's learning, I'm teaching her. I love her."

He really does love me, I know I love him. Why can't I bring myself to say it?

We get outside his apartment block, "Walk me to my door and wish me a good day Belle." He orders softly.

We both get out of my car, I walk him to his door, he pulls me to hi for a long, passionate kiss.

When we pull out of it I say, "Have a good day Parker."

"Have a good day Belle, I'm counting down the hours until 2:30, I love you."

"I can't wait to move in with you. For now I am going to have to go. I'm going to be so late."

"Alright, I will see you later."

He lets me go, and I walk back to my car and make my way to work.

Chapter Twelve

Belle

AFTER DOING SOME PAPER WORK which is always boring, I'm getting ready for my meeting with Daniel McDowd, which I am nervous about, I haven't seen him since the first meeting.

My phone rings, the only time the phone in my office rings, is when my appointments are here, "Hey Darla."

"Miss O Neil your 10:00am is here."

"Darla how many times, call me Belle, don't make me sack you." I joke, she laughs, "Alright send him up please. See you later."

I straighten out my desk, get myself a coffee and sit down, when Daniel comes in and saunters over in a grey suit, "Belle." He greets.

"Daniel please have a seat." He sits, "So are you still having your promotion party at The Ritz or have you changed your mind about that also?"

"No, no I'm settled with The Ritz. You look lovely this morning Belle."

"Thank you." I fake a smile over my cup of coffee.

"So your boyfriend seems a little intense."

"We're here to discuss your promotion party, not my personal life. Or my boyfriend."

"I recognised him, Parker Wilson, he's younger than you. I thought you went for older men."

"Again this is my personal life. Do you still want the ice sculpture to be in the centre of the room? And the chocolate fountain to be near the buffet table?"

"Yes to both. Parker Wilson is said to be the most sought after man in England, he could have any woman he wants, but he's picked the Queen of Seduction, The Marriage Killer, the woman who's been fucked by over a hundred men."

"Mr McDowd! My personal life is none of your concern and as for Parker, I have given him plenty of opportunities to leave me alone, because I am well aware that he could do better, yet he chooses to stay with me. Which I am glad because I just so happen to care about him a great deal, and I plan on moving in with him, today as a matter of fact. Now either let's get on with planning you're promotion party, or get out of my office."

"Belle O Neil the ice queen has a heart." Mr McDowd declares, "Has the great Belle O Neil settled down I wonder."

"Yes Mr McDowd I have! With a man I love." Oh my God, I said it, I actually said it out loud, to a stranger nonetheless.

We sit and go over the plans for his promotion party, how he can sit and act like nothing has happened is beyond me, I'm tense and frustrated with the whole thing and as soon as he's gone I call for M.K.

"Hey boss." She drawls.

"Can you and Bailey come to my office? I need you."

"Alright on our way."

By the time they get to my office I'm pacing it, "Oh fuck. What happened?" M.K asks, she knows me pacing is never a good thing.

"McDowd he knew Parker's face when he came over and kissed me, he was questioning me like a fucking journalist."

"Belle he is a journalist." M.K reminds me.

"Oh yeah." I sigh, "Oh shit, what if he publishes it?"

"Well he can't publish anything, he wasn't here to discuss your personal affairs, he was here to discuss business, if he publishes anything you can sue the paper and get him sacked."

"It's not that, it's what he said."

"He's upset you?" Bailey asks instantly wrapping her arms around me.

"He wanted to know why of all the women in England, Parker chose me. And he was right, I don't deserve him, I don't deserve someone like Parker. Not after all the things I've done."

"Belle if those men didn't fuck you, then they would have found another woman to cheat on their wives with. Does that mean you don't deserve to find love?" M.K challenges.

"Possibly." I shrug.

"Do we need to call Parker?" Bailey asks.

"What? No, no, don't do that." I plead.

"Belle if we don't then you're going to spend the rest of the day telling yourself you don't deserve him, and probably talk yourself out of moving in with him."

"No I still have work to do, I'll be fine."

"M.K's right you do need him."

"Look if you call him, he'll insist on me moving in with him as soon as possible, and I have a christening to oversee, I have put up with worse than Daniel McDowd, I can't run to Parker every time my feelings get hurt."

"Fine we won't tell him, but Belle, Parker loves you. Fuck your past, that's where it belongs."

Parker

After doing some tidying round, I am now dressed in a pair of black jeans and red vest top.

I'm now at a loose end, I hate being at a loose end, so I decide to go and see what Ashley is up to, she lives in a block of flats not too far away from me, so I just meander down to see her, she's just leaving by the time I get there, she has on a pair of black trousers and a white vest top.

"Hey Ashley!"

She turns and smiles, "Oh hey bro, to what do I owe the misfortune?" She jokes.

"I was waiting for Belle to finish work, then I remember you telling me that you have a day off today."

"So you thought you'd come bug me. Alright come on, we'll go for a coffee your shout."

"Of course." She links arms with me, "So how's work going?" I ask.

"Work is work, the hours are long, the pay is shit, we can't all be models like you." She jibes. What she isn't saying is she could have been.

"But yet you love your job."

"I love my job when people actually let me do it." Ashley's biggest bug bear is when people take matters into their own hands.

I decide to change the subject, "So you know M.K, Belle's friend?"

"Not really, I have only seen her once."

"Oh really? When?"

"When I went to warn Belle not to hurt you, it's what older siblings do."

"What did you think of her?"

"I could tell she's the protective one, a bit uptight."

"According to Belle, she's had a very tough life."

"So have a lot of people Parker, if she got through it then good for her."

"She's gay." Why did I tell my sister that? We walk into the coffee place.

"Good for her knowing who she is, and for being honest about it."

My sister is a very tough crowd, "We should arrange a family meal, with Belle's family and our one."

"And by Belle's family, you mean her friends and her Nan."

"Yeah it will be good, give us a chance to bond."

"And give you gay sister a chance to see if she and your girlfriend's best friend hit it off." She jibes.

"No it makes sense for us all to get to know each other."

"M.K hardly strikes me as the sort to do family meals."

"And Belle does?" I half ask half state.

"You have a point." She relents.

We get to the counter, "What will you have?"

"A large latte with an extra shot please."

"Can I get a large cappuccino, and a large latte with an extra shot please?"

As soon as the drinks are served we go and sit down, "I think it's worth giving them all a shot." I muse.

"Their choice, if they are down for it, then fair enough, if I am at work when it's arranged, then it will be a shame, but if not the I'll be there."

"Hey Parker." I turn to see M.K. In a pair of grey trousers, and a white low cut blouse, I can't help but notice that she keeps her arms covered.

"Oh hey M.K, I believe you two have met."

"Yeah, hey." She smiles at us both, and then turns to the counter, "Hey can I get a large latte with an extra shot to go please." I look at Ashely and she glares at me, "Have you been at work today?" M.K asks me.

"No. You?"

"I'm on my lunch and craved coffee. Something tells me it is going to be a long afternoon. Nan is dragging ME shopping because Belle is otherwise engaged." She's joking, it's in her eyes.

"I would apologise but…." I smile, "I'm not sorry."

She shoves at my head gently, "Not it's cool, I just hate shopping and crowds, I'm usually alright with Nan."

"Belle says you're all really close." I say.

"I honestly don't think I would be here if it wasn't for her."

"Here's your coffee." The waitress passes M.K a to go cup.

"Thanks darling. Well I had better scoot. I'll see you guys later."

I turn to face Ashley, "See she's alright. Takes her coffee like you do."

"So? That's just a coincidence."

"Come on, she's exactly your type."

"I don't know her."

"So? Get to know her."

"Parker drop it." She warns.

"You need to move on from her."

"Parker it's not like she left me, she fucking died."

"Yeah and it was sad, but that was six years ago, come on Ashley are you going to beat yourself up forever?"

"You know what? None of your business."

She goes to leave, "Ashley, Ashley." I take her hand, "I'm sorry please sit back down."

She relents and does as I ask, "Please don't try and set me up."

"I won't I promise, but promise you'll embrace love if you find it."

"I'll try." I leave the conversation at that, I know she means it.

Belle

I'm sat in my office finalising some paperwork, what Daniel said to me is playing on my mind, just like the conversation with M.K and Bailey is as well.

Do I deserve happiness after the things I've done? Should I stop this whole thing right now? It's not too late, if I just back out of moving in with him, if I just back out of this whole thing right now, before we get too far into this.

But we are too far into this, he's telling me he loves me, and even though I haven't told him, I love him so much it drives me crazy.

I put my head in my hands in the hope to relieve some tension, all of this is getting on top of me, suddenly I find myself caring about what people think, but not for my sake, for Parker's.

I hear the lift ding, I lift my head and carry on with the work I have been staring at for the last ten minutes, I see Parker walk out, give him a little smile he looks so handsome in his black jeans and red vest top.

"Oh wow you look exhausted Belle." He picks up his pace, circles around the desk, takes the pins out of my hair, kisses my shoulder, and starts a light massage. I tense up. Sensing this he spins my chair around, and places his hands on the arms of my chair, "What's wrong?"

"Bad day." I smile, but it soon fades, "Parker are you sure me moving in with you is what you want? There are women out there far more worthy of you. That haven't had affairs, that wouldn't cause so much controversy when their relationship comes out."

He puts his hand on the back of my neck, "Yes, yes Belle. I can think of nothing I want more, than to come home to you every night, and yes people are going to cause trouble, but that is not going to change the way I feel about you. Nothing will change that."

"There are better women out there." I repeat, "Who didn't used to be slags and have affairs."

"You're the only woman for me Belle."

I gently push him away and stand, "Parker I can't let you do this, the idea of you loving someone like me terrifies me. I am only going to hurt you. And while I love what we have, while I love what you do to me and how you make me feel, I have no choice, I have to let you go."

He approaches me, I should be backing off, but I secretly want this to happen, he's pissed off, I can see it in his eyes, he puts his hands on my arms, "The hell you are! I have no idea what the fuck happened here today Belle, but I tell you this, you might be willing to let me go, but I am far, far from willing to let you go. So you are going to shut down your computer, we are going to leave this office and we are going to pack your things, so you can move in with me. And tomorrow you ARE going to come with me, so that we can tell the journalist from Cosmopolitan that we are together. And no you don't get a choice, you either come willingly or I drag you there. Now stop with this nonsense before I pry the name of the person that put these thoughts in your head and beat the fuck out of them."

He plants a hard kiss on me, my brain turns to molten lava, my legs turn to jelly and my insides do cartwheels, he pushes me away from the kiss as abruptly as he pulled me into it, "Sorry." He says, "But for fuck sake Belle, never do that again, I love you, you stupid, infuriating woman."

"Sorry." I kiss him tenderly this time, "I'm sorry Parker, I'm just terrified you will get hurt."

"Belle there's nothing the papers can say that I don't know already, and here I am loving you regardless. They can't hurt me, they won't, stop worrying. Come on baby. I need to get you home, the sooner you leave here, the sooner we can forget the world for a while."

I do as he says, shut down my computer and then walk to Parker, he drapes his arm over my shoulders, "So are you going to tell me what happened today that nearly ended in us breaking up?"

"The client you kissed me in front of. He said some honest things, really Parker all he did was give me taste of what's to come.

And I do mean only a taste, I am going to have some bitter pills to swallow."

"Oh on a lighter note, I was having coffee with Ashley, and we bumped into M.K, she seemed pretty happy with herself."

"Did she? That's weird. She was pretty pissed off at what the client said, I thought she was going to take it upon herself and call you."

We get out of the lift, I say bye to Darla as we leave, "Why didn't you call me?"

"Because I didn't know if you were busy or not, and you would have dropped everything to be here for me, I'm a big girl, I have put up with a lot worse than what he said to me, so I am not going to call my boyfriend, every time my feelings get slightly hurt."

We get into my car, he spins round to face me, "But you will tell me about it? I don't expect you to call me right away, but I would like to know."

"If that's what you want, it's what I'll do Parker."

We get into my car, "Tell me. Are you always this accommodating or is it a new thing you have developed just for me?"

I smile at his cocky tone, "I told you before I have never been in a relationship, I know that they come with requests and compromises, so far everything you have requested has been pretty simple, straightforward and easy. Make a stupid request and you will see what the unaccommodating me is like."

"Is it stupid that you have been all I can think of, from the moment I met you in the bar? Is it stupid that I want to be around you all the time? Is it stupid that when I'm not with you, all I can think about is the next time I'm going to touch you, kiss you and sleep with you? Is any of that stupid Belle?"

I pull up outside my gate and look him in the eyes, those dark, serious eyes, I love the way they change shades when he is serious and intense, they go a deep shade of green, when he is sober and content, they become a shade of grey, and when he's playful and happy, they are almost blue.

"No." I smile, "None of that is stupid Parker. My turn. Is it stupid that in the couple of weeks that we have been together, you have made me so deliriously happy? Is it stupid you have terrified me? And is it stupid that I fell in love with your family the first night I met them? Because they are everything I never really had?"

"None of that is stupid Belle."

Again I smile, "Now that we have established that the way we feel about each other isn't total nonsense, I think there is one more thing that needs to be done before we go home, and that's pack my bags."

I push the button to open my gate, make my way up the drive, step out of the car, and look around my estate, I'll visit, my sisters are still here, this is not goodbye.

Parker

Belle has no idea how fit for murder I felt when she tried to 'let me go as she calls it, I don't know what I was angrier about, the fact that someone clearly put these ideas in her head, or the fact that she thought I was going to make it easy for her, I hate the fact she thinks she doesn't deserve me. So what? She has done some questionable things in her time, but she was not the risking her family, the men she fucked on the other hand were. If it wasn't Belle they cheated on their wives with, then it would have been someone else.

"Is there anything you would like to bring from downstairs?"

"No your place is actually more equipped than mine in the furniture department. So that's cool, I just need my clothes, shower gel, tooth brush, you know."

"I get the gist."

We both head upstairs, she kneels on the floor, to get her suitcase from under her bed, liking the view of her bum I tilt my head to get a better look. I love the way all of her clothes hug her figure just right, I can't help but smile and wonder if there is silk underwear underneath that dress.

She grabs her case, gets one look at my face, smiles and says, "Yes by the way."

"Yes what?" I ask baffled.

"There is silk underneath this dress."

She goes to her underwear drawer and starts packing those first, as soon as I clock a material that isn't silk, I'm over there, I dive into her suitcase, and get out all of the none silk materials, "Nope, nope."

"Parker what the fuck are you doing?"

"Taking out all of the none silk items, silk is the only underwear you're going to have on." I dump the discarded items on her bed.

"Ok now that's stupid, you can't dictate what underwear I put on." She scoffs.

"Just answer me this one question, and I promise it will be the last time I bring up your past. Did you used to wear silk underwear when you met the men you fucked?"

"No, never not even when I was with Fox."

"So I'm the only man to see you in silk underwear?"

"Yes Parker you are."

"Well then I am dictating your underwear, silk is the only underwear I'm going to allow you to bring into my apartment."

It sounds ridiculous, but there is method behind my madness, every time she has seen me, she has been wearing silk, I am the only person man she has worn it for, so that makes the material special to me. It's my material.

"Then that means I have six bras and six panties. And what about when I am on my period?"

"The underwear accommodates that, it's not like they are thongs. We can by you more underwear, and some other things that are for my eyes only."

"I'm not buying lingerie when you're with me."

"I can look away, and not come to the check out."

"Yeah right." She scoffs.

"Anyone would think you don't trust me."

"Says the man literally going through my drawers." She's trying to sound serious, but there is laughter in her eyes. She goes over to her wardrobe and walks in, "Anything in here I am prohibited from bringing with me?"

"You can wear what you like over the silk underwear, bring the lot if you want."

She does just that walking out with an armful of clothes, dumping them on the bed, going back and getting more.

"You don't have many shoes? And no handbags?" I observe.

"How very stereotypical of you." She jibes, "Let me guess you thought, rich woman probably has a wardrobe for her shoes and handbags. Nan has this saying, 'If you don't need it, don't buy it, however there's nothing wrong with a bit of indulgence.' Handbags are targets for muggers. And as for shoes, I only have two feet, so I have two pairs of shoes, work and…" She holds up a pair of designer trainers, with zips indicating right and left, "Play."

"You're a very intriguing woman."

"Not sure if that is a compliment or not."

"Compliment definitely a compliment."

She then gets on folding her clothes, putting them in her case, she's precise, neat and slow while doing it, I just kick off my shoes and lay on her bed.

"Make yourself at home." She chuckles.

"I plan on it. You're slow."

"I think the word you're looking for is precise."

"No the word I am looking for is slow."

"You just want to get me home so we can have sex."

"Like you don't want to do the same."

She closes her now full bag, "Right let's get me moved in."

Chapter Thirteen

Belle

So Parker has everything he has ever wanted, as he told me last night several times while we were having sex, I never thought the move would be quite so hard for me.

Don't get me wrong I love Parker, but I am so used to being my own woman, in my own house, and although his attitude is what's mine is yours, I find myself longing for my own space again, my own stuff. The only thing in this apartment that I can call mine, is well my clothes there is nothing else. Nothing feels like mine.

What did I expect? I have been on my own for years, only having to provide for me, only having to rely on me, now here I am under someone else's roof, with no mortgage to pay, no bills, my name is on nothing to do with this place, Parker can deal with that, and I thought that I could too, no I can't. It's easy for Parker, this is his home, his stomping ground, and I know he wants it to feel like mine, but I don't know how he can change that.

I guess I just have to fake it, let's see how that works out for me. The only thing I know that's mine in this apartment, is the man I am living with.

Parker

This is a dream come true for me, I have wanted to settle down with a woman I love for a long time, and finally Belle that amazing woman is letting me, it felt amazing while we were having sex last night, to know that from now on, it will only happen here, in my apartment, in our home.

Belle is sleeping soundly beside me, neither of us are real huggers when we're in bed, but I do love the feeling of one of us being half awake and embracing the other while they sleep peacefully, I beam at the sheer beauty of her.

After a few minutes she stirs, "I can feel your eyes on me." She murmurs, "I hope watching me sleep isn't a habit of yours, I don't like the idea of being watched."

"Sorry I can't guarantee that, you looks so fucking gorgeous when you're asleep, I could watch you sleep all day." I run my hand up and down her thigh, "I'm so happy you're here."

She smiles, "I gathered from the million times you told me last night baby."

"I meant it every time." I kiss her cheek.

"I need a coffee." She shoves me off, walk over to her wardrobe, puts on a silk dressing gown and heads to the kitchen.

I stay where I am for a moment, thriving in the fact that the woman I love is in the kitchen, my kitchen, no OUR kitchen, and that I'm going to find her in there, in a material that I just love.

Not being able to resist much longer, I get out of bed and slip on a pair of black boxers and make my way into the kitchen.

I can't say I'm surprised by the fact that she's tense and unsure, I might not like it, but I'm not shocked by it, her shoulders are hunched, and her movements are forced. She doesn't feel at home yet, I need to nip that in the bud and soon.

I'm quick to approach her, she keeps her back to me, not aware I'm there, I just wrap my arms around her and kiss the back of her neck, "You have a habit of scaring the crap out of me." She sighs.

"You're tense, I think I get it, I just want to hear you say why so I know we are on the same page."

She turns to face me and puts her hands on my chest, I can't resist moving my hands down to her bum, "It's just I'm just so used to looking after myself, paying my own way, I mean sure I lived with Bailey and M.K, but I KNEW everything was mine, everything was what I had worked for, I'm used to providing for myself."

"You're used to taking care of people, you're not used to it being the other way around. I want to take of you Belle."

"It's just, I'm not used to being take care of by a man. My Dad always taught me to be self-sufficient, self-reliant, this is so out of my comfort zone."

"All good lessons to learn, but Belle when two people are in love, they like the idea of taking care of each other. And I like the idea of taking care of you, just like I'm sure you like the idea of taking care of me."

"But fact of the matter is Parker, I've never had to take care of you, you're so strong, you have done plenty for me, but I don't see what I have done for you."

"Plenty." I put my hands on her cheeks, and gently make her look at me, "You have done plenty for me Belle."

"I'll take your word for it."

"My word is all I have Belle, and I love you so much, it drives me mental, and maybe it's because no man has ever taken real care of you, that makes me so determined to."

She takes my face in her hands and kisses me lightly, but it's lingering.

Belle

Fuck this man is so intoxicating, he has such a way of saying things, he has such a way of making me feel like the most important woman in the world, "I'm sorry, I should be happy, instead I'm being difficult."

"Baby I get it honestly, I do. What would make you feel better? How can we fix it?"

"I would feel better if I could pay my way." I say honestly.

"Alright." He contemplates, he's never going to agree, "How about we go halves on the bills?"

Oh wow I never thought he would agree, "Yes I would love that."

"Alright then it shall be done." I take his words and relax, "By the way we're meeting the journalist from the Cosmopolitan at one."

Again I automatically tense up, "You're still hell bent on that happening huh?"

"Yes Belle. I'm still hell bent on that happening."

Sensing my tension he turns me round and starts massaging my shoulders.

He kisses my shoulder, "Look baby I get why you're afraid, but nothing is going to change the way I feel about you."

He keeps kissing my shoulder and my neck, I tilt my head on a light groan, "It's really hard to concentrate when you kiss my neck like that."

"Am I killing your concentration?"

Oh fuck killing my concentration is one word for it, "Oh God yes." I murmur.

He runs his hand down my dressing gown, slowly, seductively, while still kissing my neck and my shoulder, my breathing becomes hurried and shallow, waiting for Parker to do whatever he is planning.

When he reaches my lower stomach, he pushes the material of my dressing gown to one side, and with his other hand turns my face so that he has access to my lips.

He pushes into me with his fingers, I gasp into his mouth as he keeps up his movements, my legs turn to jelly, and I place my hands on Parker's arms, it's either that or fall on the floor. He stops kissing me, but keeps his hand on my cheek so I can look at him.

"Today we're going to sit in front of a journalist, and I'm going to tell them we're together and that I love you, and that yesterday you moved in with me. And no matter how it goes, we're going to come back home and forget the world exists. Because Belle, as long as we're together, the world doesn't exist."

He doesn't give me a chance to speak. He just kisses me again and keeps up his delicious thrusts with his fingers, "Oh fuck Parker." I gasp into his mouth, I love what he does to me.

"Say you agree Belle." He orders gently.

"I agree Parker. Whatever you want."

"Right now, I want to focus on you."

I say nothing, I just let him focus on me, I dig my fingers into his arms, the closer I get to climax the more hungrily I kiss him.

And when it comes, I break out of the kiss abruptly, "Oh fuck Parker!" I groan loudly. When he's eased me down, as I'm catching my breath I just say, "Do me a favour, keep hold of me for a moment, I don't trust my legs."

"Am I the only man to make your legs turn to jelly?"

"Yes." I answer honestly, "You're the only man that has made me so physically weak from pleasure, that I need you to hold me up, in case I collapse."

"Baby, you have no idea how happy that makes me. You have given me so many sick kicks." He nibbles on my ear, "Do you want a bath before we go and meet the journalist?"

"I wouldn't mind one to be honest. Are you going to join me?"

He turns me to face him, "Baby you can guarantee, that every time you have a bath and I'm here, wild horse wouldn't stop me from bathing with you."

We share a slow, loving and mind numbing kiss.

Parker and I are now on our way to his studio so he can be interviewed by the journalist, I have on a pair of tight black jeans and a Burberry lace top, with my designer trainers. Parker has on pair of medium blue jeans and a tight black t-shirt.

The closer we get to the studio the more nervous I am, as we get level to a nearby alley, I pull him into it, gently push him against a wall, and plant a hard kiss on him, I hope that my kiss makes him as drunk as his does on me.

When I pull away, his eyes are dark with need, I run my hands up and down his chest, "What do you say we skip the interview, go to Victoria's Secret, so we can buy some underwear? And I can get some lingerie to surprise you, and we can spend the whole day in bed, and I can seduce you in a way I've never seduced another man."

I nibble on his bottom lip, and kiss his neck, he trembles, at my notion and shudders slightly, "Oh fucking hell Belle. What do you reduce me to?" He puts his hands in my hair so he can take possession of my mouth, he pulls away slowly, "Nice try babe, but we're doing this, and then we're going to do what you suggested."

"No, no this isn't multiple choice." I joke.

He cups my bum in his hands, "I would do something to change your mind, but it's not gentlemanly to have sex with a woman until her brain turns to mush in an alleyway. Come on we're late."

He takes hold of my hand. I tense up, I know I'm going to be seeing my step family, so that's something I'm not looking forward to.

Parker

Belle's tense, but she's nervous, she has never sat for an interview before, and to top it off her step family, my bosses are probably going to be there as well, which may only add to her discomfort.

When we get into the studio, Imelda is these in a royal blue long dress, the moment Belle sees her, she tries to release her hand from my grip. "Parker let go. Please." She begs.

"No Belle." I say plainly, "She can't hurt you anymore. Do you hear me? I won't let her."

As soon as Imelda sees us, she gets a look of confusion on her face, and marches over to us. I've never known Belle cower, but she does just that, she shifts slightly so that she is behind me.

"Parker what is this?" She grimaces at Belle.

Belle actually now tightens her grip on my hand, I have seen her stand up to her step mother, seemingly without fear. Is this the way she really feels?

"What does it look like?" I ask simply, releasing my hand from Belle's so I can wrap my arm around her shoulders, keeping her close to me.

"Well it looks like you're canoodling with my step daughter."

"Then it's exactly how it looks. Problem?"

"It's just that…"

"It's just what?" Belle fires back as she takes hold of my hand that's draped over her shoulders, thank fuck for that, I was worried about her for a moment.

"Well it's just Parker is the most sought after man in London, because he renowned for his looks and for his respect for women, and you are renowned for being well a slag." That comment puts my back up, and I tighten my grip on Belle's hand. "How long has this been going on for?"

"A few weeks, long enough for us to have had dinner, make love, me to declare love, and for my family to see a side to Belle, that hasn't been seen by the papers."

"I think you're making a huge mistake, but the journalist is here, and you're late, she's proving to be a bad example already."

I hear Belle snigger beside me, "Not my fault for once." She utters.

"I'm my own person, if I'm late it was my choice to be, Belle had nothing to do with it."

We walk to the part of the studio that models use when they are not doing shoots, and there's a journalist, she's young, hot, blond, with a triangle jawline, petite long bridged nose, deep set blue eyes, she's in a black leather skirt and a white designer low cut blouse.

She beams a smile at me, and practically runs to shake my hand, "Parker Wilson, Elsa Doyle." She then clocks Belle, she's aware of her reputation, I can see that from the look in her eyes, "Right let's get started then."

We all go to sit down, I deliberately wait for Belle to sit down first, so I can sit and snake my arm around her, she leans forward so I can put my hand on her hip, I kiss the side of her head in a silent show of gratitude for her co-operation.

Elsa sits down in the armchair, which has been moved so that she can sit opposite me, she turns on the recorder and sets it on the table in front of her.

"So judging by the looks of things, we have a budding romance in our midst."

"Budding is one word for it." I state, "Belle moved in with me yesterday."

"I'm shocked that there has been no mention of this in the papers."

"Which is odd." I admit, "Because there have been plenty of times when we've been walking hand in hand, kissing in public, dates in restaurants. It's safe to say that the only time we have been careful is when we're making love."

Belle sniggers beside me, and Elsa blushes at my bluntness, but she soon pulls it back, "So Parker Wilson, the most sought after man in London, and Belle O Neil the Queen Of Seduction together. It's a bit like a power couple thing really. I bet Parker was a shock to your system huh Belle?"

I feel her tense up, this is what she was really worried about, she doesn't want to be questioned. She doesn't want to be in the spotlight.

Belle

This is what I was afraid of, I hate being questioned by people, I hate being in the spotlight, Parker rubs his hand on my hip, and suddenly I feel like I can do anything.

"Yeah actually God, meeting Parker has been a major shock to my system, I've never met ANYONE like him."

"I hate to say this Belle, but there is going to be plenty of people out there that will want to see this fail. Like the men you have had affairs with, their wives, their ex-wives and their families."

"Let me tell you this, I have given Parker plenty of opportunity to just leave me, he chose to stick around, and I'm not going to lie I'm glad he did. He makes me so happy."

He kisses the side of my head, "People need to stop blaming Belle for their husband's and ex-husbands infidelities it's not like she had a family or anything to lose, people need to remember, if the men didn't cheat on their families with Belle, then they would have done it with someone else. So who is really to blame?"

"Aren't you worried that she might cheat on you?" Elsa asks.

I don't give Parker a chance to answer, "I would never do that, I care for Parker, I'm not being funny but if people cheat on their partner's then that's their lookout, I have never actually cheated on anyone, and I never would."

"Well wow, I don't know if you guys have exchanged the love word yet. But I know a couple in love when I see one. One more question though. There is a five year age gap. Men are more immature than women. No offence there Parker. But are either of you bothered about the age gap?"

"Please there is not much of an age gap." Parker quickly answers, "I've had an unsettling life because of modelling, I've travelled, I have a lot of money, I'm ready to settle down which is more than what I can say for a lot of men my age, there's not much difference in five years, and as for the men she has been with, I think Belle is glad to now have a man that want to treat her well, and not like some sort of convenient fuck."

"What about you Belle? Does the age gap bother you?"

"No Parker is right there isn't much of a difference in age. And Parker is very mature and respectful, he has been raised right, it helps to have parents who clearly love and respect each other, he comes from a very close family, so he has high family values. Parker is all round amazing."

"Alright well this has been very interesting and very different from what I was expecting, but thank you for allowing me to interview you both, I will let you get on with your day."

Elsa gathers her things and then leaves the room, "Well that wasn't so bad." I state, "But wait until it's published."

Parker takes my face in his hands and kisses me deeply and lovingly, "Is the offer of us shopping for you underwear and lingerie still open?"

"You know what? Yeah it is."

Chapter Fourteen

Parker

As Belle and I walk into Victoria's Secret, I suddenly understand why men tend to avoid coming in here with their partners. If I don't leave the store with a raging hard on, then I'll be majorly shocked. But at least I'll be going home, where I can do something about it.

As we're heading to the silk, I spot some nice lingerie, which I think would look perfect on Belle, so I pull her to a stop, "Now that would look amazing on you."

"I already told you, I'm not buying lingerie while you're with me."

"I could get it for you, you could wear it tonight."

"I think I'm the one who deserves a reward for today don't you? That journalist put me on the spot. Scared the hell out of me."

"You really hate journalists."

"Not hate, scared of." She informs, "When my father announced he was campaigning to be the new police commissioner, journalists flooded the house, I was home from school, and one day he was taking me shopping, as a bribe because I knew I was at boarding school because he wanted me out of the way. Anyway the moment we were out of the house, journalists were on us, cameras flashing, questions being yelled out, I clung to my Dad, I was terrified. I had nightmares for weeks, Bailey one night climbed into bed with me, and I found having someone with me really helped."

"How old were you when that happened?" I ask.

"I was ten." She states plainly.

"You were ten and you knew your parents sent you away to boarding school because they saw you as in the way?"

"Yep." She nods on a slight smile. But her eyes are sad. Thinking about it Belle really does have quite a heart breaking story, she has been made to feel in the way all of her life, she was made to feel in the way by her own parents, and then by her step family.

I can't help myself, I gather her into my arms, and bury my head into the crevice of her neck.

"Hey why are you crying?" She asks bringing her hand up so she can stroke my hair.

I didn't realise I was, I don't let go until I have gathered my composure, then I pull away slowly, she puts her hand on my chest. I bet she isn't used to being concerned about men. But that is the look on her amazing face now.

"Sorry." I sniff, "Sorry." I rub my hands up and down her arms, "You've had such a horrible life, everything I've taken for granted, family, a home. You never had it. It upsets me how badly you grew up."

She smiles and strokes my cheek, "I didn't grow up badly, I had M.K, Bailey and Nan. And I tell you Nan hated me going to boarding school, I remember they had an argument, she and my mother had this massive row one day, Nan said, 'If the girl is too much trouble, then I'll take her, she can live with me, don't send her to a place she doesn't know, imagine how she will feel a few years down the line.' My mother was upset I remember her replying, 'Do you think I chose this? I don't want her to go.' Nan fired back, 'So your husband is making you choose and you're choosing wrong, no child deserves to be separated from their family.' But I'm glad because I made two amazing friends who are my REAL family."

And again here come the tears, "Oh Parker." Belle soothes wrapping her arms around me, "I'm fine. I might have turned out a little but fucked up. But I have to admit meeting you has helped me no end."

I look her in the eyes, "Do you mean that?"

"Yes Parker. I mean it. You've helped me so much. You have no idea. I don't know where to begin to tell you."

"That makes me so happy." I kiss her like a man deranged.

She pushes away slightly, "You know we could skip this go home and…make love? Is that what you told Imelda we do? Is that what we do?"

I laugh a little, "Well yeah I love you more, each time we do it."

"You're so sweet." She doesn't have the courage to say she loves me back yet, "What's your choice?"

"Oh stay, definitely stay."

"Alright. But remember it was your choice."

Alright so just LOOKING at underwear is no fun for me, however I have concluded that, picturing Belle in the underwear is a lot more fun.

I hook my arms around her waist, "So hey here's an idea why don't you model them for me?" I suggest.

"I can do that at home." She turns to face me, "Unless you think you can handle it if I model them right here."

"On second thought model them at home, because at least then I can ravage you without someone feeling the need to call the police."

She giggles at that, "I have all I want. So we can go to the checkout now. I bet you can't wait to get out of here."

"At least we can go home and forget the world for a while." I kiss her cheek.

Belle

Parker really is a sensitive soul, but I couldn't stand seeing him cry, it broke my heart in two.

As we make our to the checkout I notice a lovely dress, it's a little on the short side, and low cut on the cleavage side, but it would look amazing on a night out, I stop in my tracks and feel the material, it feels nice too.

"If you think you're buying that, you have another thing coming."

"But you said I could wear whatever I want over the silk."

"I'm making an exception for this."

I pout, "It would look amazing on a night out."

"Belle let me make this perfectly clear, if you ever wear a dress like that on a night out, I'll strangle you."

"Aww." I run my hand down his chest and tug a little on his top, "But you love me."

"I do, but that dress will invite other men to touch you, and that simply isn't allowed to happen. Understood?"

He's utterly serious, "Alright fine, I won't buy the dress."

I will get it when he's not with me, and I will keep it at my old place.

We go and pay for the underwear, which comes out to quite a bit, over a hundred pounds.

When we leave the store Parker says, "Fucking hell, a hundred and ten pounds, that has got to be the most expensive underwear in the world. And I couldn't help but notice the lack of lingerie."

"For the third time, I'm not going to buy lingerie when you're with me, it's going to be a surprise. Now stop sulking and let's go home."

We get home and as soon as we're in the lift, Parker backs me into the lift wall and kisses me wildly, "I'm so proud of you for today. You were amazing. You ARE amazing Belle."

The lift opens we stumble out, he picks me up and carries me to the bedroom, we both fall onto the bed, I go to remove his top, "No, no. Not me, just you." He states, "You had a point when you said you deserve a reward for today, this is only the beginning."

He moves down my body, removes my panties and takes me in his mouth, "Oh fuck!" I shout.

He puts his hand on my stomach so I don't buck my hips too hard. He's so amazing, I always associated a reward with something a child got for being good, but this is so much better.

I love the way he really does make me feel like the world doesn't exist when we're together, the only people in the world are him and me.

"Fuck Parker." I gasp.

But he doesn't stop, he never stops, and I love him so much for that. I grip the duvet like a vice, my breath keeps hitching and I'm quivering with pleasure.

"Parker." I groan, as I climax, I pant as he eases me down. When he's done he looks me in the eyes, he stays there for several minutes just looking at me. What is he thinking?

Parker

She's so beautiful, the way her hair has fallen over her shoulders, the way her eyes have closed with pleasure, the way she's fighting to catch her breath, the way her hands are ever so slowly relaxing on the duvet and the way she's smiling slightly. And the knowledge that all of that is happening because of me is elating.

I crawl up her body slowly, trailing my lips along her skin, that's now damp with sweat.

"Fuck Belle, you're so amazing." I kiss her deeply and quickly, "So fucking amazing." I murmur against her lips.

"So are you. You make me so happy Parker, I'm so glad I've got you."

"You'll always have me Belle. I love you so much."

She strokes my cheek, "I wish I was ready to tell you the same thing. I'm sorry."

"Don't apologise, I know you love me, that's enough for me baby. You telling me I make you happy tells me all I need to know. I am willing to settle with that."

"It has never been something I'm used to hearing or saying."

"I get it baby, I do. Don't worry." I place my cheek on hers, "Are you tired? Do you need to sleep?"

"I am a little bit yeah. And some rest will do me good. Stay with me?" She snuggles closer.

"Always." I murmur, I kiss the side of her head and wrap my arms around her.

Chapter Fifteen

Parker

IT'S THE DAY AFTER THE interview, Belle's sleeping soundly beside me, after countless calls from Imelda, which have been ignored, and in the end I turned off my phone.

Belle turns and snuggles into me, placing her head on my shoulder and her hand on my chest, right over my heart, it's like she knows it belongs to her.

I kiss her head, "I love you."

"You too." She murmurs sleepily.

"That's the closest you've come to saying 'I love you' back to me." I smile.

"I do." She murmurs again.

"You do what?"

"Love you back."

"What did you say?" She's half asleep, I'm being ridiculous, she can't know what she's saying, but I'm desperate to hear it again, "Belle wake up. What did you just say?"

She moans grumpily, "What are you talking about?"

"Just now, you said you love me back."

"Did I?" She's genuinely confused, but I want so badly for her to remember.

"Yes Belle you did, you snuggled up to me, so I said I love you, you replied with you too, which is the closest you have come to saying you love me, which I expressed that, you then said you do, which I ask you do what, you then said you love me back."

She still has no recollection, "Parker I was half asleep, I say all kinds of stupid shit." I try not to act bothered, but it has bothered me, "Oh baby I'm sorry, I know how much hearing me say it means to you. But we're out in the open now, the Cosmopolitan is an international magazine most of the world knows we're together."

It should be enough but it's not.

I kiss her softly, it's time for her to admit how she really feels, even if it means dirty tactics.

I run my hands down her lace night dress, I slip two fingers into her, she gasps softly into my mouth, I know she loves me, but I need to hear the words, I give her a few strokes to build her anticipation.

"Just three little words Belle."

"Oh Parker." She gasps from both pleasure and exasperation, "I can't not yet."

"I already know in my heart you love me Belle, you just need to say the words. I'm doing this for you. In telling me you love me, you'll be admitting it to yourself."

"I'm scared of opening myself up to love Parker. I never said it to a man only my father. Please, please don't pressure me. Not when I've come so far with you."

I slip my fingers out of her, she whimpers, "Shh, I'm not going to stop." I remove my pants and slide into her.

Belle

I should have known he would try and use sex to get me to say I love him, he used the same tactic to try and get me to move in with him.

"Parker you can't use sex to get what you want."

"Belle is this an appropriate conversation to have while we're having sex?"

"Well then stop."

"Are you serious?"

"We need to talk, so yes I am."

"Can't we talk after?"

"What when I'm so blissed out from pleasure to even think? No we talk now, have sex after."

"What if I'm not in the mood?"

"Please I'm the Queen of Seduction, I will get you back in the mood, now let me go so we can have a serious conversation like adults."

He actually scoffs in my face, "Oh please, don't use that line like I'm a petulant child."

"Then stop acting like one and let me up." I order.

He let's me go, and I get up off the bed, "You can't attempt to use sex to get what you want Parker, so far every major decision I've made when it comes to you, you have tried to influence with sex. Me to move in, an admission of love, it is not a fair thing to do."

"I do it to help you Belle."

"Help me? Really?" Now it's me scoffing, "It's manipulation, to use my pleasure against me, if I had of admitted I loved you then. Would you have been satisfied? Knowing it wasn't actually me saying it, it was the pleasure ripping through me, driving me, not my own thoughts."

He goes to answer right away, "No, no think about it first."

He does as I ask, and after a bit he says, "No you're right, if you're going to say you love me, then to come when you're clear headed."

I go and sit down on the bed, "Parker I promise you, the day I tell you I love you, my head will be one hundred percent clear, and I will never stopped saying it. Just be patient please."

"Alright." He smiles, "I'll wait. I know it'll be worth it." We share a mind loving kiss.

We would have gone a lot further if my phone hadn't have rung, "Oh it's M.K." I answer, "Hey M.K."

"So the article about you and Parker is in the Cosmopolitan, paparazzi are going to be all over your arse from here on in."

"I know, I'm ready for it."

"So I've been thinking, we should all go on a night out, let people see the happy and settled side of Belle O Neil, might be good for business."

"Worth a think about yeah."

"Alright cool laters." She hangs up.

"So that was M.K, the article is out, the world will know that we're together by the end of the week." I look at Parker, he's boiling mad about something, he has his phone in his hand, "Parker, Parker." Nothing, for a moment I just sit and wait for him to snap out of it.

Parker

As Belle is on the phone to M.K, I decide to switch mine on and when I do, I find I have six missed calls from Imelda along with a text saying, 'Stop ignoring me! I need to speak to you ASAP!'

Along with three missed calls from Scarlet, along with a text, 'Seriously? For years I've been throwing myself at you, and you settle for that bitch?! I have always lived in her shadow.'

And finally a missed call from Dylan, and a text saying, 'Mate you could get anything from her, she's the biggest slut going.'

I'm boiling mad. Why can't they just let Belle be happy? I don't realise she's off the phone to M.K until she takes the phone out of my hand, to see what's got me so boiling mad, I go to take it off her to spare her feelings, but she holds it out of my reach.

"Well that's just rude." She looks at me, "Alright to clarify, you're the only man to have sex with me without a condom, also I'm on the pill, also top it off if ever one of my endeavours had a mishap and the condom split, I went to make sure I was clear of any STD's or I's, and I was clear."

She then realises that she has my phone in her hand, "Shit I'm so sorry." She hands it back to me and flies into an explanation, "I tried calling your name, but you were so mad your jaw was pulsating, so I figured, 'Let's see what's got him so boiling mad.' I have no excuses, I was out of order, I'm sorry."

"No, no Belle, I'm not mad at you, I just didn't want you to get hurt, also I should have discussed contraception with you before we slept together. I've never used a condom with you. Anyway that is beside the point, thinking out loud there." I place my hands on her shoulders, "I don't mind you reading my texts, I have nothing to hide, just like you took your call in front of me. No secrets. That's the way I like it."

"Certainly makes a change to the way I used to live, I feel comfortable enough to have a phone conversation in front of you, to tell you my plans for the day, how my day was. I feel settled…stable. I'm not used it, but I love it."

"It makes me happy you feel that way Belle, I want you to share things with me, your life, your love, whatever you give, I'll accept."

Belle

Whatever I give, he's willing to accept, there's so much I want to give him, so much I have given him already. However I've given him everything I'm willing to give him for now.

I know he wants to hear I love him but, I'm so scared. Once I open myself up to that emotion, what else could I open myself up to? Love often leads to heartbreak. I saw it when my mother died, my father never got over it, Imelda was someone to fill a physical need, my father was still human after all.

"What are you thinking about?" Parker asks kissing my shoulder.

"My father." I say plainly.

"Oh what about him?"

"Just how much I'm like him, he was a very hard man, he wanted a boy, I know he felt stuck with me, but when my mother died he became softer with me, he started talking to me a lot more, he wanted to spend time with me, he wanted to share my day, he wanted to teach me." I drift off into a day dream.

"He rarely told my mother he loved her, but she knew he she would sneak affection, cuddle up to him on the sofa, kiss his cheek or his lips softly. When he told her he loved her, he said it with such affection, you knew he meant it, his eyes were full of it. Before my mum died he occasionally told me he loved me, but there was no affection, no look in his eyes. After she died there was. I was all he had left of her, so he grew to love me then."

He wipes a tear from my cheek, which I wasn't aware had fallen, he then places his hand on the back of my neck and kisses me tenderly.

He shifts slightly so he is on top of me, he starts caressing me softly, lingering where he needs to linger to arouse, I gasp into his mouth.

"Belle." He murmurs as he slips into me, I groan lightly as he keeps up the lazy pace, "Every time you tell a story about your life, it breaks my heart."

I go to speak, but wind up groaning from the pleasure he's providing me with, "You don't need to speak, just listen baby, the way you've been treated, I'm surprised you have feelings at all, but you are more capable of feelings than I thought. I think it shows how amazing and strong you are. Every day I love you more and more."

He then says nothing, he keeps the lazy pace, and now I notice no matter how slow or fast the sex is, the result is always the same, we always end up a sweating heap of uselessness. My mind always winds up like lava, Parker always collapses on top of me, and lays there for a good few minute. We both wind up breathless.

We climax together, "Oh fuck Parker." I groan.

"I love you Belle."

After he's eased us both down he collapses on top of me and we drift off for a nap.

Parker

Both Belle and I are due at work for the first time since becoming exclusive, and the press have jumped on the story a lot over the last two days, I'm feeling alright about it, Belle on the other hand isn't, but she's been in the spotlight from a young age, every time she put a foot wrong, the press jumped all over the out of control police commissioners daughter.

I wake up and find Belle isn't beside me, so I'm up like a rocket to find her, she's in the lounge area pacing, to my disappointment, she dressed and ready for work, in a pair of black trousers and a hot pink top that's probably designer, she's showing some cleavage, but she nearly always is, I find myself having a problem with it, especially with her reputation as being the Queen of Seduction, but I'm not going to tell her, I just hope the feeling goes soon, her damn hair is in pins, I fucking hate that.

"Alright, yeah that's great...No it's cool, I'm not worried...Just meet me at work, you know the drill." She hangs up.

No prizes for guessing who she was on the phone to, I just go and sit on the sofa, as she keeps her phone in her hand, I don't like it when she's in business mode, she's detached at the best of times, but in business mode, nothing exists but her company.

"What times your first appointment?" I ask her.

"Nine thirty." She doesn't even look up.

I get up and take her phone off her, "When we're talking, your eyes are on me, got it?"

She's silent as she holds her hand out for her phone back, she simply holds my challenging stare, I put the phone in her hand, and she slips it into her bag.

"M.K and Bailey have been by both the studio and my building, both are swarming with press."

"That was to be expected." I wrap my arms around her, "I don't like you in business mode."

"I don't really like being in business mode, but I run the company so when I'm there I have no choice but to be in business mode." It's almost like she reads my mind, "And if you think of touching ANY of the pins in my hair, I'll murder you."

I kiss her neck, "But you..."

"But I'm pretty fond of you."

"That'll do for now." I kiss her cheek, "What time are you home?"

"Four." That's a long time to be without her for, "What time are you at work?"

"Eleven, I finish work at two. What does your day consist of?"

"First consultation, final meeting before an event, which means going to the place."

"Which is?"

"Chelsea. And then another consultation, so really four is a rough estimate, it depends on how long that runs. But the amount of time I spend with them is rounded up, and added to their bill, they know all of this."

So she could be gone even longer? "What if I wanted to cook dinner?"

"Then tell me and I will make sure I'm home on time. Parker I might be new to this whole relationship thing, but I'm pretty sure when someone's partner says, 'Hey babe I plan on cooking dinner tonight.' It's common courtesy to make sure they're back on time."

"Alright so if I were to prefer you to be home on time every night?"

"I would say, that would be all well and good, but doing what I do, there isn't really a set time for us to finish, I like leaving work when the work is done, it would mean me bringing work home with me, and you having to put up with Business Belle more often."

"Point taken and received."

"Right I have to get back to work. You don't plan on cooking dinner tonight do you?"

"No, not tonight, I just wanted to see what you would do."

"Alright." She gives me a quick kiss on the lips, if she thinks that's enough, I march up behind her, "I will be in touch, and will let you know if I am going to be late."

I spin her round and kiss her passionately, taking total possession of her mouth, all she can do is put her hands on my hips.

"That's how you kiss someone goodbye, especially me." I inform, "We kiss goodbye like that from now on."

"Alright." She stutters. "I really need to go."

She then leaves I'm heading into work, and M.K and Bailey weren't lying when they said that the place was swarming with paparazzi, they're on me the moment they see me, I'm in a pair of camo jeans and a forest green t-shirt.

They're shouting questions, cameras are flashing, I just keep my head down and keep walking.

Thankfully I wasn't far from the studio when they pounced on me, I quickly go in to find Imelda stood there, waiting for me, in a pair of red leather pants and red designer blouse.

"Are you crazy?" She shoots straight away.

"Maybe, but you're going to have to specify what you mean."

"I mean you being with my step daughter. Are you crazy?"

"Only about her." I muse.

"She's going to break your heart. She's a woman who hurts people for a hobby."

"ENOUGH!!" I yell making her jump, "So far the only hurtful people I have seen is you and your two children, and all the hurt you targeted towards her. Now Imelda, I love Belle, either get used to it, or I walk."

"You wouldn't." She challenges with her arms folded.

"You know that other modelling agencies would kill to have me. And would be willing to pay me more money."

"I'll pay you any figure you want, if you break up with my step daughter."

"If you ask me to do that one more time, I walk."

"I'm only trying to look out for you."

"Imelda I'm twenty years old, I can make my own decisions. You protesting this will only make me love her more."

She then gives up and let's me get on with my work.

Belle

After one bitch of a morning, M.K told me to go home because I look like death, instead I go to Nan.

She opens her front door in a pair of white trousers and a white long sleeve top.

"Oh darling you look ill. Come in. Come here." She pulls me into her arms, I wrap my arms around her mid-section and nuzzle into her neck, "How bad was it?"

"Paparazzi everywhere, shouting questions about Parker and I. Some really personal ones."

"The article in the Cosmopolitan, it's all over the papers today darling, only that you and he are together, soon you're going to be old news."

She leads me into her living room, which is cosy, not too big, not too small, she has a red floral carpet with matching wall paper, two black and grey leather two seater sofas, along with a matching armchair, there are pictures of M.K, Bailey and I, either individually, together or od one of us or all of us with Nan.

She has a TV on top of a cabinet, with a Virgin Media box and a DVD player, there is DVD shelf to the left of her TV.

I sit on one of the sofas, "So you need your old Nan to make it all better eh?"

"Yeah, yes. I need you." I place my head on her shoulder.

"Oh darling. It'll all be worth it."

"I know, I know."

"How's Parker coping with it?"

"He has everything he always wanted, the girl to come home to, exclusive relationship. He's never had this kind of exclusivity."

"So you never know, he might have hated today, the novelty might have worn off already."

"Yeah maybe." I muse, "I suppose I had better be at home when he gets there, in case he's had as rough a day as I've had."

"I should arrange a time to come and see your new home."

"Alright I'll arrange it with Parker."

Nan rises to show me out, "See you later my darling." She says as she hugs me, "And tell Parker you love him."

"I love you Nan."

"I love you too."

I make my way back home, it will be a nice surprise for Parker to see me home before him, shame it's because of this fucking migraine.

I pull up outside and quickly make my way in, when I get in the apartment I potter around just looking for something to do, when I find nothing I give in to exhaustion, I go into the bedroom, and just lay on the bed.

I don't know how long I'm asleep for, when I feel a hot kiss land on the back of my neck, and strong arms wrap around my body.

I turn around to face him, "You're home early." He kisses me lightly.

"The paparazzi stressed me out, I got a migraine. M.K sent me home, she said I'd scare the clients because I look like death. But I went to go and see Nan. I needed her."

"And how's your migraine now?"

"Still there, but it's more of an irritation now. How was your day?"

"The paparazzi wasn't my problem, your step mother on the other hand, she really did annoy me. She offered me a pay rise if I dumped you."

I scoff, "Sounds like her." I put my hands on his chest, "And what did you say?"

"I told her to get lost naturally."

"I would have agreed, I could be your dirty little secret. Imelda never wants to see me happy. I am a thorn in her side."

"Yeah she makes that clear, I told her I love you. And that if she keeps pressuring me to leave you, then I will leave the agency, there are plenty of other modelling agencies willing to take me on. Regardless of my choice of girlfriend, and they'd be willing to pay me more money."

"And that's when she offered to pay you more if you dumped me."

"A figure of my choice, I'm already a millionaire, so there isn't a figure in this world that will make me want to leave you."

"I'm glad, this is going to sound clichéd, but you complete me." I wrap my arms around Parker mid-section and nuzzle into his chest.

He sighs contentedly, "Well that's good because you complete me too."

He tilts my chin up, so we can share a loving kiss.

Parker

It's the first weekend Belle and I have had off together. The week has been proper mad, paparazzi everywhere, but we're going to be old news soon. Some of the headlines have been quite laughable to be honest, 'QUEEN OF SEDUCTION AND HER TOYBOY', 'QUEEN OF SEDUCTION AND HER TOP MODEL', 'FROM GOLDIGGAR TO COUGAR'

She was rich when she had all of those affairs, so how is she a goldiggar? Also there's only four years eight months between us, no one would bat an eyelid if it was the other way around, and I was older than her.

Belle has taken the headlines on the chin, bless her, but the publicity has got to her. I just hope people get over it soon.

Anyway right now I'm in a peaceful slumber dreaming of Belle, now she's in my dream of the future, I dream of what I want to do with her, marriage, holidays, family, it all seems to fit with her.

My dreams are soon disturbed, by I don't doubt a very hot reality, I feel a pair of naked breasts touch my back, and a pair of hot lips touch my neck and travel up to my ear, where teeth lightly graze.

"I had better not be waking up to you saying, 'I have to go to work.' Because if I am then you are dead."

She chuckles that slow and seductive chuckle, "I'm not going to work, I just like the idea of turning you on." She nibbles on my ear, while running a hand through my hair, "Is it working?" She asks right near my ear.

I'm solid as a rock right now, "Yes." I admit.

"You want to have me? Claim me? Prove I'm settled?"

"Yes, yes and yes." Claim her? Never in my life did I ever think I would hear those words come out of Belle O Neil's mouth.

"Well then…." She says right near my ear, "You are going to have to catch me."

She springs off the bed and out of the room, me in hot pursuit… naked might I add.

By the time I get into the lounge, Belle's around the kitchen counter, smiling seductively, "You sure took your time."

"You're faster than you look."

"I suppose I'd better make catching me easy for you then, if we're both going to get what we want."

"I might like the chase."

"Well then you'd better make sure you catch me, because I'm not going to make it easy."

I sprint towards her, she runs around the counter, now that I'm awake and alert, she's not as fast as I thought, I leap over the kitchen counter, and manage to get hold of her, our momentum gets the better of us, and we fall over the back of the sofa, roll off and land on the floor.

We both cry out from shock, and because I landed on top of Belle, I'm worried her outcry was from pain, "Are you alright?" She brings her hands to her face, and her shoulders are jerking, "Belle for fuck sake, are you alright?"

"Yes." She removes her hands to reveal she's laughing uncontrollably, "I'm fine, I've never done anything like that before."

"That's because you're all adult and grown up."

"No." She links her hands around my neck, "It's because I've never had a man to mess around with. Bailey always says, 'Relationships, you fight, you fuck, you play, you love.' I know there is more to it than that, but it more or less sums us up, bar the fighting."

"It will happen. It's all part of it, we'll clash, only because we're quite different, especially when you're in business mode."

She then notices that we knocked a paper off the table, and also notices the headline about me being a toy boy, "Seriously." She chuckles, "It's not like you're way younger than me, if it was the other way around, no one would even care, it's not like you're eighteen and a virgin." She then frowns, she thinks I was a virgin.

"Belle when we first slept together for the first time, did you enjoy it?" I ask her outright.

"Yes it was amazing, you're really good in bed."

"Do you think I would be so good in bed if I was?"

"You would have needed help, you didn't need help."

"So we've established I wasn't a virgin when we first slept together."

"Phew." She then opens the paper to read the story.

Her mouth drops open, "What?" I ask her.

"Have you read this?"

"No." I answer honestly.

"If I ask you not to. Will it make you want to?"

"It will make me want to take the paper out of your hands, straddle you while I read it, so you can't move or squirm away. And if I like the story, we can make love, if I don't we can argue about it."

She gives up, "Looks like I have no choice."

She hands me the paper, I take it and begin reading:

'A VOW OF LOVE, DANIEL MCDOWD

Belle O Neil, Queen of Seduction, ex-mistress to some of the most notorious and successful names in London, destroyer of countless marriages. Has finally settled down, with a man she admits to love. Her admittance of love can be found on the papers website. But her exact words when I asked her if she has settled down were, "Yes Mr McDowd I have with a man I love." Match made in heaven? Or a walking nightmare? But the Queen of Seduction and the Most Sought After Man in England, are the newest power couple.'

I toss the paper to one side carelessly, "You told him you love me?"

"Yes I did, I wish I could use I was pissed off as an excuse, but I can't, I told him the truth."

"You told him you love me, but you won't tell me?"

"I know it's stupid, but Parker I need you now." She caresses my cheek, "You make me feel alive, and I'm scared without you, I'm going back to the shell I was before you. I need you Parker."

I slip down her body, "You need me?"

She nods, "Please believe me." She pleads.

I take her in my mouth, she tastes divine, automatically one of her legs go over my shoulder, her breath is catching, she let's out a series of low moans, her body is working with my mouth, I put my left arm on her stomach so she doesn't buck her hips too hard. With my right hand I caress her body, tracing my fingers over her breasts, causing her to cry out from pleasure.

"Oh fuck Parker." She cries. Never in my life have I ever been so happy to hear a woman call out my name, "I love what you do to me."

I bet she's never said that to anyone in her life, I'm so desperate to hear her say she loves me, I want so badly for that to happen. I love her so much, I want her to admit she feels the same way.

"Oh Parker!" She yells as she climaxes. I take it all as I ease her down.

When that's done, I kiss my way up her body, I waste no time thrusting my fingers into her, "Oh fuck." She gasps, I kiss her hungrily, if she were to say she loves me now I wouldn't care, it doesn't matter how she tells me, only when, she's already said it, she just needs to say it to me, the sooner the better.

Her hands fist I my hair, as she deepens the kiss and slows it down, her body, her body's hot and sweaty, she sighs sweetly into my mouth on every thrust of my fingers.

When she climaxes, she clamps her teeth on my bottom lip, grazing them along my lip when I've eased her down.

Her body's trembling as I straddle her, I trace my fingers along her body, lingering on her breasts, which causes her to moan weakly.

"So beautiful." I murmur, I lean down to kiss her, "So amazing." I say as I push into her, she quivers, her body is trembling against mine, I keep the pace lazy, take my time.

I kiss her breasts, nibble on her nipples, she arches her back as she cries out, "Fucking hell Parker."

I don't stop, I kiss her neck, nibble on her ear, she turns her head to find my mouth, I oblige and let her have it, the kiss is as slow and lazy as our love making, our hands are careful with our caresses but at the same time effortless.

"This is us Belle. Pure and simple. As long as we have this, we're always going to be alright."

She gives a light quiver, "I couldn't agree more, this is amazing." It takes all of her energy to speak. Her body is still trembling beneath me, and probably will be for a while after we're done making love.

"This is the way love is made Belle, the emotional connection is established like this, both of us sharing mutual pleasure."

She moans this time, "I've always wanted this."

"Stay with me Belle, and you'll always have it."

"I'll never leave you." She declares.

"Why not?" I challenge.

"Because you complete me."

It's not what I want to hear, but it'll do for now.

She whimpers from pleasure this time when she climaxes.

"I love you Belle." I say as I do the same.

We stay right there on the floor for seemingly an eternity.

Belle

What the fuck has gotten into Parker? He provided me with three mind blowing orgasms, one after the other. And now we're both sprawled on his lounge floor, both completely naked and unashamed by our blatant state of undress. I'm totally blissed out, Parker is toying with my necklace beside me.

"Was all of that an attempt to get me to say I love you?" I ask, I can't be anything other than calm, I'm too full of pleasure to be anything other than calm.

"No, I wanted to pleasure so I did, I wanted us to make love, so we did."

"I don't think I was much use."

"You were, you so were." He kisses my cheek.

"Parker I couldn't move. You tired me out. Did you really get pleasure from that?"

"Of course I did. All of the men you slept with, were only out for their own pleasure, they didn't care if you climaxed or not."

"They did when I told them, if they didn't make me scream I would dump them, and just go and find another endeavour."

"At least you don't have to tell me."

"I feel selfish, I had three mind blowing orgasms, and you only had one."

"I enjoy pleasuring you Belle, as a matter of fact, I'm making it a hobby. I like knowing I'm the only man to WANT to pleasure you and to have the honour to."

I toy with his hair, "You're pretty amazing, now I'm going to sound very selfish indeed, but out of all the women in London that you could have had, I'm glad you picked me."

"I would do it again in a heartbeat."

Parker's phone then rings, he grumbles as he reaches up to the table to grope for it, when he gets it he answers, "Hey Wayne, you're on loudspeaker, say hi to Belle." I shoot him a dubious look, he nibbles on my ear lobe, I elbow him off on a giggle.

"Hey Belle."

"Hey Wayne. You alright?"

"Yeah I'm good, just finished a shoot, and wanted to check in on my main man. How are you?"

"I'm good thanks, Parker on the other hand is indulging himself on my neck."

"Sounds like him, he could never keep his hands off the women he was with, so I'm used to it. Parker question for you brother."

"Go on." He says kissing my neck.

"You coming out for drinks tonight?"

He doesn't hesitate, "No not tonight."

"Old ball and chain already?" Wayne replies.

"He can go out for drinks if he wants to." I look at Parker, "You can go out for drinks if you want to."

"I know. I don't want to, this is our first weekend together since you moved in, I want to spend it with you."

"Alright then dude, another time." Wayne hangs up.

I put my head on his shoulder on a giggle, "Did you have to put it on loudspeaker?"

"I wanted him to hear your light hearted side."

"You mean my post sex blissful side."

"That too. Now where were we before we were interrupted?"

"I was about to tell you I don't deserve you."

"Why not?" He asks kissing me lazily.

"Because I have done so much wrong."

He moves down my body, "Really? You have done so much wrong." He lifts my feet and kisses then individually, "You've never been seduced have you Belle?"

"No I haven't."

"Well then it's about time someone did." He starts massaging my feet, "This is something that takes years to perfect, I changed my technique a million times. I'm going to show you my most effective way to seduce a woman."

He moves up my leg and then works on the other side.

"Lay on your stomach Belle."

I do as he says, he straddles me, and begins to massage my back, "Oh God." I sigh, I'm already relaxed, but wow. He kisses the small of my back, runs his lips up my spine to my shoulders, when he deprives me of his lips, I shudder in despair, but he soon replaces them with his hands, and wow they are pure magic.

He lifts his weight slightly, "Turn around Belle."

I do as he asks and face him, when I do he lowers down to kiss me.

He then moves down my body, kisses my stomach causing me to quiver, he runs his lips up my stomach, kisses my breasts, nips at my nipples, which causes me to cry out.

He continues his journey up to my neck, he nibbles on my earlobe.

And finally when I am a quivering bag of need, he kisses me, I can't let him do all the work, not when he's been so good to me.

In one smooth move I flip him over and straddle him, placing my hand on his chest, "Whoa second wind?"

"What can I say? You deserve this baby."

I lower onto him, he lets out a strangled groan, I keep the pace, after a couple of minutes I decide he's mesmerised enough to listen.

"This might not be the words you want to hear, but believe me what I say that they are the absolute truth."

"Oh fuck Belle." He groans, "We don't have to talk, not now, let this do the talking."

"No let me say this. You saved me Parker, before you I was this cold hearted, calculating bitch, who fucked married men for a hobby, but now I can say, I'm your girlfriend, your lover and one day your wife. I'm yours Parker."

He climaxes at that, sitting up, fisting his hands in my hair and nuzzling deep into my neck.

When he's done he removes his face from my neck quickly, "You didn't orgasm."

"Doesn't matter, I didn't want to, that was for you." I kiss him lightly.

"I does matter Belle."

"Three." I point to myself, "Two." I point at him.

"I told you I like pleasuring you."

"Parker it's only one time."

"No Belle, it's the only time, you don't do that again. Understand me?"

"What's the big deal?" I shrug.

"The big deal is, sex is a mutual joining of two consenting adults, both of them have the right to feel pleasure from their encounter."

"And if one should choose only one to feel pleasure?"

"That's how sex slips, if you do it once then the man might think it's acceptable to do it all the time."

I hook my arms around his neck, "And if you were like those other men, then I would be worried, but you're not, you're Parker Wilson, the man who has made pleasuring his woman his hobby."

"Damn straight. Best way to keep a girl, is to treat her like you're still trying to win her."

"And how do I keep you Parker?"

"Just be you." He smiles sweetly.

God I love him so much.

Chapter Sixteen

Parker

REALLY I SHOULD HAVE KNOWN people would try and make trouble for Belle and I, but the naïve part of me thought that they weren't going to bother. But people have been going to the press saying that I am making a huge mistake, Belle's going to break my heart, the usual old news shit that I've paid no attention to.

I soon break out of my dream state, when a sky blue bra come in view, I look up to see Belle holding a white short sleeve polo shirt open.

"Oh good so now I have your attention." She starts buttoning her shirt, so Business Belle is capable of having a little fun. She looks very sexy in her grey skirt, black tights, and the shirt as well, the top button needs doing up, she's showing cleavage.

I pull her on to my lap, "My undivided attention." I muse as I kiss her neck.

"Parker stop, I'm being serious."

"Business Belle is in the house."

"Business Belle is also going to be late home, because she promised the girls she was going out for drinks with them."

I remember her telling me this at the beginning of the week, but in all fairness to her, she only tends to be late home twice a week, and that's because she goes to her Nan's twice a week both by herself and with the girls.

"When will you be back?" I ask.

"No idea, I might wind up staying with them." She puts her hands on my cheeks, "You trust me right?"

I think of everything she said to me last weekend, and everything she said, and everything we have done together since then, "Yes Belle I trust you."

"Good because I love what we have too much to wreck it." She gives me a long kiss, "I have to go to work, text me so I don't go insane. See you even have an effect on Business Belle, even she needs you."

"Just wait on moment." I do up her top button, and she rolls her eyes, "Oi these." I cup her breasts in my hands, "Are now for my eyes and hands only. You're in an office on your own with men."

"What about when I'm out with the girls?"

"If you dress anything like you did when I first met you, then you are usually quite elegant on a night out."

"Alright then." She kisses me again, "I'm going to be late if I don't go now. See you later handsome."

"I love you."

She smiles and blows me a kiss.

Well if she's going on a night out with the girls, I might as well see if the lads want to meet for some drinks, I call Wayne, "Hey brother."

"Hey man, so Belle is out tonight, so if you want to go out for drinks tonight, then it'll be sweet."

"Old ball and chain huh."

"It's nothing like that, I got it bad bro."

"Alright lads night, The River at seven, be there or be square bro."

"Alright man cool."

Belle

Now that Parker isn't with me, I go back to Victoria's Secret to buy that dress I noticed last week, I also buy Royal blue silk lingerie, to soften the blow of my disobedience.

As I leave the store I nearly run into Ashley, who has on a pair of black skinny jeans who has on a red vest top, "Oh hey Ashley."

"Hey." She blushes, "Wow this is awkward knowing that you probably have something for my little brother in that bag."

"Yeah, I guess it probably is. Tell you something really awkward, your best friends partner waiting for her to come home, in what she thinks is her room, when really it is your room, and she has nothing on but some skimpy lingerie."

"So M.K likes that kind of thing?" Weird thing to ask.

"Every now and then she's a bit spontaneous."

"Oh right. She seems to like Parker."

And you seem to be very interested in my best mate, "She just glad I've finally settled down. Although she never said anything about the way I lived my life, I could tell she was getting sick of it. All of my family really like Parker."

"He's a good guy, but I have to say that, I'm his sister."

"Do you want a lift anywhere?"

"Speaking of which, I'm meeting a friend for coffee at the Starbucks opposite your building, so only if you don't mind."

"Don't be silly get in." We get in my car, "So have you met Bailey yet?" I ask her.

"Not officially, I know she was in your office when I came to talk to you about Parker, but I was too busy staring out M.K to notice."

And checking her out, but I decide to leave out that minor detail, "Out of all of us, M.K has had the crappiest life. She protects and cherishes what's hers, mainly because she's not used to having anything, she fairly protective, and she's already given Parker the 'if you hurt her, I hurt you' talk. She did that a couple of weeks before you came to see me."

"She takes matters into her own hands."

"Ashley I once witnessed a police officer tell her, 'You're a kid in the system, if your own parents don't care what happens to you, then why should I?' She was only twelve."

"System?" Of course she wants me to elaborate on that.

"Care system, foster kid, Nan's foster kid to be exact."

"Well that's a terrible thing to say to a child, poor M.K she must have thought no one ever cared about her. How did she wind up in the care system?"

"Long story, and sorry Ashley, I've already gone over the line here, but I think you like her, so I am going to throw you a bone. She's rough around the edges but once you get through them, she's a big softie with a heart of gold."

"What are you telling me all this?"

That is the million dollar question, "Because you both need to give love another chance." I pull up outside my building, "Well here we are, look we're going out for drinks tonight, if you want to come then feel free, if not then some other time. If you want to come then meet me out here at four, we usually go to my old place to get ready, listen to music and chat, you know."

"I'll think about it."

I pass her my card, "Let me know." We both get out of my car, "Oh and Ashley."

"Yeah?" She says turning back around to face me.

"If you do come tonight, then come as you, M.K likes people only being who they are."

She smiles and I go into my building, I call Bailey, I need to tell M.K what I have done, she's not going to be happy, and Bailey can usually talk her down, "Hey, hey, hey girlfriend."

"You and M.K meet me stat, need to talk to M.K and need you to referee."

"Oh fuck, what have you done?"

"Let's just say, it begins with A ends in Y, and is a relation to my boyfriend."

"Ashley? The cop? M.K hates cops."

"Apparently not this one, and apparently the feeling is mutual. I'm getting in the lift now."

"Alright meet you there."

I push the button for M.K and Bailey's floor, when I get there Bailey practically bounces in, M.K saunters in behind her.

"Seriously?" She arches her brow, "You know I hate being summoned."

"I do, but this is important, Bailey's here so you don't kill me."

"Depending on what you tell me, depends on whether she can stop me." She drawls. When the lift opens she steps into my office, "Alright so what is this about?"

"You have an admirer." I say sitting on my desk.

"Who?"

"Ashley Wilson."

"As in Parker's sister and cop?"

"Yeah her. I saw her this morning on my way to work, I also bobbed into Victoria's Secret, she said she felt awkward knowing that I had something in the bag intended for her little brother, so I told her about what Laura did for you, and because she thought my room was your room I walked in on her, suddenly you were the topic of conversation."

"Fucking great. And what was said?"

All good things M.K, that you were in the care system, which she would have found out if she did a check on you, I also told her that Nan fostered you. That was it M.K."

"So you thing she likes me?" M.K asks.

"She certainly takes a lot of interest in you, but if she accepts my invitation for drinks tonight, you shall see for yourself."

"Belle you badass." Bailey beams.

M.K approaches me, "You take a lot of liberties, but this one might pay off, she's pretty nice."

"I told her that you're rough around the edges, but when you get through the edges, you're a big softie."

"Just ruin my reputation completely." She muses.

"Right now get out of my office and get to work." I joke.

M.K kisses my cheek, "Thanks pal."

"You're welcome. Love you."

M.K wraps her arm around Bailey as they walk out.

After what has been a bit of a trying day, with journalist posing as clients, to get up to my office so they can interview me about my relationship with the man dubbed, 'The most Sought After Man in London.'

Let's just say a night out with the girls is just what the doctor ordered, so at four I don't hesitate in shutting down my computer, and going to get M.K and Bailey.

I get out of the lift and walk into M.K's office, Bailey is in there too, they have their own office right next to each other, but when they don't have clients, they either ring up to see if I feel like company and come and do paperwork in my office, or they work in M.K's.

"The one time you two are bothered about paperwork." I muse, as I look at them with the same love as you would sisters, "I've been doing some thinking."

"Uh oh, that's dangerous." M.K laughs but then she glances up and clocks my face, "Oh you're serious. What is it?"

"It's not something to discuss here, come on guys shut down. Come home, I really need to talk to you two."

"Alright we're coming."

They shut down their computers, Bailey puts her laptop in the top drawer of the cabinet.

"Is something wrong?" Bailey asks laying a hand on my arm.

"No something is very, very right, and I'm kicking seven shades of shit out of myself for not thinking about it sooner, it's so obvious."

We step into the lift, "Going to give us a hint or keep guessing?" M.K asks impatiently, she hates being kept in suspense.

"We can discuss it when we get to my place, your place sorry."

"What are you apologising for? You're still paying for the stuff, it will always be your place Belle."

As long as they are there, it will be, they make it home.

The lift opens and we step out, Ashley is sat waiting for us in the lobby in a short sky blue lace dress that compliments her figure, she has on a little makeup but not too much, she looks lovely.

"What's she doing here?" M.K asks trying not to check her out.

"Oh I told her that if she wanted to come out with us tonight then she has to meet us here." I smile and wave.

"Wait, what about what you want to tell us?" M.K asks.

"I can say it in front of her." I shrug, "Hey Ashley glad you could make it, you look really nice."

"Thank you for inviting me. And thanks for the compliment. I like to make an effort in a night out, Wilson's are famous for their appearance on nights out. Even though it's only Parker that is really famous, he sort of made his whole family figures in the spotlight." She resents that, but not him, I don't think she could ever resent him.

"Right well if you come with me, I'll drive you to my place, we usually have a meal, and then get ready, but before we do anything, I want to talk to my girls."

M.K and Bailey separate to go to Bailey's car, I know Bailey makes some quip about Ashley to M.K, I don't hear what is said, but I see her get shoved for her trouble.

I shake my head and smile, "Bailey is the joker of the group." I say as we get into the car, "But she's serious when she needs to be."

"What's her story? You don't have to go into details, just the basics will do."

"Both of her parents died when she was young, her adoptive mother sent her to boarding school, because there were no decent schools in the area, but then again she also fostered, it took Bailey and I a while to settle in to boarding school. M.K on the other hand, she settled in right away, which made us kind of like worried in a sense. Bailey's adoptive Mum was cool, she took us all in, she saw the way my step mother could treat me, but then she died pretty suddenly, Bailey and M.K then only had Nan and me, she took us all in."

"Wow everyone she cared about died, but she seems so bubbly."

"Oh she was messed up, don't get me wrong, I am not going to go into detail, but she had her messed up moments, but Nan straightened her out, Nan straightened us all out. Look Ashley, we're all individually strong in our own right."

We get to my house, I push my Bluetooth button to open the gate, "Oh wow." She muses, "This place is huge."

"My pride and joy, I bought this place for Bailey, M.K and I, like I promised."

I pull up outside the house, and get out of the car, Ashley follows, "So you all live here?"

"Yeah it's big enough to be able to avoid people if wish, which is good."

We go into the house, M.K and Bailey are close behind Ashley and I.

"So where do you want to talk?" M.K asks me, with impatience still hinting in her tone, she really hates suspense.

"Straight to the point as usual." I smile at M.K, "The lounge." I walk in there and turn the fireplace on low, I stand before the fire as I usually do when we're discussing things, Bailey sits on the sofa, "Pick a place Ashley, there's no standing permitted in this room, especially if you're a guest."

"And unless you're me, the rules don't apply." M.K shoots me a challenging look, as she leans on the back of the sofa near Ashley, "So what's this about?"

"I want it to be made legal that you two are my sisters." I declare.

"Why legal?" M.K enquires.

"Because we're family in every other way there is, but not in the eyes of the law. I want to make it legal that we're family, and I was hoping that you two would want the same thing."

"To add an effect we could change our names, make it more realistic." Bailey suggests.

"Which may be hard for you." I say to Bailey.

"But not so much for me." M.K snipes, "Because let's face it, I was abused and abandoned but my family." Ashley looks at M.K at that, she's tempted to reach out to her.

M.K winces, "Fuck." She curses softly, "Bailey if you're happy with it, then I'll do it, my name is not something I take any pride in."

"Bailey O Neil." Bailey muses, "Good ring to it. Certainly has a better ring to it than Moxxam. Alright why not? I mean we're so close people think we're related anyway and we never correct them."

I look at M.K who is trying to shake off the memories of her past, "M.K do you need a minute?"

She shakes her head and starts pacing, "Townsend, whenever I say, write or hear that name, I'm reminded of everything I've been through, how far I've come. But I do wonder how it would feel to hear a name that doesn't make me tremble with hatred first. M.K O Neil." She tests the name, "I like it. Alright let's do it."

I smile at them both, Ashley hasn't taken her eyes off M.K since she blurted out she was abused and abandoned.

"Now we have something to celebrate when we go out. I'll go and make a start on dinner."

"I'll take that moment now." M.K says, she looks at Bailey, I walk over and kiss her cheek before I leave.

I then go into the kitchen Ashley is close behind me, "Where's Bailey?" She asks.

"M.K wanted her to stay." I go into the fridge, get out some salsa and sour cream, and put them both in the microwave, I then go into the pantry to get out three big bags of nachos, I set them on the counter and then go into a cupboard, I find a huge plate, and set it on the counter, I pour the nachos on it and spread them out evenly.

"Her past really hurts her." Ashley says, she seems to be thinking out loud.

"Best to forget about that." I say getting the salsa out of the microwave, "She doesn't like to talk about it, so if she tells you it means that she cares about you a lot. And you can't ask, she has to tell you."

M.K and Bailey then walk in, I'm silent as I go over and hug M.K, "I love you." I whisper in her ear.

"I love you too."

Parker

So it's been an alright day, the lads are over for pre drinks we tend to get a little wild, Belle will probably be glad that she isn't here, the big kid in me tends to come out when I am with the lads, we rough house, play stupid games, that usually involve shouting.

Right now, Sam and I are wrestling on the floor, Wayne is too worried about wrinkling his clothes to join in, he has on a pair of Italian shoes, charcoal trousers, a white t-shirt and a charcoal jacket.

Sam has on a pair of grey jeans and a white t-shirt.

I have on a pair medium blue jeans and a white t-shirt.

It's nearly time to head out.

All of a sudden my lift opens, my head pops up as Belle strolls in, in the same clothes as she had on this morning, she has a Victoria's Secret bag in her hand.

She clocks me, "I thought it was only me you liked to wrestle." Her eyes are swimming with amusement.

I get up and go to her, "Well it's more fun with you." I pull her to me and nuzzle her neck. "Want to show me what's in the bag?" I kiss her slowly.

"No, not yet." She grazes her teeth along my bottom lip, "I'm saving it for a special occasion."

"Oh come on, just a peak." I turn to the boys, "I'm just going to ravage my woman for a moment."

"Alright bro, just keep it down. Some of us haven't been laid in months." Sam moans.

I drag her into the bedroom, "You can't be serious?"

"Oh I am deadly." I kiss her again, "What's in the bag?"

"I'm not telling you."

"Do I have to look myself?"

"You do that and I'll cut it."

"You're a mean woman." I pull her top up so I can get my hands on her skin, "I could sulk, I always get a little bit childish when I am with the lads, I could always give you my famous pout."

"It won't work." I brush my hands up to her breasts, "Oh fuck." She gasps.

"Or I could seduce you. And have you put it on or no sex."

She hooks her arms around my neck, and presses herself against me, "You wouldn't punish yourself like that." She murmurs against my lips, "And pleasuring me is your hobby, unless that was a lie."

She has me there, "Call me a liar again, I really will ravage you."

"I'll have to remember that later."

"Oh and Jack text me earlier, he said congratulations on bagging the fittest bird in London."

"Typical bloke." She smiles, she plants a hard kiss on me, "I've got to go." We walk hand in hand out of the bedroom, "See you later handsome." She purrs, "I'll be thinking of you doing all kinds of amazing things to me."

She kisses me again, gives my bum a hearty squeeze, and before I can really pay her back, she running and summoning the lift, I still have some time, I go over to her and back her into the kitchen counter, "You're really asking for that ravaging."

"And you're really asking for a knee in the groin."

"You wouldn't do that, you love me too much."

"You're right I do." She agrees. She agrees that she loves me, she just needs to say the words.

"I'll take the affirmation for now." The lift opens and I groan my dissatisfaction, "I could get rid of Sam and Wayne and we could stay in."

"No, I have a promise to keep. Rain check." She kisses me again, "I got to go."

I let her go, I blow her a kiss as the lift door is closing and she does the same thing.

I then go and sit with the fellas, "Whoa." Wayne exclaims, "You weren't even like that with Chelsea. You really do have it bad bro."

"I know bro, it's amazing, but so fucking painful at the same time."

"Well take your mind off it for tonight big guy."

Belle

I have just got back to my friends, I walk into the lounge, "Well that took longer than expected, Parker had Wayne and Sam over but that didn't stop him trying to ravage me in the bedroom, your brother is certainly a randy one Ashley, not that I am complaining."

"Where do you think he gets it from? My parents are like it, surely you noticed when you had dinner with us."

"I noticed they were a bit hands on with each other."

"Times that by ten, they were reserved because you were new, when they get to know you, they will not be so stingy with the PDA's, trust me."

"I once walked in on my Dad and step mother having sex on the couch, nothing is worse than that, trust me, but that wasn't love, it was need."

"What are you like to be with Ashley?" M.K asks, I shoot her a look wondering what her game is.

Ashley looks directly at M.K, "I like to think I'm a good partner, I learnt a lot about relationships from my Mum and Dad, and they have been together over twenty five years and still madly in love, my ex and I were good together but it didn't work out."

Something bad happened, you can tell because there was a flash of sadness in her eyes when she said that, it was brief but it was there, whatever happened she isn't going to go into it, "Yeah well that doesn't reflect badly on you, some things just don't work out." Bailey muses.

I know we all saw the same thing, "My ex left me for another woman, and turns out I'm too bitter for a relationship."

"Your ex was just using you anyway, you're better off without her." Bailey chirps.

"Right let's go and get ready. Are we doing the usual routine of convening in my room, you two coming in with a selection of clothes and us taking a vote?"

"Yeah." M.K nods. We head upstairs, "Let me guess you already have your outfit picked out."

"Victoria's Secret, along with a little something for Parker as well."

"Ew seriously." Ashley grimaces, "It's bad enough seeing you walk out of there with a bag in your hand KNOWING it's for my brother, without hearing you admit it."

"Aww." M.K runs her hand down Ashley's arm, in a gesture that I can't tell is friendly or flirty, "We have a shy one here guys."

"Ashley if you want to come in my room with me, the girls will be with us soon." We do just that, "Looks like both you and my sister have parts of you past you don't want to go into." I observe.

"I'm not sure I know what you mean."

"When M.K asked about the kind of partner you are, you sort of froze when you spoke of your ex."

"Oh I…"

"Was hoping we wouldn't notice."

"Thanks for not asking."

"It clearly hurts you, whatever happened, so we won't pry."

"You really are nothing like the papers make out, when I saw you and Parker on your first date, I wanted to kill you right there on the spot, I thought you were using him."

"I don't blame you for thinking that."

M.K and Bailey then walk in, Bailey in her undies which consist of sky blue satin underwear.

M.K is in a black long sleeve jumpsuit that shows some cleavage and hugs her butt really well, I know it's for Ashley's benefit and that she's noticed, "It's just miss picky shit, I got my outfit sorted, there is a plus side to not wearing dresses."

"Picky shit." Bailey repeats sticking her tongue out.

"Children let's not squabble, this is supposed to be fun. Alright Bailey show me the options."

"The thing is with all the dresses I want to wear, are I need to wear hair extensions."

"Here's an idea, grow your hair." M.K jibes.

"I do agree with M.K, longer hair would suit you, but M.K there are extensions in the bathroom, if you go and get them, Bailey can start modelling the clothes for us."

M.K does just that, and Bailey gets a black dress and holds it against her, "You own something black?" I ask her in awe, "I thought you hated the colour."

"It would look good for dates."

"She's right." Ashley agrees, "It's very seductive."

"I like her." Bailey smiles.

"If the dress was bought for dates, then it should be used for that, it could be like a celebration." Ashley advises.

"You're right."

She that dress down and picks up a mint green number, "Too plain, you need something to bring out your eyes." I say.

She purses her lips and wiggles her nose in consideration, she looks at her pile of clothes, "I think I have it."

She dives into the pile, and pulls out a nice little red number, she holds it against her, it's low on cleavage, short enough to show some thigh, but not too short, it will hug her figure when she has it on, "That's it." Ashley says enthusiastically, "That's the dress."

I laugh at her enthusiasm and then look at Bailey, I nod my approval, "She's right you look hot."

M.K then walks in and tosses the hair extensions to me, "What do you think? Ashley picked it."

"I think she has very good taste, considering I told you that was the dress you should wear." She glances over at Ashley, she clearly approves of her in a lot of ways.

I then get out the dress I plan on wearing, "Oh wow." M.K gasps, "That dress is killer, you should save that Parker."

"No way, he said I couldn't get it."

"He actually said that?" Ashley can't believe it.

"Yeah, he said if I bought the dress, he would kill me. So I went back when he wasn't with me, he also doesn't let me show cleavage."

"He's never been like that with a woman before." She then drifts off into a daydream.

"It's alright, I know my past, I knew that when I eventually got into a relationship, they might be a little paranoid."

"As long as he doesn't hurt you." M.K shrugs.

"He wouldn't do that." Ashley is quick to stand up for her little brother, "He flies into a meltdown at the thought of hurting someone he loves."

"I know he wouldn't hurt me, he's nothing but gentle, it's why I love him. Relax Ashley." I lay my hand on her arm.

"I will talk to him about the clothes thing."

"It's really not a problem, I was only kidding." Family is important to her, she really is the protector.

I go to put on the dress, when I come out Bailey is sat on the bed, "They're having a moment, family is a sensitive subject to Ashley."

"And M.K is playing agony aunt? Wonders never cease."

"More like protector to protector chat."

"I was careless, family is important to the Wilson's, we joke about family because we never really had one, they do, we should have known better."

"Well we know for next time. First time remember, still learning." M.K and Ashley them come in from the balcony, "Ashley I'm so sorry. I was careless."

"We all are." Bailey put in.

"Honestly it's fine, I was being stupid."

"No you weren't don't do things like that Ashley." M.K scolds, "Feelings are never stupid."

"Shall we go out?" I ask, "Clean slate from here on in, only fun is permitted now."

"Sounds good to me."

We walk to the pub, it's not far from my house only about half an hour.

When we get to the pub, we head straight to the bar, I order the drinks, "A bottle of Bulmers Pear Cider, a large Jack Daniels on the rocks, a Southern Comfort with lemonade." I turn to Ashley, "What will you have?"

"Oh just a glass of Pinot Grigio."

"A glass of your finest Pinot Grigio."

"It didn't have to be the finest." She says, "I doubt I could even afford that."

"Well you're out with us, it's my round, and you can order none finest, when it's yours." I smile.

"Best not to argue." M.K states taking hold of Ashley's arm to lead her to our favourite booth.

"Alright then." She shrugs to taste her wine, "That really is very good actually."

"See and you were complaining." M.K gives her leg a friendly pat, "Stick with us kid you get used to fine dining."

I can't help but wonder how long it will be before M.K is asking her to stick with HER.

Parker

So my friends and I are now at The River, laughing, joking and playing pool. Which is all standard lads night out stuff really.

"Sorry bro, but I got to ask this." Wayne says, "Belle does she live up to her Queen of Seduction name?"

I smile, "Oh mate, she surpasses it, those guys didn't do her justice, she's new to the whole relationship thing, but she is amazing, everything I have ever wanted."

"And is she as good in bed as they claim?" Sam asks, I should smack him in the mouth for that question, but I'm in too much of a good mood.

"She really is bro, she's amazing to sleep with, she takes command without you even realising it's happening, she can change the gear of a kiss, of sex and make you think it's all your idea, and I bet a lot of naïve men think it is their idea, but I'm not naïve, and she knows that. She is completely amazing."

"Anyway." Wayne shifts awkwardly, "The idea of this was to take his mind off his woman."

"First of all you started it, second of all, the man has been daydreaming about her since we came out, he's like spell bound. I think the woman is a witch."

"She certainly has me spell bound." I admit.

"Don't look now bro but your woman has just walked in with her posse, and it looks like your sister has joined them." Wayne informs me.

I turn my head and see that he is actually right, my sister is with them, she seems comfortable with them as well, they are sat in a booth laughing, she seems very at home. I can't help but love Belle even more now, Ashley might finally move on from Laura.

They all look lovely, Bailey in her red dress, that hugs her figure nicely, and shows some cleavage and thigh.

M.K in a nice tight jumpsuit that too shows cleavage.

Ashley in a mint green dress that flows at the legs and hugs her upper body well.

And Belle...she is in a dress I specifically told her I wouldn't want her going out in. That little black dress from Victoria's Secret, it's so tight I'm shocked she can breathe, I can see all of her curves.

Fucking hell how can I be so pissed off and so turned on at the same time? She looks amazing, but she didn't wear the dress for my eyes, she wore it for other people.

I can't really blame her, she had no idea I planned on coming here with the lads tonight, I never told her I planned on coming here, and I know that this is her local, so if I go over there now, she will think that I am here to spy on her.

"Whoa brother, your woman looks killer." Sam nearly chokes on his pint, good saves me choking him.

"Remind me again how did you two meet?" Wayne begins, "How did you two meet?"

"Here, not last time the time before that, Friday night, a night like this one."

"She looked hot then." Wayne remembers, "You actually came up to us then and said, 'Sorry fellas love calls." I thought you'd gone nuts."

"He had, for her."

I smile at that, Sam's right, I was nuts for her the moment I met her.

I see Belle and the girls start to get up, they move on to the dance floor, all four of them dance together, as a cohesive unit. All of them using seductive moves, even my sister, never in my life did I ever think I would ever see my sister dance seductively with a group of women and look likes she's enjoying it. I just watch them, well Belle mainly, I'm thinking of ways to persuade her to give me a private dance.

All of a sudden there is a man approaching them, I'm up like a shot, Sam grabs my arm, "Mate you do that, you will prove you don't trust her, which will kill your relationship, just see what she does first."

The guy takes Belle in his arms, M.K, Bailey and Ashley start telling him to back off, Belle elbows him in the ribs, he releases her, she rubs her hip, "He's hurt her."

Now no one stops me, I walk up to the guy, he's in his forties, slick brown hair, triangle jawline, uneven lips, big eagle like nose, big round grey eyes, he's a business type in a grey suit and a pink shirt.

"You like hurting defenceless women do you?" I grab his collar and hit him once, "Walk away, before I beat the fuck out of you." I shove him away, turn to Belle, I bring her into my arms, I need to hold her a moment.

"I didn't know you were going to be here." She states.

She pushes out of my embrace, I wrap a lock of her hair around my index finger, "Clearly." I state, "Me and the lads always come here when we meet up."

"You didn't have to hit him. We had it handled."

"He hurt you." I put my hand on her hip, "I told you not to buy this dress Belle."

"You can't control what I wear."

"I did it for your benefit Belle, not for mine, you look lovely, too lovely, men like him take it as an invitation."

"We would have looked out for her." M.K sticks up for Belle.

"Yeah Parker we had it handled." Ashley states, "What's with the caveman impression? This isn't like you."

203

Belle puts her hand on my cheek, "Is this because of me? Are you like this, controlling and possessive because of me?"

I don't answer, I can't answer, I fear it, if I do I'll lose her.

"You've told me all I need to know through your silence Parker, if I bring this out in you, then I'm not worth it. Goodbye."

She runs out of the pub, me in hot pursuit, she hails a taxi and is in it before I have the chance to catch her, Bailey, M.K and Ashley soon appear on the pavement behind me.

I turn to them, "Where will she go? Her old place? Where? Someone answer me!"

"Nan!" M.K states plainly, "She'll go to Nan, but you both need space, some time to cool off."

"M.K's right." Ashley puts in, "Go to Mum and Dad Parker, you're a mess, you need to speak to them."

"I don't need Mum and Dad. I need Belle!"

Ashley marches up to me and takes my chin in her hand roughly, "You listen to me, I have no idea what's gotten into you, but you are going to go to them, tell them what happened tonight and they are going to help you make sense of it, so tomorrow you can sort things out with Belle. Got it?"

I nod.

"Good, go to them."

I do as she says.

I arrive at my parent's like Ashley told me to do, I'm a mess, when Mum opens the door, in her hot pink nightgown, I practically fall into her arms sobbing, "Oh my boy, what's happened?"

"I messed up Mum, I messed up bad."

"Come inside honey, come on." I don't let her go, I just walk forward, she shuts the door behind me, "Darling you're going to have to calm down and talk to me."

I let her go and we sit on the sofa, "What's all the commotion? I'm trying to put Skyla to bed." Dad says in a pair of green and black plaid pyjama bottoms, his top half is bare, he's in good shape for age, he as a tight, lean physique.

"I'm trying to work that out, this might be a job for the both of us darling."

Dad then looks at me, "What's the matter son?" He asks placing a hand on my shoulder.

"I messed up dad, I messed up really bad."

"Just give me a moment, I'll ask Julian to put Skyla to bed." He then goes upstairs.

"It can't be that bad, the girl is besotted with you, whatever you've done, I'm sure she'll forgive."

Dad then comes downstairs, and leans on the back of the sofa, "What's happened son?"

"Belle was out with her friends, so I went out with Wayne and Sam, Belle, her friends and Ashley came into the same bar, she didn't know I was going to be there, she had on this really hot dress. She looked so amazing, she and the girls got up to dance, all of a sudden this guy grabs Belle, she handles it fine, but then she rubs where the guy grabbed her, and I got really mad, I march over to the guy and I hit him."

"Sounds like a reasonable reaction to me, seeing her hurt is what made you mad." Dad says.

"There is something you're not telling us." Mum states.

"I told her not to buy the dress she had on because she told me she planned on wearing it for a night out. I also have a problem with her wearing clothes that show cleavage, I even do up her buttons if her clothes have them."

"Alright son, when your mother is reading the news, she sometimes wears low cut tops. Do you think I like the idea of millions of men ogling her? I mean look at her, she's still got it, men in their twenties have tried it on with her."

"And so you think I like it when your father and I attend parties, and women in their twenties are coming up to him kissing his cheek with a fuck me look in their eyes?" She gives my Dad a challenging look, she knows he hates her swearing, "No I want to stab their eyes out."

"How do you handle it?"

"I revel in the knowledge that at the end of the day, it's me that your mother is going to be coming home to, it's me she's going to kiss, me she's going to cuddle, me she's going to be going to bed with, and me she's going to love."

Mum caresses Dad's cheek, "And I revel in the knowledge of knowing, that I'm the only woman your father looks at with pure love in his eyes, and the knowledge I'm always going to be that woman, and that look will never change."

"See my boy, even after nearly thirty years of being together, we still have stints of the green eyed monster, a bit of jealousy proves you love the person you're with. As for the clothes the next time you see her like it, revel in the knowledge that it's you she's going to be coming home to. The girl has settled with you Parker, she loves you, treat her right, and she will always come home to you."

"Stay here tonight." Dad suggests, "And tomorrow go and fight for her, calmly, coolly and remember everything we have told you."

"Thank you, I have no idea what I would have done without you two."

"We love you Parker, so much." Mum kisses my cheek, "I'll get you some duvet."

She then goes upstairs, "How do you keep the love alive?"

"Compromise, respect, trust, honesty and some good old loving. You have a good woman in Belle son, I know she became the way she is because of people assuming the worst of her all the time, I feel sorry for her really. But now she has you, she's happy Parker, which is more than I bet she thought she ever would be, that's because of you."

My parents are right, I have to fight for her, I'm not letting her go, tomorrow I'm getting her back and never letting her go again, she can push, she can run, but she can't hide, I will always find her, I will always catch her and I will always keep her.

Chapter Seventeen

Belle

I**T WAS THE HARDEST THING** in the world for me to do. But I couldn't bear the idea of turning Parker into someone he's not, he's not possessive, he's not controlling and he's not violent. But all the time he is with me, he is. What else was I supposed to do?

I'm sat in Nan's kitchen in a pair of pyjamas that are sky blue with small coffee cup all over them, which say 'Need More Coffee' on the mugs, I'm literally crying into my coffee.

Nan then walks in, wearing a long pink dressing gown, "Oh my darling." She sits down beside me and brings my head to her breast, "I knew you were upset last night. Why did you lie?"

"Because I had no idea how to tell you the truth." I still have no idea how to put it nicely, so I just decide to rip off the plaster and put it bluntly, "Parker and I broke up."

"Oh sweetheart why?"

"Because of that fucking dress." Getting to Nan's is a little bit of a haze, but I do remember the first thing I did was take it off and put it in the bin, "I'm sorry for swearing, Parker didn't want me to wear the dress, I did it anyway, there was a man last night, he grabbed me while I was dancing, I didn't know Parker was there, I didn't know he was there until all of a sudden he was THERE, and he hit him Nan, Parker has never been violent or controlling in his life, I did that to him, so I had to let him go."

"No, no lovey, love did that to him, a little bit of possessiveness is normal, not liking the idea of other men ogling you and touching you, that is normal, and if you tell me that M.K wouldn't have done the same thing, then I'll call you a liar."

"He's never been like that before." I sob.

"Then he's never been in love before. What he did last night was normal, and you honey, you are just looking for one last ditch attempt to save yourself from the wonder that is love. You won't be able to stay away and he won't be able to let you."

Maybe she's right, but I'm not taking that risk yet.

So when there's a frantic knocking at her front door, I run to the spare room, I know who it is, and I'm surprised he hasn't come sooner, "Please Nan I beg you, you haven't seen me."

"You were here, you left early." Nan clarifies.

I kiss her cheek, "I love you."

I then go into the spare room and hide in the wardrobe. I know it is a stupid and childish thing for me to do, but I'm not ready to face Parker yet, I don't think I am ever going to be ready to face him, but I also know that eventually he is not going to give me choice.

Parker

I haven't slept, but everything my parents said to me last night has been going round in my head all night, and I have been fighting with every fibre of my being to give Belle the space M.K told me to give her, but now it's driving me mad.

I'm at her Nan's house frantically knocking on her door, her Nan answer in a light pink dressing gown, "Is she here?"

"You look shattered, come in honey." I do just that, "Belle was here but she left early."

"How was she?"

"Heartbroken, she told me what happened last night, I told her your reaction was perfectly normal, that a little bit of possessiveness is normal in a relationship, not liking the idea of other men ogling and touching you is normal."

"I love her so much. I've never felt this way before, it's driving me so nuts, I feel like I'm going crazy."

"Well then my dear, you fight for her, and don't let her go."

"If I knew where she was then I would."

"She's in her room." Her Nan rises slowly to show me her room, "She's probably in the wardrobe."

I open the door, the wardrobe and the window are both open, Belle is hightailing it away from the house, in her pyjamas. I bellow her name, I sprint out of the house and pursue her, but by the time I have her in my sights, she's getting into a cab.

Belle

I can hear everything from the bedroom I'm in, he loves me so much I drive him nuts, that can't be good for him.

I should have known Nan would cave, that she wasn't going to let me throw away the best thing that happened to me, but I can't cave on this.

I storm out of the wardrobe and climb out of the window, my feet work like rockets, getting me away from the house, I hear him shout my name, I don't look back, I can't. I also know that I can't stay on foot, if I do that then he'll catch me, he's way too fast.

I find a parked taxi, "Are you working?"

"Yeah hop in love."

I get in and tell the driver where to go, I then call M.K, she answers quickly, "Hey you good?"

"Not really." I choke on a sob, "I'm on my way to you, I need you to get my purse and get some money for a taxi home."

"Alright see you in a bit."

I hang up and try to stop crying, but I can't.

When the taxi gets outside my house, M.K is at the gate, in a pair of black skinny jeans, and a red long sleeve crop top, "How much?"

"Fifteen." The driver replies.

M.K hands him a twenty, "Keep the change." She knows I like to give people tips.

I get out of the taxi, M.K wraps her arm around me as we walk to the house, "Ashley stayed here last night, in the spare room before you jump to any conclusions."

"Did I say anything?"

"No but I know what you're like."

We step into the house, Bailey sprints out of the lounge to hug me, in a hot pink onesie, "Oh honey."

"I'm alright." We walk into the lounge Ashley is in there, it looks like Bailey gave her some clothes to sleep in, she has on pair of black lounge pants, and a white baggy vest top, she looks the most casual I have ever seen her, "Hey." I smile weakly.

"Hey. You alright?"

"I will be."

"It's not going to be that easy you know. Parker has never been in love before."

"Nan said his reaction was totally normal, that a little bit of possessiveness is normal." I turn to M.K, "Remember how your ex could get with you?"

"No that was too possessive, she hated me spending time with you two, blew up my phone when I did, and then fucked off to another woman when I refused to ditch you two."

"Look." Ashley begins, "I have been in love and had my heart broken, but I do know it is really different with different people, Parker loved Chelsea, but she treated him like shit, she only wanted him for two things, his money and the sex. Now he's found someone who genuinely loves him, who he's in love with, and he has no idea what to do about it, so he made a mistake."

"If that's what love does to people, then surely it's better to stay out of it." I slump in a chair.

"You would think so wouldn't you?" Ashley tilts her head on a smile, "Other than what happened last night, how is Parker better off without you?"

"Because I break people's hearts, eventually I will do the same to him." I sigh.

"If you believe that then you're stupid." Ashley replies bluntly.

Ashley's remark earns a smile from M.K, "Can we keep her around? Because she says things I would usually say, and it saves me the trouble."

"Can I be saved the lecture please? I've made up my mind, Parker is better off without me, I'm going upstairs to brood and sob, whatever I need to do to get over this."

I then go upstairs, fall on my bed and sob.

Parker

I'm outside Belle's old place, I know her friends like me, but I also know how loyal they are, they are never going to let me in, so I'm going to let myself in, I scale the gate, years of climbing trees paid off, the ascent is easy enough, the descent on the other hand, is not easy but I manage it.

I walk to the front door and knock.

M.K answers, "How did you get in?" She asks in pure shock.

"I scaled the gate."

"You could have killed yourself." She scolds, but she steps to the side, she clearly respects my effort, "You look like shit, you had better come in. Go into the lounge."

I walk into the lounge and Ashley is there, "What are you doing here? In lounge clothes?" I add.

"I stayed here last night, in the spare room before you ask, I figured you would come here and it would probably be early, so M.K suggested that I stay the night. Did you see Mum and Dad?"

"Yes I did."

"A bit of jealousy is normal, Mum and Dad both witness things that make them jealous, but they both revel in the knowledge of coming home to each other."

Ashley knows what makes Mum and Dad jealous she's been through this herself, "So you have come to what conclusion?"

"None of this is Belle's fault, I've never been in love before, so I reacted badly to a situation."

"Well we agree on one thing to say the least, love has done this to you, so you're here to get her back."

"Yes I am." I go to leave the room.

M.K blocks my path, "I have to at least make it look like I tried to stop you. Shoes off." I take off my shoes, and she moves out of my way, "Tell Belle I tried to stop you."

"I will. Thank you M.K."

I make my way upstairs, I'm quite, I just want to hold her, I quietly open her door, she's asleep on her bed, her backs to me, she fell asleep crying, her breath is still trembling.

I can't bear it, I need to hold her.

211

Belle

I fell asleep crying, I wish I could stop dreaming of Parker, but I can't, all I can think of is what I'll be missing out on, I don't know if I'll ever move on from this.

I jump awake when the feeling of familiar and secretly much needed arms snake around me, "You shouldn't be here." I try to sound cold and unattached, but I know it won't work with him.

"I'm exactly where I should be." He nuzzles into the back of my neck, "I've missed you."

"You're better off without me." I sob, I can't help myself, and this man opens me up to a string of emotions all the time.

"No, no Belle, I'm not better off without you, these last twelve hours have nearly killed me, I lost you both last night and this morning. I know I shouldn't control what you wear."

"I shouldn't have worn that fucking dress, I know a bit of possessiveness is normal in a relationship. But Parker, is it love that's doing this to you? Or is it because of WHO you love?"

"I've never been in love before, not really, all of this is as new to me as it is to you, I've fallen in love with you Belle. Madly, gut wrenchingly, amazingly in love with you."

Tears run down my face, I turn to face him, he looks as drained as I do, "I'm going to destroy you."

He shakes his head, "Only if you leave me baby." He kisses me sweetly, "This isn't over Belle, I'm not going to let you end it, I love you too much." He nuzzles into my neck and tightens his hold, "Please, please don't end this. I'm begging you." He's crying, I can feel his tears on my neck.

I can't help but shed some tears of my own, "I don't want to hurt you Parker, I love you."

"You love me?"

"Yes, I love you so much it hurts."

"It only hurts now because we came so close to losing each other It won't hurt while we're together, it will never hurt while we're together."

He shifts so he's on top of me, he runs his hands up my top and shudders, "I've missed the feel of your skin."

He takes total possession of my mouth, his teeth are nipping and grazing over my lips, I sigh my surrender, and allow my hands to make their own journey up his top.

"I was wrong for being controlling." He says, he stops kissing me, "I was wrong for telling you what can and can't wear, and saying how you should wear your clothes, but that man hurt you last night Belle, I'm not sorry for hitting him."

"I'm sorry for wearing that dress, I shouldn't have bought it."

"Yes you should have, I have no right dictating your wardrobe."

"Only the silk underwear." I smile, "We can make an exception for that, well I can."

He smiles and kisses me lightly, "That is the only thing I will demand, well that and mind blowing sex."

"We both demand that. Shut up and make love with me." I pull him to me for a kiss.

I pull his top over his head, he does the same thing to me, he removes my pyjama bottoms, I arch my back to let him.

In one smooth move I flip him over and rain kisses over his neck, his chest and his stomach.

He groans his approval, "When we've finished making love here, I want to take you home and make love to you endlessly."

I undo his trousers, remove them and his pants, I crawl up his body, and push onto him, I lean down to kiss him, "You need more hobbies." He's now the one to take control, he flips me over and grinds in deep, "Oh fuck." I groan.

"I love the way you swear when we do this." He muses.

"Don't believe in God, so can hardly call out to Him."

I wrap my legs around his mid-section and pull him to me, "Oh fuck Belle."

"See now you're doing it."

"You really know how to test a man's control."

He grinds in deep, I groan loudly, "You nearly lost me, are you sure making love is on your agenda? Show me I can have it rough and not be marked."

"You want to be fucked?"

"Yes." I say plainly, "Make me scream."

Parker

She wants it rough, alright I can do that, we share one last tender kiss. Before I slam into her, "Fuck!" She screams, I don't let up, I just carry on, this time I slam into her and grind in deeper, "Oh Parker!" I'm so happy to hear that sound.

I keep it up, slamming and grinding, slamming and grinding, her nails dig into my shoulders, and she drags them down my back, she drags my head down so that she can give me a rough kiss and bites down on my bottom lip, when I slam into her and grind again, she then licks where her teeth grind in.

I then slam into her one more time and she climaxes, "Oh fuck Parker!"

I moan loudly as I do the same, I'm gentle as I ease us both down, and then collapse on top of her, we're both trembling after that.

"Please say I didn't hurt you." I say as soon as I have the ability to talk.

She chuckles and nibbles on my ear, "No baby you didn't hurt me." She slurs.

"Are you slurring?" I ask amused.

"Yep, I feel drunk, that's what you do to me."

"Are you sure you're not hurt?"

"I'm not hurt, you might be though, I dug in pretty hard there."

"I'm alright."

"Let me see."

"Belle I said I'm alright."

"And I said let me see, come on Parker, I'm going to see you naked at some point, we live together, have sex regularly, if I've marked you, I'm going to see whether you want me to or not."

I relent and turn around, I hear her gasp, "It's a fucking mess, your shoulders are the worst, I did a number on you there. Do they sting?"

I shake my head, "No I wouldn't have known they were there."

"We're not doing that again." She spits, she's so cute right now, my amazing woman.

"Whoa, whoa, let's not be hasty."

"I'm not being hasty. Parker you hate the idea of marking me, I also hate the idea of marking you, we're not having sex like that again."

I think for a moment, "What if I hold your hands like this?" I hold her hands above her head, and intertwine our fingers so it's still intimate.

"It doesn't stop me biting you."

I smile, "Doesn't stop me biting you either." To prove my point I nibble on her neck.

"Alright you've made your point." She giggles, "So have me made up now?"

"Yes baby, we've just had makeup sex for the first time. Now are you going to come home so I can pleasure you endlessly?"

"I still think you need a new hobby."

"No, no." I nibble on her ear and toy with her nipple, she arches her back on a groan, "I like this hobby, this will do nicely."

"I love you." I will never get tired of hearing her say that, "All I have to wear are those pyjamas."

"Good thing they look quite fetching on you then. Get dressed I'm taking you home O Neil."

It doesn't take long to get dressed, both of us are eager to get home, but before we leave we say bye to the girls.

We walk into the lounge all loved up, because well we are, "So it looks like you two crazy kids are back together." M.K says with a smile.

"Looks like it." Belle replies, placing her head intimately on my shoulder, "I'm going home."

"I'm happy for you." Ashley says rising and walking towards me, she stands on her tiptoes, so she can kiss my cheek, "Look after each other, and forgive the fuck ups, they happen in love. See you around little brother."

It's been a couple of days since Belle and I made up, and Belle's at work so I'm doing a little tidying around to get rid of the boredom that surrounds her not being here, so when my intercom rings, I'm hoping it's her saying she's forgotten her card, and needs me to let her up, but when I answer, Sam's voice sings through, "Hey brother going to let us in or what?"

I buzz them in, when the lift dings, both Sam and Wayne stroll out, Sam in a pair of white jeans and a black long sleeve shirt.

Wayne in a royal blue suit.

"What are you two doing here?"

"We came to check you're alright, you and Belle have split up haven't you?" Sam asks.

"No, where on earth did you hear a thing like that?"

"The papers. Wayne show him."

Wayne holds up the paper, I take it off him, 'THE MOST POWERFUL COUPLE IN LONDON BUST UP!'

With a picture of Belle getting into a taxi and me running after her.

"It's total bullshit." I say, "Look guys sit down, let me level with you." They do as I say, "Look guys you saw what happened the other night. Didn't you?"

"Yeah we saw a guy grab Belle, and you go and hit him, you and Belle exchange words, her run out, you go after her and not come back."

"Alright so what happened was, Ashley basically said my reaction wasn't like me, Belle thought it was because of her, but it wasn't really, I went to go and see my parents, and they said my reaction was normal, and they also said that they both have bouts of jealousy, but they deal with them. All I have to do is revel in the knowledge that it's me Belle is going to come home to."

"Oh man your parents." Wayne shakes his head on a smile, "Your parents are the most randy couple ever. They can't keep their hands off each other, you're mum is hot though, is there any wonder they're so on."

"Wayne seriously bro, don't refer to my mum as hot, especially considering the last woman you fucked was Imelda."

"And I think Parker and Belle take the title for the most randy couple we know." Sam nods at me, "We have seen how they are together, I've no doubt they both get some good loving." Sam turns to Wayne, "And what's with that anyway? You've slept with Imelda, now you want Scarlet, have you got a mother-daughter thing going on or what?"

"Hey, hey Imelda was throwing herself at me for months, a man can only resist so much."

Wayne does have a point, she did practically put it on a plate for him, and willpower has never been a strong suit with him.

"So all is good in paradise now?" Sam affirms, "You've made up and everything."

I nod, "Several times, she's so irresistible, not like I even try, there's no point in trying, she's so seductive."

"Well she's not referred to as the Queen of Seduction for nothing bro." Wayne points out.

"Yeah you're right there brother. But now she's MY queen."

She refers to herself as mine, and I feel like I'm hers, and have felt that way since I first saw her in The River.

Belle

The last couple of days have been eventful, paparazzi have been practically stalking Parker and I, they know something went off the other night, and they're trying to pump for a comment.

I must remember to thank Parker's Dad when I next see him, he wrote an article with The Mirror on our behalf, it's only because of M.K telling me that I found out about it, so I'm on my way home, I hope Parker will be there, I'm eager to see him after the day I've had.

Wearing a royal blue dress, that's low cut and sits just above me knees, I get in the lift, swipe my card down, and lean back against the wall and shut my eyes on an exhausted sigh.

When the lift opens, I hear laughter of more than one person, then I see that we have company, in the form of Sam and Wayne, Parker is sat on the form in a pair of black jeans and a grey vest top, I love it when he wears vests top, he looks so ripped.

I put my stuff on the hook near the door that leads to the stairs, "Hey babe how was your day?"

I lean on the back of the sofa, between Sam and Wayne, "Mad. Paparazzi got wind of something happening on Friday night, they wanted a statement, if the headlines aren't questioning whether we're still together, they have jumped to the conclusion that we're not. Your father is my hero, he's published an article about our relationship, I only found out because M.K told me. I went out to buy it. Do you want to read it?"

"Why not sit down near me and read it to us?"

I grab the paper, and do as he says, going to sit near him, I find the article, "The headline is pretty to the point. 'MY SON AND THE QUEEN OF SEDUCTION, BY JOEL WILSON,

I must say I was shocked when my boy dubbed 'The Most Sought After Man In London' brought, 'The Queen Of Seduction' Belle O Neil home for her to meet the family. But I must also admit, I was very humbled, she is nothing like the papers, including my own made out. She is actually a very kind, loyal and loving individual, with a very heart breaking story for those who choose to hear it. She was a hit with my youngest child Skyla, and I think I speak for my entire family when I say she stole our hearts.

My son and Belle are very much in love, so Belle O Neil is living proof that leopards CAN change their spots. I look forward to getting to know Belle further, and am glad to call her a member of my family, we welcome her with open arms. We couldn't be happier for the both of them.'"

"A glowing reference." Parker smiles.

"Hopefully it will make them fuck off and leave us alone."

"Probably not, but we'll weather the storm babe." He shuffles behind me, moves forward so I'm between his legs and wraps his arms around me, kissing my temple, I hold his hands, welcoming the contact.

"Paparazzi are vultures, remember what they were like at the idea of Wayne and Imelda were sleeping together."

"Difference is that was true." Wayne smiles.

"Oh God I don't even want that image in my head. I wasn't surprised when I saw the article."

"You should have heard the ribbing he got for it." Parker says close to my ear, "Toy boy."

"Look who's talking." Wayne smiles smugly.

"Five years difference." I gesture to Parker and I, "Over twenty years difference." I point to Wayne. "You still hold the title for the biggest toy boy in the room honey. I see the attraction though, and you do strike me as the sort to have a thing for older women."

"My girlfriend the analyst." Parker muses, taking the pins out of my hair, and moving it to one side to kiss my neck.

"Your girlfriend the business woman, analysing people is part of my job. Are you two going to stay for dinner?"

"Only if that's alright." Sam says.

"Yeah, it's fine with me. I'll make a start."

"Babe you've been at work, why don't I cook?"

"Because you can probably entertain our guests better than me, I don't mind babe."

"What are you planning?" Sam asks.

"Something quick. Egg fried rice or noodles. Your decision. With chicken, oriental sauce and cashews. So the only decision you have to make is, noodles or rice?"

"I'll have rice please." Sam answers.

"I'll have the same please honey." Wayne replies.

"Belle cooks amazing food, so whatever. If you're having noodles baby then I will too. She does amazing noodles, aren't I lucky." He nibbles on my ear.

"Not as lucky as me, but I can't cook unless you let me go."

"Give me a kiss and I'll think about it."

I tilt my head back on his shoulder, he keeps the kiss light and sweet, nibbling on my bottom lip before he pulls away, "That'll do for now."

He let's me go and I start cooking, I feel much more at home now, so cooking in here should be a breeze.

Parker

She looks so natural in my kitchen now, I can't keep my eyes off her, "Dude I don't know if I will ever get used to this version of you." Wayne declares.

"What version of me?"

"The in love version, it's so surreal."

"Is that a bad thing?"

"No, it's actually a very good thing, so good I might never get over it, I've never known you not be able to keep your hands or eyes off someone, you actually remind me a lot of how your Dad is with your Mum."

I watch as Belle moves fluidly around the kitchen, she keeps on glancing over and blushing at being under such close scrutiny.

"Go to her man." Sam sighs, "You haven't seen her all day, and you've wanted to go to her since she went into the kitchen. So go to her."

I do just that, I waste no time taking her in my arms and kissing her neck, "You keep blushing every time you catch me watching you."

"Because I'm not used to being watched."

"Well then get used to it, it's hard to keep my hands and my eyes off you. You're irresistible. You're MY queen."

She turns and links her arms around my neck, "Oh your queen. What does that make you? My king?"

"No your knave. I'm at your service."

"You don't see yourself as equal to me?" Her brow furrows.

"We're equals, but I worship the ground you walk on Belle. I love you."

"I love you Parker. So much."

"Well then you're my queen."

"Hey Wilson!" Wayne shouts, "If your missus burns my food because of you, I'll kill you."

Belle shoves me off her playfully, "You heard the man. Now let me cook Wilson."

I go to sit down as she carries on cooking.

"Now there is a woman in love." Sam muses.

"I know right, I'm so lucky."

Belle

After a successful evening dining with Parker's friends, they are now leaving, "Tonight has been fun, look forward to doing it again sometime, thanks for the feed Belle it was lovely." Sam says.

"Next time, I'll make sure we have wine, and do something special. Good night you two."

As soon as the lift closes Parker kisses me lovingly, "That was our first meal with my friends, you were a hit. And after all of the madness of today."

He unzips my dress, draws me up to standing, tugs at the dress so it falls down, he lifts me up and carries me to bed, his lips stay locked on mine in a passionate kiss.

He seduces me with his kiss, as he unhooks my bra and then slithers down my body, he removes my panties, "You deserve this baby."

He takes me in his mouth hard, I scream instantly, Parker has to put a lot of pressure on my stomach to stop me bucking my hips too hard, "Fuck Parker!!" He runs his hands up to my breasts and tweaks my nipples, I give a long throaty scream, "What do you do to me?" I whimper.

He stops for a second, "I treat you like a queen." He says shortly, then he carries on taking me in his mouth.

I moan on every movement of his delicious mouth, "Oh fuck! Don't stop!" I cry.

He takes me harder, I'm burning with desire and need, I know he isn't going to stop until I'm quivering and whimpering from pleasure, I scream, "PARKER!!!" As I orgasm he takes his time still, I can only gasp at every luscious movement of his mouth.

He moves up my body, captures my mouth, I tug greedily and impatiently at his top, drawing it roughly over his head so he can possess my lips again.

I undo his belt, "A little impatient aren't we?" He murmurs against my lips.

"Yes, I want you, let me have you Parker."

"You have me Belle." He pushes his finger into me, he's gentle now, I choke on a moan, "You'll always have me Belle."

"Fuck." I gasp, "You're no knave. You're a God."

"I live to pleasure you Belle, to love you, I'm not your God, I'm your subject."

"I'm your queen?" I tug on his hair so he meets my eyes.

"Yes baby you're my queen."

"You make me so happy." I gasp.

"Marry me." He says as he kisses me.

"What?" I choke out as he plunges his fingers deep inside me.

"Marry me." He repeats the word and his movement.

"You're nuts." I gasp.

He removes his fingers from me, only to thrust his arousal deep in me, "Only for you Belle. Marry me." He says again.

"Parker, I've only just said I love you."

He grinds in deep again, "Marry me Belle, say you will."

"Fuck Parker." I gasp, "You're impossible. No, no yet. Let me get used to loving you first."

He captures my mouth with his and draws us both to climax, "Marry me." He gasps out.

"Fuck, I love you." I moan, he eases us both down. "Dirty tactics baby." I say when he lays on top of me.

"I'm sorry." He kisses my neck, "I'm so in love with you, I couldn't resist, say that we will be married though Belle."

"I will give you everything you want, I promise in time though baby, I love you to the moon and back. You're the best thing to ever happen to me."

"So wait back up." M.K, Bailey, Nan, and I are on our weekly shopping trip, "He actually proposed while you were having sex?"

I have on a sky blue pencil dress.

M.K has on a pair of grey trousers and a salmon pink polo shirt.

Bailey has on a pair of light blue trousers with a white shirt.

Nan has on a long red dress.

"That's a good way to do it." Nan laughs.

"You actually condone that?" I ask in awe.

"Oh darling, you should have known that Parker isn't the sort to do things the conventional way. It's not in his nature."

"But I wasn't expecting marriage proposals during sex, all one at all right now if I'm honest."

"Why not?" Bailey smiles, "Anyone can see that you two are nuts about each other."

"We've only been together a matter of weeks."

"By the sounds of things his parents had a bit of a whirlwind romance." M.K points out.

"And how long before you and Ashley go out on a date?"

"And who is Ashley?" Nan asks.

"Parker's sister."

"Oh is she nice?"

"M.K seems to think so." I nudge her and M.K blushes. "And look she's all embarrassed. It's shocking how one so tough can he embarrassed so easily."

"Will you shut the fuck up?"

I wrap my arm around her mid-section, "She'll be different babe." I look at the time, "We need to head to the Depol, and get you two registered as O Neil's."

"That was the longest fucking time of my life." M.K moans.

"At least it's over and we're officially family." I smile.

"So you leave me for a fucking model!"

We all turn to see Fox storming towards us, in a grey suit.

Instinctively we all stand in front of Nan to protect her.

"Fox." I roll my shoulders coolly, "I didn't leave you Fox, we were never together."

"If you had of asked, I would have been with you properly, dammit I started to fall in love with you Belle."

"Really? Surely if you love someone you treat them with tenderness and care. We never even made it to the bedroom Fox, you were always so rough. How can you call that love?"

"If you had of said that bothered you, then I would have changed it Belle, you don't just go into a relationship with another man, dammit Belle you never even gave me an explanation. When did you start seeing this kid?"

"He's not a kid! Just walk away. Fox don't do this to yourself."

"Just tell me!"

"After the last time I saw you, he came to my office, offered to take me out and I said yes, as model who wants to treat me with tenderness and care. What kind of woman would say no?"

"So a few hours after we had sex, you were with him."

"On a date, we shared a kiss at the end of the night that was it, we went on a few dates before we slept together. I love him Fox."

All of a sudden he lunges at me, he grabs my arms in a vice like grip, "People like you don't know what love is, you only want to be fucked." He plants a hard kiss on me.

I try to push him off, but he's too strong, M.K intervenes and tries to yank him off me, he elbows her in the face, this time she punches him in the face, he now lets me go and touches his bloody lip, "You fucking bitch!"

"Yeah I am, take another swing, go one."

He gives her a back hander this time, M.K takes it, and with pain driving her, she punches him again, this time sirens ring out. There's a police car, Ashley steps out, "What the hell is going on here?" She shouts.

"She assaulted me!" Fox yells.

"He did the same thing, look at her." Bailey argues.

Ashley calls for backup, "Until we find out what happened, you're both going to have to be arrested." She puts cuffs on M.K while reciting her, her rights.

Her partner who must be in his mid-thirties, with round grey eyes, a small bulb like noes, sharp lips and defined square jawline, puts cuffs on Fox, "I'll escort M.K to my car."

Now I shove Fox, "You bastard!"

"I've never laid my hands on a woman before." Fox says wide eyed, "She didn't even flinch."

"She used to it." I turn to Nan, "She should have left it alone, now she's hurt."

"M.K will be fine, she's stronger than all of us."

As soon as the backup Ashley calls for arrives, M.K and Fox are taken to the police station.

Parker

"So you asked Belle to marry you?" Mum asks, she has on a pair of medium blue jeans and a hot pink long sleeve top, "What did she say?"

"You asked Belle to marry you?" Dad asks in a burgundy suit and a black shirt, he's just come home from work, "You don't do things by halves do you my boy." He wraps his arms around Mum and kisses her cheek, "Hello my darling."

"Hello my love." She reaches up to touch his cheek and turns her head so he can kiss her lips, "Parker was just telling me what she said."

"She said not yet."

"You've only been together a few weeks, so there is no surprise, she's a practical woman." My Mum smiles, she looks at a snoozing Skyla, who has fallen asleep playing.

"Oh yeah I forgot, thank you for the article by the way, it was really nice what you said about Belle, we really appreciate it."

"Meant every word son."

"Now as much as we love you. Why are you here and not entertaining your lovely girlfriend?"

"Because my lovely girlfriend is out with her friends and her Nan, they are all shopping, so I figured I would come and see my favourite couple."

"Oh yeah tell us about her Nan, Belle seems awfully fond of her."

"Her Nan is totally amazing, she classes M.K and Bailey as her grandchildren also, they're all super close. Her Nan welcomed me with open arms, she's just glad someone is finally looking after Belle."

"And has everything been good since the argument?" Dad enquires.

"Yeah everything has been amazing, Sam and Wayne came over the day you published the story, she cooked them dinner, and I felt bad because she's been at work."

"That was good of her, she doesn't really know Sam and Wayne, so she probably thought it was best to leave you entertaining your friends, and for her to cook the meal."

"I hope you made it worth her while." Dad says.

"You'd better have used more than sex." Mum scolds.

"Darling that's none of our business." Dad scolds kissing Mum's cheek.

"A lot of the time she instigates it."

"She a hot blooded female, like someone else I know."

My phone then rings, it's Belle, I answer quickly, "Hey babe, are you done with your shopping trip?"

"Not quite, I'm at the police station, we ran into some trouble, M.K was arrested, by none other than Ashley."

"Why? What happened?" I ask quickly.

"Fox Mason happened, I'll explain later."

"I'm coming to you now."

I don't give her a chance to argue, I hang up. "Ashley arrested M.K, I have no idea what happened, but I'm going to go there now and find out."

"Just stay calm though honey, no repetitions of what happened last week."

I move like lightening to the police station. When I get there, Belle is clinging to her Nan, she sees me, she's up and is practically flying into my arms, "Oh Parker." I keep a tight hold on her, "He hit her." She sobs, "He hit her."

"Who hit her?"

"Fox he saw us come out of the Depol, and started yelling at me, he said he was in love with me, and I just left him with no explanation, and then he saw the news about us, and he just grabbed me and kissed me, M.K tried to get him off me, but he elbowed her in the face. So she hit him, then Ashley showed up. Arrested them both."

I run my hands up and down her arms, I better be out of here before Fox Mason is released, I'm boiling mad.

I embrace Belle again, "It's alright baby, it's alright."

She tightens her grip on me, "I'm glad you're here."

M.K then strolls out, her cheek is bruised, her lip is cut and swollen, "Oh look what he did to you." Belle says on the brink of being totally distraught.

"I'm alright honey." She replies hugging Belle.

"I'm so sorry."

"Don't be, not your fault."

"M.K has been released without charge, I can take her and Bailey home if you want."

"Go home. I'll call you."

Ashley goes to leave, "Hey." Belle touches her arm, "He wasn't going to drop the charges. What did you do?"

"It was obvious that he'd hit her before we showed up, I told my partner we saw him hit her first, he went along with it, if I promised to have a drink with him."

"Are you going to?"

"It's the least I can do, he did me a solid."

We then leave the station, Belle drives us home. I'm trying not to let what Belle said play on my mind, but it is.

When we get in, she's the first to speak, "What's wrong?"

"Nothing." I say shortly.

"Something is." She states.

"He thought he could have you, he thought what you had was so good that he had fallen in love with you. Did you ever feel the same way?"

"For a while." She admits, "I wanted a life with him, he wasn't married, he seemed to like me, I liked him, I thought after a few more rendezvous', he might ask me to be serious with him that maybe would could have a future."

It's hard for me to hear, but at least she's being honest, "What changed?"

"You did." She says sharply, "You cornered me in a toilet, I slept with Fox to try and forget about you, to get you out of my head, then you asked me out, and I knew I would never have another man again."

It's not enough. Why do I feel the need to punish her? It's not like she did anything wrong.

"I need some space." I go out for a walk.

Chapter Eighteen

Belle

"I'M GOING NUTS, HE HAS barely touched me in two days, I have tried to initiate contact, but he just shrugs me off, he's been avoiding me, he only talks to me when I speak to him, and then when I do, I only get short answers. Usually he can barely go five minutes without, speaking, touching or seeking me out. What if it's over?" I'm pacing with my hands on my hips, M.K and Bailey are sat on the sofa, "It's like he's punishing me."

I have on a pair of black trousers and a red Laura Ashley designer top.

M.K has on a grey long sleeve jumpsuit.

Bailey has on a royal blue tea dress.

"Why would he be punishing you?" M.K asks.

"I don't know, that's what I'm thinking, it's not like I did anything wrong. We haven't made love, when I wake up he's gone, when I touch him he backs away as if it burns. I think we might be over."

"No I don't think that." M.K says, "Something has clearly upset him though."

"Can you think of anything that might have upset him, anything at all Belle?" Bailey asks.

"I did admit that before I met Parker, I was picturing a future with Fox."

"Oh that could be what did it." Bailey suggests.

"I also told him that all changed when I met him."

"Still it must have been a bitter pill to swallow." M.K agrees with Bailey, "I bet he was really fucked off."

"But in all fairness that's not reason to go artic on her." Bailey considers.

"No but it doesn't change the fact that he has. The real question here is Belle: What are you going to do about it?"

"In about half an hour he finishes his shoot, I want to beat him home."

"Bailey and I will handle McDowd. You have a plan?"

"Yes I do, I obviously have to remind him why he wanted me in the first place."

"The Queen of Seduction is in the house." Bailey smiles.

"Have you heard from Ashley at all?" I remember her telling me about drinks with her partner.

"Why would I hear from her?" M.K says bluntly, "No and I'm glad."

"Oh M.K don't be too hard on her, she did what she had to do."

I kiss both of their cheeks and make my way home, so I can fix things with Parker, I know just the way to do it.

I get out of the lift and go straight to the bedroom, I find the Victoria's Secret bag that I had hidden from Parker and pull out the piece of lingerie he pointed out, I quickly go and shower and change into it.

I then sit on the sofa and wait for Parker.

Parker

It has been a long couple of day, I have no idea why I have felt the need to punish Belle and effectively punish myself, so I'm going to fix that as soon as she gets home.

I get in the lift and question if I should have made going to Belle my first port of call, oh well I'm in the lift now, I'll shower, change and then go to her.

The lift opens then I get the shock of my life, Belle is stood in the middle of the room, in the red lace lingerie I pointed out to her in Victoria's Secret.

My eyes widen.

What's her game?

"Oh so you are still attracted to me then? I did wonder."

"Why on earth would you think I wasn't?"

"Because these last couple of days, you haven't kissed me, touched me, made love with me, and you have barely spoken to me, and when you have it is because I have spoken to you first, and they have been short comments."

"I was mad, it's not easy hearing that you were picturing a future with a man like that."

"But then I met you." She says exasperated, "The moment I met you, you invaded my head, and nothing, NOTHING I did could change that, not fucking Fox, not getting incredibly drunk, nothing worked, you were still there and I was still empty, then I let myself have you, and now I'm not."

I go to her now, I wrap my arms around her mid-section and nuzzle into her neck, she sighs in relief and wraps her arms around my neck, "Thank fuck I haven't blown it."

I pull out of the embrace and kiss her sweetly, "You want to be touched?" I say as we kiss.

"Yes."

I place my hands on her bum and squeeze, "Here?"

"Yes."

I move my hands up to her breasts and squeeze gently, "Here?"

"Yes." She gasps.

I move my hand between her thighs and find her hot and ready, "Here?"

"Fuck, yes Parker." She deepens the kiss, starts undoing my shirt, she rips it from my shoulders, she then moves on to my belt, "It's only you Parker. You're all I need, I love you. Only you. I'm yours." She moves on to kiss my neck, "Make love with me. Please."

I take her down exactly where we are, remove my trousers and pants, and drown us both in an intoxicating kiss.

Something comes over me, I deepen the kiss, make it hungrier, I draw Belle's hands over her head, and interlink our fingers, and slam into her.

"Fuck Parker!" She screams.

I don't stop, I keep up the merciless pace, making her scream, pound after pound after pound. I have no idea what has come over me, but Belle clearly doesn't mind, although I never asked if I could go down this route.

"Fuck Parker!" Belle screams again.

I grunt with effort, we're both soaking with sweat, it's dripping off me, my muscles are burning, I have to finish this soon.

After a couple more pounds, Belle climaxes on a loud scream, I send out a loud roar that resonates around the apartment, it takes everything I have to ease is both down.

I practically collapse on top of Belle, we're both trembling, neither of us move for an age.

Eventually I ask, "Are you alright?" She doesn't answer, "Belle baby." I kiss her neck and she whimpers, "Are you alright?"

"Fine, just tired. What was that?"

"That was making up." I say tentatively. "Both for the argument and for lost time."

"I didn't do anything wrong. I had nothing to make up for."

She's right, I took her like that to claim her, remind her she's mine, I didn't need to do that, "I'll make it up to you baby. Now please answer me. Are you alright?"

"I think I saw stars."

"Is that a yes?"

"Babe, I'm fine you didn't hurt me, but if you say we have to move then I might hurt you."

I laugh, "We don't have to move." I snuggle back where I was, and we stay on the floor.

I have no idea what got into me yesterday, but I do know it was amazing for the both of us, I wake up and find that we fell asleep where we had sex and I can't help but chuckle to myself.

I nibble on Belle's ear, "Baby." She murmurs something, I have no idea what, "Belle wake up."

She stirs, "What?"

She's so sexy when she's only just woken up, her voice is full of sleep, it's such a turn on.

"We slept on the kitchen floor last night."

"We're so randy, I'm surprised we ever make it to bed." She says matter of factly, "Now either make coffee or shut up, I want to sleep."

"Or I could just do this…"

I push my fingers into her, she's awake and alert on a gasp, "Or you could just do that." She muses, I do it again and she moans, "Parker you do such amazing things to me."

"Marry me Belle."

"You can't be serious."

"I am, I'm sorry, I know we agreed I wouldn't do this, but you're too practical when you're clear headed."

"It's who I am Parker."

I kiss her neck and keep working her up with my fingers, "And I love who you are baby, you're my amazing woman, my love, my life and mine. Marry me Belle."

"Parker." She moans, "Don't I make you happy?" She gasps out every word.

"You do, you do baby, so, so happy." I kiss her deeply, she arches her back on the next thrust of my fingers.

"Then why rush? Will it make the sex better than it is already?"

I smile at that, "Probably not."

"Well then what?"

I don't know what to say, so I just kiss her brains out, and let her focus on the pleasure I'm providing her with, she arches her body to me, throws her hand in my hair and lets out broken little whimpers of pleasure.

When she climaxes, she places her head on my shoulder, "Parker." She gasps.

I ease her down and kiss the top of her head, "You make me irrational." I say half thinking, half aloud. She lifts her head to look me in the eyes, "I'm never really in my own head around you. From the moment I cornered you in the toilet, at The River, straight thinking hasn't been my specialty, especially when it comes to you."

"You have had the opposite effect on me, since meeting you for the first time in my life, everything has been so clear, it scares the hell out of me sometimes."

"I wish I could explain why I took you the way I did last night, or why I'm so desperate to marry you, but it's difficult to explain, you might think I'm crazy."

"I think you're crazy for wanting me Parker, no matter how you explain it, or how many times you do explain it, I still think you're nuts. So try and explain the need for marriage, because no matter what you say, I'm going nowhere."

She can't physically go anywhere, because I'm on top of her.

I prop up on my elbows and look her in the eyes, "I wanted you Belle, from the moment you had your first affair, you looked so sad, so drained, and it was the same thing with every single one of your affairs, and all I could think was, 'I wish someone would make her happy.' And then I would think, 'I could make her happy.' And I hope I am."

"You are. You're making me so happy. And what is the reason behind the sex last night? Because it was more than making up."

"Having you say that you were thinking of having a future with Fox, even though you hadn't met, or been out with me yet, that hurt especially how he'd marked you, hurt you. I wanted to remind you, you're mine, not that you needed reminding, but that's what I wanted to do."

"It was very good sex. And the need for marriage?"

"Sex claims someone physically, communication claims someone emotionally, and I have all of that with you, marriage claims a person..."

"Legally." She interrupts, "It's just a piece of paper Parker."

"Not when we get married, I feel so connected to you both physically and emotionally, I want to cement that connection through marriage."

"We could get eternity rings."

"But would they be legally binding"?

"No but they would cement OUR eternal connection, privately, the way love should be celebrated."

"I might want our family to celebrate our love with us."

"Then we have an eternal ring exchanging ceremony, where you announce me as your queen, and you as my knave."

"You have an answer for everything."

"Which is why you..." Oh she's playing my game.

"Want to marry you." I plant a hard kiss on her lips.

When I break away she frowns, "Unbelievable man."

"Stubborn woman."

Belle

"So he's deadly serious about wanting to marry you?" Bailey asks in her grey lounge suit.

"Yes and it's so fucking annoying." I moan, I'm at my old place in a pair of black trousers and a grey Burberry designer blouse.

"Aww I think its sweet. Why don't you say yes?"

"Because it's a piece of paper, it means nothing. My dad married Imelda, and he didn't love her."

"No but he was a very sexually active man, and she fulfilled his needs. Isn't that what he told you when you asked him why he did it?"

"Is that grounds to marry someone?"

"No. Are you saying that is why you would marry Parker?" Bailey asks smugly.

"Of course not!" I spit.

"I already knew that Belle, I just needed you to hear yourself say the words. Why would you marry Parker?"

"Because I love him."

"Well then there you go. Now ask yourself this question." She says taking my shoulders, "What's stopping you from marrying him?"

Then it dawns on me, "The amount of time we have been together."

"There is one way you can fix that."

"How?" I shrug.

"Go and see his parent."

My phone the rings, it's Parker, "Hey babe."

"Where are you?"

"I just have some things to take care of, last minute work stuff, the charge for the call out fee is too much to refuse."

"Ever the business woman baby."

"It's how I stay rich, I won't be long."

"You better not be, I miss you."

"If I said I love you, would that make it better?"

"It might." He's smiling, I can tell.

"I love you."

"I love you too baby."

I hang up, "Right I had better go, before he starts hunting me down."

I kiss Bailey on the cheek and make my way to his parents house, I stop off at the florist and get his mum a bunch of red tulips, working on a hunch, I just hope it's a good one.

I get to his parent's house, and when I knock, his mum answers in a pair of grey jogging bottoms and a black vest top, she's bouncing Skyla who has on the same outfit.

"Oh Belle, you caught me in my lounge wear I'm afraid, my husband thought it would be cute for Skyla and I to wear the same outfits."

"And it really is. Swap you." I take hold of Skyla, and pass Caty the tulips.

"Oh red tulips, they are my favourite. But what are they in aid of?"

"They are a thank you actually."

"What are you thanking me for?"

"Your son." I say matter of factly, "Your amazing, beautiful, loving and respectful son."

She comes over and kisses my cheek, "That's just lovely of you, I can see why he fell for you."

"I also came by to ask you something. If that's alright?"

"Would you like a coffee while we talk?"

"Yes please that would be great."

She makes the coffee while I entertain Skyla with my necklace, while sitting on the sofa.

When his mum comes in with a tray of cups and coffee, milk and a bowl of sugar, she sets it down on the coffee table, "Take what you like."

I pour some milk and add two spoons of sugar, when she does the same I can't help but smile to myself, "So what would you like to ask?"

"You know Parker has proposed?"

"Yes." She smiles, "You said not yet."

"I was wondering how long you were with Joel before he proposed?"

Again she smiles, she remember the story of her relationship well, "Three months, it was a bit like you and Parker really, he sees me from a distance, I see him, but my parents want me to be with another man, a posher less rougher looking man, Joel was rugged in his looks, he still is really, except he has traded in his leather jacket for suits. This other man I was with, was doing law and is also studying politics. At first I was desperate to please my parents, but Joel was fresh, endearing, he made me passionate, he made me feel desirable, in the end I disobeyed my parents, and I just followed my heart, right to Joel, thirty years later, he still has it."

"And you have no regrets?" I ask.

"Belle the man I was with before Joel, had an affair with you two years ago."

"Oh." I remember the man, "Miles Henly? You got a lucky break there, he was crap."

She then laughs, "No arguments here, but you see my darling, if I had done what my parents wanted, it would have been me, Joel saved me in more ways than one. The only regret I have is not finding him sooner."

"See I can't say things like that, because then I would really be approaching cougar territory."

She then laughs again, "Oh you're a funny one, your visit has made my day Belle, I'm glad Parker has found you."

"More like the other way around. Mrs Wilson." I stand up, "I am going to marry your son."

"Miss O Neil." She also stands, "Welcome to the family."

Parker

I'm at home waiting for Belle to come back from whatever errands she has to run, so I'm laid on my bed, in a pair of black jogging bottoms.

When my phone rings, it's Mum, "Hey Mum."

"Hey baby." She sounds really happy, "I just called to tell you, you have such an amazing girlfriend."

"I already know, but I'm intrigued to know why you feel the need to remind me."

"She brought me flowers to thank me for you. Did you tell her red tulips are my favourite?"

"Mum I had no idea she planned on doing that, she told me she was running errands for work, I had no idea she was planning to surprise you with flowers, to thank you for giving birth to me."

"You hold on to her my boy, that girl is a total gem."

"Plan on it Mum."

I hang up the phone and pace around my apartment waiting for her to come home, when the lift opens, I rush to her pick her up, spin her round, sit her on the kitchen counter and give her a smacking kiss, "I should run errands for work more often." She muses.

"Really? I got a rather interesting call from my Mum a moment ago, telling me how you brought her flowers to thank her for how she raised me."

"I might have." She says coyly, "I might have had an ulterior motive."

"Like?"

"Like to ask her how long she and your Dad were together before he proposed. And I also want to go and see Bailey to clear my head."

There is something she wants to explain, "And now your mind is clear? Would you like to share those thoughts with me?"

"Yes, and I promise the end result is good."

"Alright baby, fill me in please."

"When my father married Imelda, I asked him why and he said, 'Belle I'm a sexually active man, I need someone to fulfil my needs. Imelda does that.' Not one mention of love."

I put my hand on the back of her neck, "Baby that is different with us. I love you."

"I know, I know it is, it's just I didn't want to rush anything." She takes my hand and kisses my palm, "But I do want you to ask me again. Please."

I lift her off the counter, and carry her to the sofa, "I can walk you know." She giggles.

"Your weight feels nice in my arms, and this is more romantic." I sit her on the sofa, kneel on the floor, run my hands up her legs, and look her in the eyes, "Marry me Belle."

She frames my face in her hands and kisses me wildly, "I would love to marry you Parker."

Belle

After a blissful night making love with Parker, to celebrate our engagement privately, I'm cooking Parker some breakfast before I leave for work, I have on a pair of black trousers and a white designer polo shirt.

I'm cooking him some cinnamon toast, I have Katy Perry Unconditionally playing in the background, and it's not long before I am singing along, and thinking of Parker while I am.

Parker is soon out of the bedroom in the same black joggers he had on last night, "You should have woken me." He says accusingly, he circles around the counter, wraps his arms around my mid-section and ravages my neck.

"I thought you would have had enough last night." I snigger, "Parker that tickles."

"Good, punishment for thinking I could ever have enough of you. Say it again."

"Parker you've heard me say it a thousand times already."

He nibbles on my neck, "Either say it again or I'm going to get you naked and make you very, very late."

To add emphasis to his threat, he takes a pin out of my hair, "No, no don't baby, I have back to back meetings all day, I have to look professional."

"Well then tell me what I want to hear."

I turn and put my hands on his chest, "I want to marry you, but you need to get me a ring."

"I will do that."

"Right babe, I have made you breakfast, I'm going to have lunch with the girls and Nan to tell them we're engaged, and you can tell your family."

"They will want to celebrate." He informs me.

"So will my Nan and sisters, we could all do it at Clarks or The River, we all like it there." I put my hand on the back of Parker's neck and kiss him deeply, "I will text you, I love you, see you later baby."

"Hey I'm going to cook dinner tonight, your favourite, so please be on time."

"I will, I promise." I kiss him again, "Love you."

"Love you too baby."

As I'm heading to my car, I nearly bump into Ashley, who has on a lovely black dress, "Hey Ashley." I smile.

"Hey Belle, how's M.K since…"

"She's alright, it's water off a ducks back with M.K, you have nothing to worry about."

"I still feel really bad."

"You lied for her, risked you job, you didn't have to do it, you chose to. And your partner, does he have a thing for you?"

"A little crush, nothing I can't, and haven't handled. I'm going to head up, see my little bro, he's requested my assistance with something."

"Oh cool, I have to get to work, I'll see you later."

I get in my car and start the drive to work, I call Bailey on the way there, "Hey." She practically sings out.

"Hey are you and M.K available for lunch? I'm going to call Nan and see if she's available as well."

I hear a muffled exchanged between Bailey and M.K, "Yeah we can make ourselves available."

"Good see you then." I hang up and call Nan.

"Hello my darling. How are you?"

"I'm good thanks. How are you Nan?"

"I'm alright honey."

"Are you available for lunch at one? I can pick you up on my way back from Hammersmith."

"That will be good darling yes. Starbucks?"

"You know it."

This morning has been the longest morning of my life, I've had meetings in East Acton, Bedford Park and Hammersmith. Top it off the events I'm dealing with are either getting married or arranging a funeral, so all I have going around my head right now, is flower arrangements, catering arrangements, seating arrangements and event locations.

Only a couple more hours to go and then I can go home to Parker.

So right now I am on my way to see my Nan, and take her to lunch with the family.

I pull up outside her bungalow, she steps out as soon as I pull up, I get out of the car, rush over to her, and link arms with her, "I can walk myself to your car."

"I know, I like walking you though." She looks nice in her long purple dress.

I open my passenger door, Nan climbs in with the grace of a deer.

I walk around to the driver's side and hop in, Nan leans over and kisses my cheek, "Hello my darling." She smiles.

"Hello Nan."

"What's all this in aid of?"

"I'll fill you in when we get to the girls."

I drive to Starbucks, M.K and Bailey are waiting outside.

M.K in a pair of black trouser and a burgundy long sleeve jumpsuit.

Bailey is in a pair of snug black jeans and a royal blue designer Burberry top.

"Hey you two. Shall we go in?"

"Only thing we can do if we're going to find out what's wrong with you." M.K points out mildly.

"Oh M.K straight to the point as usual." Nan touches M.K cheek, "Don't ever change."

M.K kisses her cheek, Bailey does the same, and we then walk into Starbucks.

I pick up a salmon and cream cheese sandwich, Nan picks up the same thing, I'm always in awe of our very similar taste. We both order a caramel latter, and take two packs of sugar.

M.K picks out a bacon and egg panini, and orders a large latte with an extra shot.

And Bailey picks out a tuna salad and orders a large cappuccino.

We go upstairs, "So what's all this about?" M.K asks the moment we're all sat down.

"Parker and I are engaged, he asked me to marry him again last night, and I said yes."

"Well newsflash we kind of knew that was going to happen eventually." M.K snorts.

"We should celebrate. Both families." Nan suggests.

"That's what I told Parker. So we will arrange something."

"I can imaging his friends will want to come." Bailey considers.

"This is a dream come true." Nan beams, "One of my granddaughters is getting married."

Parker

When my lift dings and Ashley strolls out, she looks as fresh as a daisy, "Hey so what did you want to see me about?"

I now have on a pair of grey jeans a black polo long sleeve shirt, "Have you spoken to M.K since you arrested her?"

"No, Belle asked me the same thing."

"Is something going on between you and her?"

"No why would there be?"

"But you want something to be?"

"Parker what's with the twenty questions about my love life?" She snaps.

"You're my sister, M.K is practically my sister in law. It's my business to know."

"No and nothing is going to happen either."

"Why not?" She want there to be something with her though, I can tell.

"Because she's dangerous."

I fold my arms, "Dangerous?" I almost snigger.

"Yes dangerous, everything is a game to her. I won't be played."

"And you think she would do that to you?"

"Yes I do, it's not her fault, it's the way she was brought up. I feel sorry for her, but she's a player and I'm not interested in players."

"Alright but you do have to try and get along with her, she is also Belle's sister."

"Anyway please tell me you didn't just call me here to talk about my love life, or lack thereof."

"No come on, I want your opinion on something." We walk out of the apartment block and get into Ashley's car, which is a black Ford Fiesta Golf 2014.

"Where to?"

"H. Samuel."

"Ohh getting Belle a present?" She asks as she starts driving.

"Yeah, something like that."

"Don't tell me you're thinking of proposing." She glances over at me and clocks my face, "Oh fucking hell you are."

"Ashley I already have, we got engaged last night, only I forgot the key ingredient, which I ordered a week ago, and it's arrived today."

"You really don't do things by halves do you?"

"Nope it's the whole log or nothing, but I'm going to ask her again properly tonight."

Ashley pulls into the carpark near the store, "You're paying for parking, little brother."

"We're only going to be two minutes, in and out."

"In and out he says, you just had to get the damn thing insured didn't you? And you didn't need me, so that..." She punches me in the arm, "Is for getting me out of bed just so you can grill me about M.K. Go on, let's see it."

I get it out of my pocket open the red velvet box, to reveal a sterling silver right with a ruby as the jewel, which is shaped like a heart. "Oh Parker." She gasps, "Can you propose to me?" She realises what she said immediately, "Second thoughts don't bother. But wow it matches her necklace, of course that was probably your intention." She fans her face with both hands to ward off threatening tears, "Oh fuck it." She lets the tears fall as she hugs me, "It's not every day my little brother gets engaged. Is she really the one?"

"She's really the one."

"You need to tell Mum and Dad. Mum's going to be worse than me."

We head to the car and she makes the drive to Mum and Dad's house, we don't bother knocking, we just walk in to Dad in a pair of medium blue jeans and a light blue polo shirt, he's bouncing little Skyla on his knee, she has on a hot pink tracksuit.

"Oh look it's your big brother and sister, not been squabbling have you?"

"Oh you know this and that." Ashley kisses my dad on the cheek and then holds out her arms for Skyla, "Aww hello baby girl. Have you been good today?"

"Ran her poor Mum ragged, she went for a lay down."

"Which is code for, 'we got a little randy during Skyla's nap and she always needs to go for a lie down after we have had sex.' I would ask what you do that makes her so tired, but I've gone twenty six years without picturing my parents having sex, and would like to continue sleeping at night, if it is all the same."

"Probably does the same thing to her as I do to Belle."

Ashley punches me in the arm, "Gross I don't want to hear about your bedroom habits."

"Parker stop weirding your sister out." Mum says coming downstairs in a light blue dress, she goes to my Dad and kisses him lovingly, "Thank you for watching Skyla while I took a nap, it was very much needed."

"No need to thank me darling, she's as much mine as yours, I'm doing my fatherly duty."

Julian then walks in, he has on his all black uniform for school, "Hey how was school?" Ashley asks passing him Skyla when he holds out his arms for her.

"Hello baby." He kisses her cheek, "School was school, there was a fight, kid got a bloody nose, his mum is threatening to press charges even though he started it."

"Sounds eventful." Mum muses.

"Not really. Full house." Julian notices, "Why is there a full house?"

"Sit down fella, I have some news."

"Belle's pregnant?" He guess.

"No I'm in love not stupid, I want a good couple of years with her before we bring a baby into the mix. Just sit down."

When he's done what I've asked, I begin, "I've asked Belle to marry me, she said yes. I'm engaged." I beam with happiness.

"That was going to be my next guess." Julian says rolling his eyes.

Mum springs up to wrap her arms around me, "Oh Parker that's amazing news. Where is she?"

"She had to work today, she told her family over lunch, I'm telling you guys now, we should also all arrange a time for us to celebrate together."

"What's the ring like? Do you have a picture?" Mum asks hopefully.

"I have the ring."

I pull the box out of my pocket and show Mum, she puts her hands to her mouth on a gasp, "It's beautiful, so beautiful." Tears start falling.

"You always did have good taste son." Dad muses.

When I show Julian, he makes the connection, "It matches her necklace, wow that's really romantic Parker."

I ruffle his hair, "You catch on quick kid, this is how you keep a woman. You treat her like she's your world. Anyway I'm going to head home. I told Belle I was going to cook her favourite tonight, best way to propose properly."

I give everyone a hug, plus give Mum, Ashley and Skyla a kiss on the cheek, then I head back home to begin cooking for Belle.

After what feels like forever Belle texts me, 'Hey baby, I'm on my way home, today has sucked, I'm so tired, I can't wait to see you. X.'

I smile, and check on the food in the oven, everything seems to be running smoothly.

I go about setting up candles and lighting them, and then hit another switch to have the shades brought down, so we both benefit from the candles.

When the lift dings, Belle strolls out and stops in awe, her drained face turns into one of astonishment, "Wow I wasn't expecting this, I thought you were just cooking a meal."

"I am. Parker Wilson style" I wrap my arms around her mid-section and pull her close so I can nuzzle her neck, "I've missed you."

"I missed you too. So much."

"How was your day?"

"Long, boring and draining. Telling the girls we're engaged was the highlight of it. They were so happy for me."

"My family is ecstatic, even Ashley cried which is a rarity to be honest, so did Mum, but she still cries at Bambi."

"Hey that is sad, even I cried when his mum died."

""I have got to see that." I joke.

She gives me a jab in the ribs for my trouble, "You sadistic fuck, it's a good job you're good in bed, because that makes up for your downright mean streak."

"Phew, I get to keep my woman, because I make her call out my name in sheer ecstasy."

She laughs and kisses me lightly, "It certainly is a very good perk."

"The food is ready, if you want to sit down."

She does as I ask, I dish up the meal and carry it to the table, I then take the champagne, along with a bucket of ice and two champagne flutes to the table.

I pour the champagne, pass Belle her glass and then hold up my own, "To us."

Belle clinks her glass to mine, "To us."

We start eating our meal, "Oh wow." Belle muses, "This is better than Nan's, Parker please marry me, I'll even beg."

"If I'd have known cooking your favourite meal would make you propose, then I would have done it on our first date." She smiles at that, she looks so perfect, "You look amazing in the candlelight, just stunning baby."

She beams, "You flatter me, right now I look tired, drained and feeling it more so."

"Not flattery, not in the slightest, you're the most beautiful woman I have ever seen."

"And you're the most amazing man ever, you're so much more handsome in the candle light, and I didn't think that was possible."

We carry on our meal in a comfortable silence, when we're done and I've washed the dishes, we curl up on the sofa, sharing slow, tender and love filled kisses.

"I've got something for you." I say tracing her lips with my thumb.

"Oh? I can't for the life of me think what it could be." She says sarcastically.

I nibble on her bottom lip, "Smart arse."

"It's why you love me."

I take the red velvet box out of my pocket and kneel in front of her, "I know I already asked, but I should have waited, because this makes this moment so much more special. Belle O Neil, in the words of your great grandfather, 'I can't give you my heart, but I can give you the next best thing. Will you marry me?"

I open the box and she gasps, "It matches my necklace. This must have cost a small fortune."

"Money isn't an issue, you know that. Your answer?"

She pulls me to her for a long and passionate kiss, "Yes, a thousand times yes." She kisses me wildly, "Come with me."

She stands, takes hold of my hand and leads me into the bedroom, she wastes no time stripping off my top, she lets me take off her trousers and her top, but when I get to her underwear she says, "Stop. This is all about you baby." She shoves me onto the bed, takes off my trousers and pants.

She sets about devouring my neck, licking, nipping and kissing, she moves down to my chest, then my stomach, I have no idea what she is thinking, but I don't want her to stop.

She takes me in her mouth, "Oh fuck." I roll my head back my mind starts to spin, this woman does such amazing things to me already, and now she's doing this, she moves her hands up my stomach, and gently drags them down, her nails are digging in, but not enough to leave marks, "Fuck Belle, don't stop, please don't stop." I beg.

Have I ever begged for anything in my life? Have I ever felt the need to? No but yet here she is making me beg for more, whether she intends to or not.

And she answers, taking me harder, quicker and with more urgency, "Fuck Belle!" I shout.

Does she know what she is doing to me? How crazy she makes me? Can she ever truly understand how in love with her I am?

I climax, "Oh fuck Belle." I give some low moans as she eases me down, when she's done, she slowly and seductively crawls up my body, trailing her hot tongue and lips over my flesh.

When she reaches my lips, I capture her mouth, "My majesty, my queen." I murmur.

"Tonight you're my king."

"No tonight I'm still your knave, that has only made me worship you more. Please tell me you have never done that to another man."

"I've never done that to another man."

I kiss her again, "When I recover, we'll make love."

"Not tonight, it's been a long day, just hold me Parker, until I fall asleep in your arms. That's all I need from you right now."

I do as she asks, wrapping my arms around her, I kiss the side of her head, "Then it will be done." I promise.

Belle

So tonight is the night of our engagement party, and I have decided to surprise Parker, so a couple of days ago I went out to Victoria's Secret, and found a lovely royal blue silk dress, it's a little on the sort side, but silk is Parker's favourite material on me, so knowing that I'm wearing the dress for him, I'm sure he'll make an exception.

I make my way out of the bathroom and to him, he's pacing in a sky blue suit, he has his back to me, "I never had you down as a nervous man."

He turns around, "Oh wow you look incredible." He approaches me, "Silk." He runs his hand over the material of my dress, I don't think I'm going to be able to keep my hands off you."

"When do you ever try?" He starts to well up, "Oh baby come here." I wrap my arms around him, "Well I'm marrying a man who doesn't need Bambi to cry."

He chuckles a little, "Sorry tears of joy."

"Don't apologise for loving me, I love you Parker. I've got something for you." I go into the bedroom I go into my wardrobe and get out a Hugo Boss bag, I go back out and pass it to him, "Here open."

He does that and pulls out a bottle of Boss The Scent, "You always hone in on my neck when I wear this stuff."

"I love this fragrance on you, you wore it the first night we met. It was one of the most captivating things about you, one of the reasons I knew you were different to the rest. I couldn't stop thinking about that smell. About you."

"I love you so much."

"I love you too, so much, my sensitive man." I put my hand on the back of his neck and kiss him lovingly, again he runs his hands over the material of my dress.

"Yeah I'm not going to be able to keep my hands off you." He decides.

"Good job I'm not asking you to. But we do have to go, we're going to be late."

He keeps his hand on my back, when we get into my car, he then puts his hand on my leg, "This is a very short dress." He informs.

"I figured you would think so, I also thought given the occasion, you would make an exception, I looked for silk especially for you, so I would soften the blow." I run my hand up his leg, to his groin which is solid as a rock, "Obviously I thought wrong." I say amused.

"The size of the dress is fine, it means I can do this." He too runs his hand up my leg, under the material of my dress, he pushes past the material of my silk panties, humming his approval at my silk underwear.

I let out a shudder of anticipation, he pushes his fingers into me, I moan, "Oh fuck." He does it a few more times, "Fucking hell Parker."

He pulls his finger out of me, "We're nearly there."

"You bastard." I scowl.

"That's not very nice." He smiles.

"You do that again, I'll show you just how not nice I can be."

I pull into the carpark of The River, "We can always go home and be fashionably late." He suggests, which I am not going to lie, it's highly tempting.

"No it's fine, I'll take my time with you later." I lean in close, right near his ear, I run my hand over his chest and stomach as I speak, "Where I can tease you and tempt you, until you can't control the desire in you any longer, and you fuck me where we stand."

He turns his head to kiss me, I back off and get out of the car, I can't help but feel very pleased with myself over that.

I walk into The River, everyone break out in cheer, I can't help but smile.

Parker catches up with me, spins me round and crushes his mouth onto mine, not caring where we are, he just takes everything he wants for now, when he pulls away I feel a little drugged.

"Let the games begin." He whispers.

"You're a child." I smile.

"You're beautiful." He looks at the crowd, "Sorry folks, just wrapping up some unfinished business with my lovely fiancé."

"More like creating some." I nudge him and look to the crowd myself, "Thank you everyone for coming and celebrating our engagement with us. I think it's safe to say, I've never been happier. I hope my amazing fiancé can say the same."

"The feelings most definitely mutual, Belle's done nothing but make me happy since I first met her. I love her with every fibre of my being."

We then set about mingling with the crowd together, then we break off to be with our families.

Parker

Belle looks amazing sat in her usual booth with her family, just talking and laughing, we have both taken opportunities to have sneaky touches and steal kisses.

Mum comes over to me, in a black pencil dress, she has Skyla in her arms, who has on a white and sky blue floral dress.

"Mum." I kiss her cheek, I take Skyla and put her on my own hip, "You look amazing." I hold Skyla over my head to make her laugh, "You both do." I kiss Skyla's cheek.

"You're a natural born father." Mum muses.

"Don't tell Belle that, she'll think I'll want to get her pregnant tomorrow. However you could always tell her the story of how you conceived Ashley and Jack, and this little monkey."

"Enjoy some time with Belle first, before children come into the mix. Why do you think our children were born quite far apart? Granted Ashley and Jack were not entirely planned, but when they were old enough to go to school, your father and I took our time together as sacred, children do strain a relationship, sometimes we did feel it, we're an active couple, and we had to schedule time together around you kids being at school."

"Do you regret any of it?"

"Not in the slightest, we would die for all of you kids, but I'm just pointing out, maybe slow down a bit, marry Belle, then treasure the time you have with her, the time you have together is sacred, don't rush into having children, especially if Belle isn't sure if she wants any, children are not something you can compromise over."

"No you're right, I just want Belle, and she will always be enough for me."

"I'm going to say hello to Belle, I love you my boy."

She takes hold of Skyla, before she goes to say hello to Belle, she rescues Dad, who has on a dark grey suit, from a young blond who is flirting with him, Mum does it, by putting her hand on the back of Dad's neck and kissing him like mad, and by doing that she makes a simple statement, 'Mine.' Then she makes her way over to my lovely fiancé.

Soon I feel a pat on my back, "Parker my brother." Wayne drawls, he has on a charcoal suit, "So she really has her claws in you deep."

"I've never been more in love brother, she's the one."

"Let's hope she really has changed her spots then, however there is a picture out there." He shows me a picture of Fox kissing Belle.

"He kissed her." I say snatching it away from him.

"She isn't exactly fighting him off though is she."

"He has hold of her arms, you can see she is trying to push him off her."

Sam then joins us in a pair of black jeans and a white and blue plaid flannel shirt, "Hey bro congratulations, a hell of a woman you have there." He clocks what's in my hands, "Oh bro pay no attention to that. You can see she's trying to pull away from him."

"Just what I was telling Wayne."

"Wayne what are you playing at?"

"Just reminding him of the kind of woman she was, and if you turn around, you'll be reminded of the kind of woman you could have."

I stupidly turn around, a pair of hands land on my face, and someone is kissing me wildly, it's not Belle, I know it's not Belle, I don't have any of the feelings she gives me, as a matter of fact, I feel disdain.

I put my hands on the mystery woman's shoulders and push her away, it's Scarlet, in a slutty black dress, "What the fuck are you doing?!" I spit angrily.

"Reminding you of the kind of woman you can have, you could be with a real woman, and not a slut like Belle."

"Belle is more woman than you'll ever be. And I love her more than anything in the world, without her I'm nothing."

All of a sudden Scarlet is being spun round and viciously slapped around the face.

Belle

I'm sat with my family in our favourite booth. Nan has on a long sky blue dress.

M.K has on a pair of black jeans and a red long sleeve crop top, showing off her tight toned abdominal muscles.

Bailey has on a lovely purple dress that flows around her legs and fits her body nicely.

We have been sat chatting about wedding plans.

And soon find Ashley approaching us, "Hey guys." She's nervous.

"Hey Ashley, join us." I say.

"Thanks." She sits next to M.K because that is the only place in the booth with room, well that is not entirely true, Bailey and I could have moved up, but then she wouldn't be sat next to M.K. And where would the fun be in that?

"Parker looks so natural with a child in his arms." Nan points out.

"Who is the kid?" M.K asks.

"My little sister Skyla." Ashley answers, "She's the terror of the house hold."

"I find that hard to believe, she's too cute."

"You like kids?" Ashley asks M.K.

"Yeah what's not to like? Why are you so shocked?"

"You just don't look like the sort of person that likes kids."

"Uh oh." Bailey smiles, "Looks like Daddy's in trouble."

Ashley looks around to see her dad being flirted with by a blond half his age, she goes to get up, M.K puts her hand over Ashley's, "Hold up babe."

"Don't call me babe." She goes to free her hand, "M.K let go of my hand."

"Just cool off and look." M.K orders.

Ashley sits back to see her mother saunter over and kiss her father like a woman possessed, that kiss was designed to say one thing 'Mine.'

"Someone's going to get lucky tonight." Bailey muses, "That was one hot kiss."

"That's one hot woman." M.K replies.

"That's my Mum." Ashley jibes.

"Do you kiss like that?" M.K asks.

"Depends on if I'm feeling possessive or not."

"M.K." I shoot her a warning look, she merely shrugs.

Caty then approaches us, we all make room, "Caty and Skyla, this is M.K, Bailey and my Nan Elsie. M.K, Bailey and Nan, this is Parker's Mum Caty and his little sister Skyla."

"Well she is the cutest thing in the world." M.K coos.

"You can have her if you want." Caty jokes.

"How are you enjoying the party?" I ask.

"Oh very well, Julian sends his apologies, he has an exam in the morning, IT, his best subject, he didn't want a night away from studying."

"Oh don't worry about it, I will get him a gift for tomorrow, to let him know I'm thinking of him."

I see Scarlet scoot by us, "What the fuck is she doing here?" M.K blurts out.

"M.K language, there are little ears present." I chastise her, I look in Scarlet's direction, to see her approach Parker, he turns around and she kisses him, "Bailey move now."

She hesitates, "Let her up Bailey." M.K tells her.

Bailey gets up, I'm up like a shot, I move like lightening, Parker shoves her off, there's an exchange of words, I don't care, I grab her, spin her round and slap her around the face.

"You could never let me have anything could you?! You fucking little bitch!"

"You don't deserve Parker. You've never done anything but hurt people."

"You're right I don't deserve him, but I'm the person that has him, people need to start accepting that, because I'll be damned if anything or anyone is going to change that." I take hold of Parker's hand, "Everyone please enjoy the party, Parker and I are going home." I wrap my arm around Parker's mid-section, "Time to finish what we started. I want you."

Parker

We get into Belle's car, she says nothing now, she's trembling with anger, she's seething mad, I can't help but blame myself, "Belle baby, I'm so sorry, I had no idea she was there."

"You did nothing wrong, but I just want to be with you now."

"Then it will be done."

She's silent the rest of the way home, when we get there, she is calmer, but I can see anger still etched on that beautiful face, she's silent a moment and then she looks me in the eyes, "She was right Parker. I don't deserve you."

I get out of the car, circle round, open her door, undo her belt, lift her out of the car and carry her inside, I just want to her get her home, so we can forget the world exists, nothing else matters when we're together, I want to remind her of that, I need to remind her that she does deserve me.

"Kiss me Belle." I order softly when we get into the lift, she obliges, keeping the kiss light and sweet, the lift opens and I carry her into the bedroom, keeping my lips locked to hers. "When Scarlet kissed me, I hated her for it, because you're the only person I want to taste and make love with as long as I live."

"I feel the same way." She sighs.

"Then it will be done, my queen."

"It will be done." She murmurs, locking lips with me again.

We lay down on the bed and make sweet endless love.

Printed in the United States
By Bookmasters